The

Nominated ~~for~~
Award f

"A charming romp. The witty repartee and naughty innuendos set the perfect pitch for the entertaining romance. Though there are serious themes and carefully researched historical details, it's the banter and sensuality that are sure to enchant readers."

—*RT Book Reviews*, 4 Stars

"A witty, seductive historical romance that is sure to gain this new author many fans… Misguided influences, colorful characters, naughty innuendos, humor, passion, romance, and true love are only part of what makes this second-chance love story so delightful."

—*Long and Short Reviews*

"A quirky but steamy historical romance…very entertaining with marvelously spirited interactions."

—*Tome Tender*

"A lovely romance…a very lighthearted romantic tale."

—*Kritiques*

"A hoot. It is

—*Junkies*

"A sweet, well-paced romance between two intelligent adults…most definitely a good read."

—*All About Romance*

"Lighthearted, highly entertaining, and fast-paced romance."

—*Bookworm 2 Bookworm*

"A good read… The dialogue was witty and the entire story flowed at an easy pace."

—*The Romance Reviews*

"Had me laughing out loud throughout the story, and I'm looking forward to reading about the other two authors of *The Rake's Handbook*!"

—*Historical Romance Lover*

"A solid beginning to a debut author and a new series!"

—*My Book Addiction and More*

"Lots of sexual chemistry, some misguided influences, and even some nefarious characters causing all sorts of problems. Ms. Orr touches all the bases…a lighthearted look at late Regency society."

—*La Deetda Reads*

SALLY ORR

sourcebooks
casablanca

Published by Sourcebooks Casablanca, an imprint of Sourcebooks, Inc.
P.O. Box 4410, Naperville, Illinois 60567-4410
(630) 961-3900
Fax: (630) 961-2168
www.sourcebooks.com

Printed and bound in Canada.
MBP 10 9 8 7 6 5 4 3 2 1

One

LORD BOYCE PARKER FELT A SUDDEN URGE TO SING.
The brisk morning air, the glorious sunshine, and the
presence of a hundred or so excited gentlemen milling
around him could only mean a remarkable day ahead.
Boyce knew he'd be mocked if he broke out in song,
but sometimes happiness just bubbled up from somewhere down in your toes and overwhelmed a fellow.
"My candle burns bright—"

"Goes without saying you learned to sing by reading a book," said George Drexel, one of Boyce's
oldest friends. "Right now I could be in bed with
the lovely Widow Donhurst. Instead, I'm standing
here amongst the rabble of London, far too early for
any sane man, following another one of your bacon-
brained schemes."

Boyce ignored him and kept his gaze fixed on the
balcony of Stainthorpe House. Yesterday, the Earl
of Stainthorpe had placed an advertisement in all of
the newspapers inviting London's finest bachelors to

gather in Royston Square. Although the details in the advertisement were few, it hinted fame and five thousand pounds might be gained by winning one of several "challenges." As the son of a wealthy marquess, Boyce had no need for the money, but he longed for a chance to impress his father. "It's not my bacon-brained scheme; it's the earl's. Cheer up. You will be the friend of the victorious Lord Boyce Parker."

Drexel turned to glare at the pressing horde of eager young gentlemen behind them. "You don't even know what the old man's challenges are. They could all be a hum, like a scavenger hunt to find his great-uncle's tricorne hat or his aunt's lost poodle." Drexel dressed in somber colors without fancy cravats or fobs, so his words had the gravity of a humorless man no one would willfully cross. This morning, his rumpled clothes, dark whiskers, and obvious lack of sleep—no doubt due to a long night of amorous adventure—made him appear grumpier than normal. "I hardly think the earl's tomfool challenges will make you famous."

"You don't sound cheerful." Boyce grinned at his old school friend. "I'm confident the earl's challenges will be significant and my assured victory will pave the way to restoring my father's esteem."

Drexel spat on the ground. "Chasing your brother's fame? Richard is a glorious war hero. I'm sure winning some silly challenge won't compete with his elevated consequence."

"You're wrong. When my name is printed in the newspapers, my father will have to speak of me with the same admiration he gives Richard."

"I don't think winning a challenge will change the marquess's opinion of you—"

"Look." Boyce pointed upward.

The Earl of Stainthorpe stepped to the edge of his balcony overlooking Royston Square. "My friends, I understand there are no great men left in England." Silver wisps of hair escaped the earl's old-fashioned queue and blew over his forehead, but he ignored them as he squarely confronted the men below.

The audience surged forward and yelled retorts to the earl's audacious remark.

Boyce had arrived an hour early so he would be close enough to hear his lordship's every word. But if this hubbub continued, he might not catch what the earl had to say. He turned to the man yelling behind him. "I'll give you a pound, my good fellow, if you can shout louder."

The man smiled and shouted.

"Definitely not louder, unfortunate loss indeed," Boyce said. "Now I suggest you hush and let his lordship speak."

Standing two steps behind his master, the earl's butler vigorously rang a handbell to gain the attention of the boisterous crowd.

"The earldom of Stainthorpe owns numerous and diverse holdings," the earl bellowed. "Therefore, upon my death, my daughter will be the richest woman in England."

The crowd cheered.

The earl waited for them to settle down. "What I'm trying to say is, Lady Sarah Stainthorpe needs a husband. But so far, none of the Eligibles paraded before

her will do. She refuses to marry and claims all the
gentlemen in London are rogues, dandies, or worse.
The point is, she's a bluestocking and might fall in love
with some bloody…a poet. I tell you, my friends, that
Byron fellow has a lot to answer for."

As the youngest son of a marquess, Boyce was
considered an Eligible. Only, Lady Sarah had rejected
him, and all the other Eligibles, seconds after they had
presented themselves at Royston House—an unfortunate circumstance, since he believed Lady Sarah would
make an excellent wife and a very pretty one too.
After a moment of reflection, he realized every lady
of his acquaintance would make a pretty wife. One
or two may have a feature some might call "unfortunate." Nevertheless, he always found something pretty
in every female countenance.

"Are all the gentlemen I see before me rogues or
dandies?" the earl shouted. "Of course not. One or
two maybe, and several of you are shockingly loose
in the haft." His lordship pointed to a young man
wearing a violet greatcoat, hanging by one arm on a
streetlight. "Especially you, sir."

With his free hand, the man doffed his top hat.

"Yes, I mean you," the earl said. "My condolences
to your poor father."

All of the Parker men possessed a fine figure, so he
knew even a poorly tailored coat hung well upon his
shoulders. The many compliments he received had
gained him a reputation as an expert in masculine fashion.
Therefore, Boyce felt his lordship should show more
sympathy to a man wearing a lamentable violet greatcoat,
since the earl wore an old square coat and baggy breeches.

"Where was I?" The earl paused to scan the crowd. "Besides an obvious bone-breaker or two, you gentlemen are the embodiment of the character traits that make Englishmen the greatest people on earth. So I am challenging you—the finest Englishmen alive—to a race. A race to Paris!"

The crowd cheered.

"This is not a race where the winner arrives first," the earl said. "No, it is a test to discover the gentlemen who possess England's greatest traits."

"Gin drinking, gov?" someone shouted.

The crowd laughed and called out a few additional "traits."

The earl ignored their comments. "And I mean *English* character traits—not British. That country was some tomfoolery created by meddlesome politicians. This is a race for Englishmen only. Now, my race will have five challenges and five winners. Each winner will win a prize of a gold cup and five thousand pounds."

The mob erupted in huzzahs; top hats flew into the air.

Under his sky-blue waistcoat, Boyce's heartbeat escalated. This race presented him with his best opportunity to distinguish himself. He would win at least two of the earl's challenges and earn a reputation as a prime example of English manhood. "Huzzah!" He too threw his beaver hat in the air.

The butler rang the handbell for a full minute before the crowd settled down.

The earl held up his hands. "Here are the details of the five—count them—five challenges. You have one month to reach Stainthorpe House in Paris. Each gentleman will write about his journey and provide the name of a witness. The man whose travels provide the best example of an English trait wins a challenge. Once the winners promise to spend the remainder of the summer in our company, they will be rewarded with a gold cup and five thousand pounds. With such excellent examples of true English manhood escorting Lady Sarah around Paris, she must certainly fall in love with one of you unlicked cubs."

The assembled men danced in circles. Each one of them was probably dreaming about how he would spend his winnings.

Eager to hear the details, Boyce frowned at the clamorous riffraff behind him. The earl was right; they all appeared to be a lot of rag-mannered coves, so he gained complete confidence that he could best any of their English traits—whatever those traits may be. Once he reached Paris, Lady Sarah would discover he was the finest of fellows and they would fall in love. Women seemed naturally to favor him over other gentlemen—wonderful creatures, women.

The earl's voice boomed across the square. "What are the character traits that make Englishmen so great, you ask?"

The young men below the balcony tendered several improper suggestions.

"No." The earl waved his hand. "Not physical features. Traits like courage and intelligence. So the challenges are thus: The first gold cup will be given to the gentleman who represents English courage. We are the country of Nelson, so bravery and courage course through every one of our veins."

Someone shouted the nature of what was coursing through his veins.

The earl continued without hesitation. "The second gold cup will be given to the gentleman whose journey represents classic English sportsmanship. Any Englishman alive can out hunt, out fish, and out ride all other races of men. So to win the second cup, some outstanding feat of sportsmanship will rule the day. Extra consideration will be given to the best example of a journey completed under difficult circumstances."

Boyce huffed. "Well, his lordship is wrong. The true nature of English sportsmanship is not victory over adversity, but our support for the dark horse and sense of fair play. We are, by nature, a generous people."

Drexel slapped him on the back. "For once I agree with you. But considering your history in the field, I suggest you don't try for the sportsmanship cup."

"Sportsmanship can be demonstrated by means other than fishing or shooting every magnificent creature—for example, by boxing or gaming. I practice my pugilistic skills at Jackson's twice a week now. You cannot tell me his place is not full of sportsmen. Or how about when a fellow loses a fortune gaming at White's and faces his loss with the grace and good humor of a gentleman? That's sportsmanship under pressure, if you ask me."

"Yes, but the earl believes boxing is for professionals and only women play cards."

Boyce widened his eyes. "In my opinion, his lordship's definition of *sportsmanship* is rather limited."

The handbell sounded again before the earl continued his speech. "The third gold cup will be given to the gentleman whose journey best exhibits loyalty to the king or service to a lady."

One man yelled, "I'd be delighted to service all the ladies on my way to Paris."

Others in the crowd shouted similar generous offers.

"If you do so, sir," the earl replied, "you will be shown the door. Loyalty means old-fashioned manners, being polite, and keeping your distance from your betters. Of all the challenges, I believe service to the Crown is the greatest honor any man could desire. And considering the manners I've witnessed here today, I'd say the challenge of this cup will remain unmet."

Jeers filled the air.

Boyce wondered how a fellow could show loyalty to the king in a race. He supposed a gentleman might salute the king's profile on a sovereign with every step of his journey, but dismissed it as an absurd notion. No, he'd be better off trying to provide a service to some lady.

His lordship nodded, and the handbell rang again. "Now quiet down. The fourth cup will be given to the man whose journey provides the best example of our English intelligence. We are the land of Newton and Davy, so the greatest brains of civilization are English. Except for that da Vinci fellow and one or two Greeks, but we can afford to be generous and let the rest of the world have a little luck now and then."

Boyce elbowed his friend. "Yes, yes, that's the cup for me. Bet I'll win too. What do you say, fifty?"

"Agreed," Drexel said. "I will also wager by the end of this whole flummery, Lady Sarah will reject all the winners out of spite. I would, if I were her."

Boyce refused to believe Lady Sarah would object to any of the winners, once she knew them well. The lady wanted to be married, didn't she? "No, no, young women are full of tender affection. I have never met one who did not want to fall in love and make her family happy."

Drexel rolled his eyes. "I suspect that is because there are so many unmarried ladies dangling after you, you cannot imagine one refusing. And from the stories I heard yesterday, I'll wager that if I throw a pebble into the crowd at the next assembly, it will hit a widow who has, or wants to be, in your bed. And believe me, those ladies are not expecting marriage."

"You're being vulgar in public," Boyce said. "All of the widows I have ever…met were delightful. Deep in their hearts, they want to be married again, I'm sure."

"So why haven't you married one of these delight-ful ladies?"

"Never understood how fellows choose one to fall in love with."

"If I know the marquess, the best way to impress him is to give him grandchildren. My father becomes unhinged with even the thought of grandchildren."

"Grandchildren? Grandchildren are far in the future. A great public achievement is my best and only chance to regain my father's respect. You'll see. When I am crowned the victor of more than one challenge, my achievements will be the toast of London. Then all of England will think of me differently. I will no longer be just one of the seven anonymous brothers of the war hero Richard. Worse yet, if people do recognize me, they remember I'm the Parker son who published a scandalous book and then received the cut direct from his father—his own father. After my victory in the challenges, everyone will have to refer to me as the intelligent, courageous Lord *Boyce*. Don't you understand?"

Drexel winked at his friend. "Tell me, which of the great English traits do you represent best? Sounds like only Service to a Lady, and believe me, your service is the wrong type as far as the earl is concerned."

"Ah, that's my secret. But you will be a witness to my victory, won't you?"

After pulling off his hat, Drexel took a full minute to smooth the beaver nap on the brim. "I'll consider it." A wide smirk broke across his dark, handsome face. "You've persuaded me to join the race too."

"No!"

The handbell clanged, and everyone faced the balcony again. "Gentlemen, there is one last challenge, the fifth cup. Since this was my daughter's idea, perhaps in jest, you never know with females, let us call it the Lady's Favorite."

Shouts and laughter rose from the rabble.

The earl leaned forward over the mob. "Perhaps there are no gentlemen in England, and my daughter is right?" His lordship waited until the crowd quieted. "Lady Sarah has a funny notion that the greatest achievements of the English race are their sense of humor, wit, and eccentricities. I mean, now really, she is fond of Sheridan's plays." The earl held up his right hand to quiet the laughing crowd. "For this cup, Lady Sarah will be the final judge."

The mob tendered several humorous jests of questionable wit.

The earl coughed several times but remained unmoving. "So there you have it. The five greatest English traits are courage, sportsmanship, intelligence, wit, and service to a lady. Now to business. I expect all who plan to take up the challenges to gather in our vestibule below. There, we will compile a list of the participants. You do not have to choose which cup you aspire to, and you may switch to another challenge at the end of your journey. Finally, you may win more than one challenge. Oh, and you must provide an acceptable witness. Anyone who observes your achievement and can testify on your behalf may be an official witness. The only exclusions are people who cannot be trusted, like paid companions or dear old mums."

Several groans were heard, and one person clapped.

The earl nodded in the direction of the man who clapped. "Good man. The race will officially start after I stop speaking and will end a month from now on the second of July. On that day, you will present your written story describing your journey to Stainthorpe House at Rue de la Chaussée-d'Antin. There, I will choose the five best stories for each challenge, and those finalists will be asked to recite their adventures aloud. Indeed, everyone here today will be invited to attend this party and hear my pick of the winners. Lastly, the five thousand pounds and gold cups will be presented at the end of the evening. It goes without saying that the victors will be appropriately recognized in all of the newspapers."

Boyce elbowed Drexel. "Yes, yes, my father reads every paper."

The crowd's cheers erupted again after the mention of the winnings.

The earl held his arms out. "I tell you, my friends, I'm excited about this race. To help defray the cost of your journey, any man who takes up our challenges will receive a hundred pounds after reaching Paris."

Shouts and applause echoed around the square.

"Gentlemen, gentlemen, Lady Sarah and I look forward to hearing the adventures of England's finest men. I am positive that once my daughter is acquainted with you fine fellows, she will fall in love. With such excellent examples of the greatness inherent in the English, how could she not? We also anticipate the pleasure of your company during our summer in Paris. The only other thing I can say is…" The earl lifted his quizzing glass to his eye and scanned the crowd. "Ready, steady, go!"

❦

An unusually warm and cloudless sky greeted Boyce the next morning as he started his journey to Paris. It took some effort to hide his disappointment that Drexel had changed his mind and agreed to be his witness for only one day. During the night, his friend had run into trouble of the female kind and needed to return to London before the day's end.

The first man out of the stable yard was Drexel, and he pointed his dappled gray south.

Boyce whistled to get his attention. "We must head north."

Drexel reigned in his horse. "But Paris is to the east and south, not north."

"No, no." He patted his horse's neck. "I will win by heading north. Why that direction, you might ask. Follow me."

Boyce and Drexel traveled northward before taking a sharp turn to the east.

After ten minutes of silence, Boyce winked at his friend. "So tell me about the female trouble you ran into yesterday."

A scowl crossed Drexel's sharp features. "I will never forgive you for coercing me, and Ross, into writing *The Rake's Handbook: Including Field Guide*. Help you with your publishing career be damned. That handbook has been nothing but trouble for all of us. Now some chit is angered over the section of the book I wrote, *The Field Guide*. Claims the wrong initials were added under 'Happy Goers.' But don't worry, I have a clever plan to deal with her." The tone of his voice, combined with his wicked smile, meant certain trouble for some unsuspecting female.

After a long gallop, followed by a conversation about troublesome women, they found themselves riding down Frog Lane, surrounded by open fields near the village of Islington. On one side, London's vegetable gardens stretched out into the distance, filling the air with the odor of manure. On the other side, several dozen people gathered around a large, wooden platform. A large balloon half-filled with the newly discovered inflammable air—created during the manufacture of illuminating gas—fixed everyone's attention. A silver-blue monster of over forty feet in diameter, the silk balloon swayed with every little puff of wind.

Drexel whistled softly. "You have more courage than I if you go up in that thing."

Brimming with confidence, Boyce straightened in the saddle. "Now you understand the brilliance of my plan. I'll win both the courage and intelligence challenge. Courage, because no other challenger will journey to Paris by balloon. Intelligence, because this balloon represents a new technology that will lead the way in transportation. My successful flight may one day prove that ordinary people can travel great distances by air."

"I'll give you courage, but not intelligence. It's too dangerous to travel far. Balloons are only used for paid ascensions or to observe troop movements."

"No, no, expand your imagination. The prince—I mean that sorry fellow who is now our king—has gone on hundreds of ascensions, so they're not dangerous at all. Think of the balloon's future on a grand scale, a way to cross deserts, find the source of the Amazon, or lift heavy cargo. Perhaps one day you will reach for your wings in the morning instead of your riding boots. Let's watch them prepare, shall we?"

Up on the platform, three people worked diligently. The youngest was a lad of eight or nine who seemed to run wherever directed. Next, a young woman dressed in a tan wool overcoat, her brown hair neatly plaited, lifted birdcages into the balloon's basket. The third person, a slim gentleman, stood next to the balloon and shouted incoherent instructions to the boy.

In a chair, by one of the many barrels that must have contained the inflammable air, sat an older man with remarkable whiskers that arched along the top of his cheeks. Boyce had met the aeronaut, Mr. Thomas Mountfloy, on the previous evening when he had made arrangements for the balloon's hire. The flight had been planned to perform several atmospheric experiments, like testing the ability of birds to fly at high altitudes. So Mr. Mountfloy initially refused Boyce's proposal. He only agreed to his scheme after Boyce paid an outrageous sum and agreed to assist with the experiments.

Boyce studied the basket. Made of wicker, about eight feet in length and perhaps five feet tall, it was shaped somewhat like a dinghy with several birdcages piled on one side.

Drexel shook his head. "What a sight. I've never seen a balloon up close."

The slim man held a long tube attached to the bottom of the balloon. The shiny silk undulated in the light breeze and quickly inflated to about three-quarters of its size.

Last night, Boyce had read that balloons were never fully inflated before ascending, because they needed room for the gas to expand at high altitudes. So when the slim man pulled the tube away, he knew it was time for his ascent. He tied a sack, containing clothing for cold weather and a tin of biscuits, around his waist before swallowing a swift mouthful of brandy from his silver flask. This movement caught Drexel's attention, but he spoke first. "You are the official witness to my ascension, remember? Now watch me."

Drexel grabbed his arm. "No! Please reconsider. You might be killed."

"Nowadays people don't die in balloons. They are

as safe as a gallop on Charity. Oh, and thank you for taking her back to the stables. Now keep your eye on me." He jumped up onto the platform and climbed into the basket. The girl had entered before him and seemed to be tying down the birdcages. He urged Mr. Mountfloy to come aboard with haste.

Mr. Mountfloy called out, "Are you ready, my lord?"

"Right ho," Boyce replied.

The girl looked at Mr. Mountfloy. "Father, please."

The slim man started to fiddle with the ropes, so Boyce wondered when Mr. Mountfloy would climb aboard. Then one side of the basket started to lift off the platform, so he shouted for the aeronaut to hurry.

After a nod in the direction of the slim man, Mr. Mountfloy waved his arm. "Good luck, your lordship. See you soon. Hang on!"

The balloon shot upward.

Two

Boyce yelled like a lunatic.

Whoosh. His hat blew off.

He clutched the side of the basket.

His favorite old hat tumbled away, far out in front of him.

Despite the blast of cold air, it was the most thrilling moment of his twenty-seven years.

He tried to lift his head, but it felt like a heavy cannonball pressed down to his chest by an unseen hand.

The wooden platform grew smaller as the balloon gained altitude. It didn't take long until the townsfolk looked like little black insects moving around in green grass. Several men on horseback followed in their direction, apparently chasing the balloon. Seconds later, the fields and hedgerows below resembled the irregular squares of a mottled green chessboard.

Boyce continued to yell as Islington shrank into the distance.

The balloon's upward movement seemed to slow, and several minutes later, it stopped.

Now certain of his survival after that remarkable

ascent, joy swelled in his chest. He laughed without reserve. Never had he felt so free. He needed to sing his thanks and praises to the magnificence of the balloon. "Away from my view fly the world and its strife, the banquet of fancy's feast is my life." He hung over the basket, spread his arms wide, and serenaded the town. "My spirits are mounting, my heart's full of glee." An odd sensation overcame his ears, and his voice sounded like he was singing under water. In the process of poking his ear with his pinky, he saw the girl.

She smiled at him before reaching up to pull the draw line, opening the spring valve. The escaping gas hissed softly. "Don't worry," she said. "We'll be on the ground in a few minutes."

"No! Close the valve." Boyce looked up at the swollen balloon. "What are you doing?"

Several strands of brown hair escaped her plait and blew around her close-fitting woolen cap. "I am releasing some of the gas. We need to land immediately."

"What? No, no, stop."

She spun to face him. "You don't want to descend? Every gentleman we take on a paid ascension wants to land soon after they retch…after such a rapid ascent."

"I didn't retch. I thought it was wonderful, and I have no desire to land." Being at least a foot taller, he grabbed the rope above her hand and pulled it out of her grasp. The valve clanged shut, and he stood with one hand holding the draw line high in the air, so she could not reach it.

"We must land and soon," she said. "Once I get you safely on the ground, we have plans for experiments today."

"But I hired this balloon to go to France."

"Of course you did." She backed away, placing both hands on her hips, emphasizing her slim figure on a statuesque frame. "Are you touched in your upper works? You need special equipment, like cork jackets, and experienced aeronauts for such a flight. Perhaps there was some miscommunication. My father did inform you this was a scientific balloon, right? I expected to take you up, then descend to drop you off—a regular paid ascension. Once on the ground, my father and his assistant will board. Then we can begin our experiments. We must hurry. Otherwise, we will land too far away for the flight to resume today."

He shook his head. "I do not wish to be dropped off. I am not like other men. How many bleaters paid for ascensions and then called off?"

She lifted a strong chin set on a pretty oval face. "Six."

"They all insisted on descending immediately?" He tied the draw line onto the rope rigging.

"Yes."

"Really? Well, I do not. I paid for this flight, so I expect to travel to France." He glanced ahead. "Since we are going in the right direction, you and I will have to make the flight together."

"No! Time is of the essence. The valve must be opened." She squinted her sky-blue eyes, like she was studying the best way to reach the draw line. Her breathing increased, and she noticeably swallowed. Leaning forward, as if to attack, she widened her stance. Her hard stare never wavered.

Her actions caught him off guard. He too began to pant, and he crouched in anticipation of repelling her charge. Under the circumstances, he found her opposition stimulating, and he stiffened in excitement. Who would move first? He returned her narrow-eyed stare.

She jumped forward to her left.

He leaped to his right.

At the last second, she dove past him on the other side and attempted to grab the draw line controlling the valve.

Picking her up by the waist, he carried her to the opposite end of the swaying basket then held her in place. "I paid your father to take me to France, and he cheerfully agreed. So when I let you go, you must not try to open the valve again."

Squirming earnestly to free herself, she only managed to turn sideways. "You're a madman."

"Beg pardon?"

"Who but a madman would…sing all the way up?"

"You expected me to cry?" He watched her eyes sparkle with ire and realized she was quite pretty. A Long Meg with her forehead currently furrowed in anger, her glare only emphasized an adorable button nose, while her almost-sneering mouth had the most delicious apple-red lips he had ever seen. The thought of sweet, angry apples made him want to taste her. So he instinctively leaned close, but then he remembered his manners. Besides, she smelled like chemicals, perhaps the gas used to inflate the balloon.

She struggled, but his grip held fast, so she stomped on his foot.

"Ow, you little hoyden. What did you do that for?"

"Let me go."

"Only if you keep your father's word and take me to France. Promise?"

She stilled, as if weighing her next response. "Don't our experiments take precedence, now that you know it's all just a *misunderstanding*?"

"You appear to be the only one suffering from a misunderstanding. In terms of your experiments, I'd be delighted to assist you. I'm sure, together, we can get the job done."

She inhaled sharply and paused. "Well...it is not appropriate that I travel without a chaperone, so we have to land. You do not want my reputation to be compromised?"

He glanced around from left to right.

"Answer the question, madman."

"Wait a minute, what a hum. You made ascensions with six other fellows. But your point is noted. I am a gentleman, so a chaperone is not required. Besides, you know full well no one can see us together up here. However, I give you my word that once we reach France, we will land in an empty field where we will not be seen. I'll then make arrangements for your return, and we can separate before anyone catches us together." He pointed eastward. "Onward to France."

"France! You really are a madman." She struggled to free herself, but to no avail. "This balloon is not an exploratory machine that just flies about, trying to break records." She glanced around her. "We have no equipment or instruments on board for such a long journey."

"But the crossing can be accomplished, correct? Last night I read all about balloons. Considering the elevations they can achieve and the fine weather today, we should be able to make it with ease. That Frenchman made the journey in just a couple of hours."

"You're a madman *and* a simpleton. The crossing to France is a major undertaking. There is a chance we could land in the Channel and perish. Father must have assumed you were liver-hearted, like everyone else, and would demand to land immediately. A journey to France is so farcical, he probably did not take you seriously."

"Sounds like your father has a little racket fleecing coves. A rapid ascent to scare a fellow to death, so he'll demand to land immediately?"

A blush appeared high on her cheeks. "He uses the money to pay for his research. As a dutiful daughter, I must do what he says." Her brows knit. "I'm curious, why are you in such a hurry? Why today? Why France?"

"I didn't know of the earl's challenges until yesterday." Boyce then explained the race and his hopes of winning multiple cups. "So, without enough time to arrange my own balloon, the only way I could triumph in several challenges was to hire a balloon already prepared for flight. I figure the intelligence, courage, and possibly sportsmanship cups are in the bag. Don't you?"

"No. A crash from lack of preparations is not very intelligent. And failing to consider the wishes of your companion is not very sportsmanlike." She glared up at him. "That Lady Sarah was right. There are no gentlemen left in London. The entire city must be populated by madmen. Now let me go."

"Now that's not very generous, is it, my daring miss?"

"Listen. Let's look at this situation logically." She paused, lifting a finely arched brow.

Boyce guessed she stopped because the wiseacre expected him to ask what the word *logically* meant. "Since you are a pretty miss dangling in my arms, enjoying my friendly embrace, you deserve a serenade too." Now, up here in this magnificent balloon, the wind whistling by in a steady melody, he could be himself and freely express—without being mocked— the happiness bubbling up from his toes. "Oh, but first let me introduce myself. My name is Lord Boyce Parker. I assume you are Miss Mountfloy. A pleasure to meet you."

She failed to answer and halfheartedly struggled to free herself from his grip.

"In your honor, let me think of a song where the last word rhymes with *floy*. Perhaps a refrain ending in the word *boy* or *toy*. Funny that, the only songs that come to mind at the moment are about candles alight, drummers, and drumsticks. Oh, beg pardon."

"No songs, please."

"Yes, yes, my sincere apologies."

"Listen. I've dedicated my life to helping my father collect important scientific data from the experiments performed during each flight. With these results, we can learn about the characteristics and behavior of our atmosphere. Future men of science will then have more reliable information with which to warn our populace when dangerous storms approach. Think, Lord Madman, we may *save humanity*."

Boyce lifted a brow. The young damsel believed this with all of her heart, so he had no intention of disrespecting her dream. Anyhow, he'd rather look at her cheeks. They had returned to that fine, pinkish sort of color that complemented the apple-red lips nicely.

"'Save humanity' might be an exaggeration," she said, "but science is important work. With data from our experiments, we hope to understand our weather, clouds, and the chemical properties of our atmosphere. So this balloon has a purpose. It is not just some easy convenience to complete the harum-scarum scheme of some bored nobleman."

"I've never been bored in my life."

"You know what I mean. Titled gentlemen who only consider themselves—spoiled, rich, foolish. I'll wager you spend most of your days swinging from your club's chandelier."

Even though Boyce had been guilty of this behavior when he was young, he refused to get vexed at the pretty package in his arms. Yes, he decided, he liked her very much. "How would a scientist define a chandelier *logically*? Must it have crystal drops?"

"You know what I mean. Drinking to excess and spending your days indoors, making foolish wagers, like black-beetle races."

"No, you're wrong. Piglets are nothing like black beetles, much faster."

"Hypothesis proved."

"Don't be so hard on your fellow man. I'm not bookish, like your father. Nor will I ever be a famous politician sitting in Lords, like my father. There are no wars, so I can never be a war hero, like my brother. Besides, I detest wars. How else can I achieve recognition and make a name for myself, my daring miss?" A wisp of her hair blew under his chin and repeatedly tickled it.

"I'm not your daring miss."

"My intelligent miss?"

"I'm not your intelligent miss."

He lifted her to direct eye level. "But those are all compliments. Don't tell me you prefer, my hoydenish cow?"

"Oh!"

"You really are very pretty. May I call you my pretty miss?"

"Pretty! I'm a-a lady of science." With renewed vigor, she struggled to escape his grip.

Boyce held tight, and it took some effort to keep her from breaking free, but he enjoyed the tussle. Like all women, her figure was an enchanting mixture of hard and soft in all the right places—hard in her heels, now kicking his ankles, and soft in her breasts, currently compressed under his forearms. He quickly learned she could gain no advantage if he held her in a firm hug and lifted her feet off the floor of the basket.

After a committed effort for a full minute to free herself, she stilled.

While she caught her breath, his hold relaxed. Her steadfast determination convinced him that if any lady could handle a historic crossing, and probably become the first female to reach France by balloon, it would be this one. "To guarantee a successful journey, I think you should be captain."

"Very well. Put me down."

One glance at her lips, and he became mesmerized by her pout.

She stared at him with an analyzing squint. "Why are you looking at me in that odd manner?"

After a moment of silence, he answered truthfully. "I'm hungry for an apple."

"This balloon is not fully loaded with the needed supplies to reach France, so no apples. No food at all for that matter. Since I understand young gentlemen have large appetites, I expect you to swoon with hunger at any minute. I insist you swoon over the side, and let me accomplish my experiments in peace." She glanced over at the boxes piled next to the birdcages. "Considering our circumstances, we lack the proper equipment for crossing the English Channel. We must descend after we finish the experiments. You can complete your havey-cavey journey some other time." More of her wavy brown hair escaped her plait, her cap tilted recklessly over one ear, and she still sported that delicious pout.

Overwhelmed by great affection for this plucky miss, he rocked her back and forth in his arms. "I have biscuits if we get hungry, and since the ground is speeding by, I'm sure we're halfway there already."

"Paris must be three hundred miles from where we started."

"I don't expect you to land us in front of Notre-Dame. Just over the Channel will do. What's that, a hundred miles? You don't want to deprive me of my chance at recognition."

"My pleasure, sir."

"So you're going to be troublesome, eh? I will give you two choices. First, I can hold you in my arms all the way across the Channel. Once over French soil, I will release you, and we can descend. This is a fetching, warm, and satisfactory choice as far as I'm concerned. Or you can pick choice number two. I can let you go now, and we can complete the experiments that are so important to humanity. Of course, your release is dependent upon the condition you promise to cross over to France. The choice is yours. Remain in my warm, friendly arms, or save humanity. Well?"

Three

LIKE EVERY PERSON OF SCIENCE WHO DEPENDED UPON logic to make their decisions, Eve Mountfloy considered the variables and weighed the possible consequences. The results fell into two groups: choice number one or number choice two.

Choice number one, she could remain a hostage in his arms. As the gas eventually escaped the silk balloon, they would slowly descend. But how long would that take? After another peek at his face, she noticed his lips sported a soft yet seductive smile. She inhaled deeply.

The problem with the hostage choice was that the madman holding her was the most attractive young gentleman she had ever seen, much less spoken to. While she was a gentleman's daughter, he was a titled aristocrat—a lord no less. Indeed, if she had to classify him, it would be as a much-admired male specimen sometimes called a "Tulip of the Goes." So if she wanted to spend time in the agreeable embrace of a cream of the fashionables, this was her chance. Because in reality, Tulips rarely noticed plain, bookish women like herself.

She stole another peek. This time his raised brow created an expectant expression. Due to their current altitude, his cheeks and nose were flushed, but that hardly detracted from his handsome face. A hint of masculine whisker growth gave him a rugged countenance, while his somewhat long sable hair had become completely disheveled. She gulped and told herself the altitude must have dried her throat.

Stop dreaming and focus.

Choice number one—to remain in his arms—did have some pleasing aspects, she had to admit. However, she would not be able to complete the experiments planned for this flight.

Next, she considered choice number two: agree to his tomfool plan but secretly change the conditions and only *pretend* to cross the Channel. This choice allowed her to complete the experiments, a definite advantage. Once she collected the data, she'd double-cross him and open the valve while he was not looking, so they could safely land in England. She glanced over to the draw line tied to the rigging. How long would it take for the gas to escape, and would the hissing gas and rapid descent avoid his detection? Of course, their descent must not be too fast, but slow enough to land gently, so as not to dash their brains against a tree.

The wind blew the madman's curls around in a mesmerizing manner, except for one perfect curl that found refuge on his cheek. She sighed over her crazy urge to softly stroke this protected curl. *Stop daydreaming and use logic.* She dragged her mind back to concentrate on the problem before her.

A new choice—number three—entered her mind.

If she continued on to France, she would become the first woman, and perhaps the first person born in England, to complete the crossing. Considering the two men that had crossed the Channel together in 1784, Blanchard was born in France and Jeffries in America. That crossing took two and a half hours, and they had suffered problems once they neared France, but Eve had confidence in her newer, more modern balloon. The odds also seemed to be in their favor, because of unusually warm weather and a significant breeze. Unless the wind died altogether, they'd reach France before nightfall. Besides, if successful, her father would likely receive the needed funds to complete his experiments for many years to come. This meant he would also cease his demands for her to frighten respectable ladies and gentlemen using overly rapid ascents. However, she had no experience in long-distance balloon flights, so choice three was risky and dangerous. She rejected this choice and labeled it a product of silly dreams and vaulting ambition, an unrealistic goal for a female in her situation.

Eve decided on choice number two. While she had no idea how she might double-cross him and land before they reached the Channel, she would think of something later—some action more cunning than bludgeoning him until he became unconscious. She took a deep breath and answered her blackmailer's question. "The only choice is to save humanity."

He flashed a broad smile for a second. "Yes, yes, France, here we come. I am going to release you now, so no tricks."

She returned his smile with great artifice and batted her eyelashes.

"I like you." He opened his embrace to release her.

This might have been easier than she had expected because of his trusting nature. Perhaps when the time came, she could tie him up with a rope before he caught on to her purpose. The box in the corner contained sufficient rope, so to be prepared, she must remember to casually remove it. The mental image of this Tulip trussed up made her gulp again.

Remember your goal is to save humanity.

She knelt to take several barometer readings. "My calculations indicate we are currently at an altitude of five thousand, two hundred feet."

He peered ahead. "So that's the address of clouds."

She grinned and pulled on the line to open the valve, so they could descend to four thousand feet, the predetermined altitude for the experiments to begin. After tying the line to the balloon's harness, she sat on a low seat and faced him. "Our first experiment will examine the capacity of air at this elevation to maintain flight. I mean normal flight—without a gas balloon. To accomplish this goal, we have cages containing various birds of different weights and wing lengths. So to test the thickness of the air, we will release each bird. If the air is too thin, they will not be able to fly. With multiple testing at many altitudes, men of science can discover the correct ratio of wing length to weight necessary for flight at various elevations. Your job will be to help me observe if the bird is able to fly away or if it falls. If the bird falls, it will be important to determine whether or not they are flapping their wings to limit their descent."

Turning sideways, he glanced at the cages. "Please let me do it. You can watch me."

"No." She placed her hand on a wicker cage. "My father designed these experiments carefully. I must follow the experimental design precisely." Opening the wooden box, she pulled out a piece of rope and big ledger book. Green leather covered the book's boards and on the front the word *Results,* embellished in gold letters, glinted in the sun. "This book is the most important item we have on board. All of the data we have collected this year is contained in this book. After our planned experiments are completed, my father and I will use the information to advance our knowledge of the air, and maybe even increase the accuracy of predicting England's weather. With routine storm prediction, many lives could be saved."

"How exactly? I mean, when the rain falls on my nose, I'm not likely to die."

She wondered if he understood the uncertain threats many people lived with every day—farmers, sailors, people other than Tulips. "My father and I started our experimentation after my brother's death. Tom was returning home from Gibraltar after the war. A nasty gale struck, and his ship foundered on the rocks." She glanced over to discover true empathy in his countenance, a soft knowing in his green eyes. Perhaps reality was not a stranger to him, and he too at one time had lost a loved one. She drew a deep breath. "Twenty lives were lost. I was six years old. I don't remember him exactly but…" A wave of fragmented memories overwhelmed her. She closed her eyes, leaned her head against the rough wicker, and recalled Tom's last farewell.

Boyce remained silent.

Several minutes passed, the only sound being the soft wind and the creaking basket.

"I know why you hold your arms that way," he whispered.

She opened her eyes and noticed she had held her arms slightly out to the side. "I didn't realize... Why?"

"When you remember Tom, what is he doing?"

She thought for a moment and remembered Tom bursting through the front door, his arms held wide ready to pick her up. "He's rushing toward me to give me a hug."

"I lost my mother years ago. Now, whenever I remember her, I first see her when I was little, leaning forward to pick me up for a kiss. We instinctively open our arms for the embrace that will never come."

She smiled wistfully at the meaning behind her gesture. "I guess holding them out in anticipation of a promised hug keeps their memory alive."

"Tom sounds like a nice fellow."

"Yes, he was." Even though the high altitude had dried her eyes, she felt tears gathering. "My father and I dedicated our lives to helping others avoid the same tragedy."

His hand stilled on the duck's cage, and he turned to face her. "I apologize, Miss Mountfloy. I did not know about the motives behind your research before now. Seems we both have sufficient reasons to continue. Don't we?"

The Tulip smiled. A charming gesture probably common to Tulips.

Nevertheless, she couldn't help but smile in return. Except, for some illogical reason, he believed the motives behind a silly challenge were equal to hers. Of course, he might be in love with Lady Sarah; that would explain his drive. But to Eve, no challenge could be more important than saving lives. "Imagine the importance of our research. When a storm brews, we can recognize the type of clouds formed. This, combined with other types of data, such as barometer readings and the behavior of air currents, will helps us be able to predict the severity of the storm. Ships can then be warned to remain at sea, or people on land advised to seek shelter. Thousands of people at one time may be saved. So now you know what I meant by saving humanity. Not nearly as important as, let's say…chasing a fortune."

He blinked—twice. "I don't need a fortune. I want to distinguish myself by besting the other gentlemen in this race. The winner's story will be published in the papers, and my father will no doubt read it. I will no longer be the cork-brained youngest son, and he'll have to respect me for my achievements." Pausing for a moment, his lightheartedness returned. "Anyhow, at the end of the race, one of the competitors and Lady Sarah will fall in love, and if that man is me, all the better. I promise to be the best of husbands. And she probably needs me right now without knowing it yet. So saving humanity means the chance to save every family, doesn't it?"

The madman spoke about love and family—unusual

for a gentleman of such short acquaintance. She suspected she might be dealing with a rare male specimen. Perhaps there was an undiscovered depth of character lurking under those jesting green eyes. Maybe the amiable, charming Tulip was a fabricated facade, one meant to hide his sharp intelligence and true heart. *If so*, she wondered, *why the deception?* "By the words 'every family,' do you mean saving future families too?"

He slapped her on the back. "Yes, yes, you understand me. Ladies of science are impressive. Are there other ladies like you interested in science?"

Eve ignored him. Their altitude had not changed considerably, the sun was still high, and only a few cumulus clouds dotted the sky. However, the once-steady wind had lessened. If the wind dropped even more, they might have to land before the experiments were completed. "Yes, there are other female natural philosophers and chemists. Not many, I grant, but some have made significant discoveries. I'm not really one of these ladies though, since my father designs the experiments. I study his books in hopes of one day learning the scholarship necessary to plan them. Besides, females are normally expected to assist men of science or instruct others upon scientific principles. For example, one of my great inspirations is the famous author Mrs. Marcet. Have you heard of her?"

"No, is she a member of the *ton*? Would I find her at Court or Almack's?"

The mental picture of the brilliant Mrs. Marcet conversing with the illustrious toadeaters at Almack's elicited a chuckle.

"Wait. Give me a chance. The Royal Society of London?"

"A good guess, but no. Mrs. Marcet is a wife, mother, and inspiration to all who study science—not just women. I am sure every young person interested in chemistry or natural philosophy is reading her books now. In the future, I'll wager one of her students will become the world's greatest chemist. That is how influential her books are."

"Books." He rubbed his chin. "I publish books. Learned all about the editing business at my brother's publishing house. Found it a great deal of fun. In five years, I've published all sorts of books, comedies, handbooks, songs. I first published a book written by two of my old school friends and even wrote one myself. Although my father was not pleased…" He paused. "No, he was not pleased."

"Really? What is the title of your book? Maybe I have read it."

He was no longer looking at her directly. "No, no, I am sure you have not. Just a limited distribution of a small tome of comical songs."

"I like songs."

"Um, songs for gents."

"Oh."

His cheeks sported a rosy blush, a lovely contrast to the shadow of dark whiskers. "Continue. Tell me about our clever wife and mother. Maybe I've read her books."

"Because she is a woman, she originally published her books anonymously, but now she is recognized as the author of my favorite book, titled *Conversations on Chemistry*. Have you read it?"

The Tulip tugged on his cravat. "Well, no. It doesn't sound like a page-turner. What's the book about? Are there knights a jousting?" He leaned close and whispered, "A lady reclining on a pile of skulls hears a noise behind her. What could it be?"

"Oh." His vivid imagination made her stare at his dark whisker growth—not a beard, more like a roughness that demanded experimental touch—and she wanted to touch. She glared at him for having such an alluring chin. "Mrs. Marcet's book is a hypothetical conversation between a teacher, named Mrs. B., and two students, Emily and Caroline. The girls pose basic questions many of us would ask, then Mrs. B. answers them. A simple format that proves to be an effective instructional tool, in fact—"

"Yes, yes. Let's get to it." He grabbed the cage with a crow inside.

Why did he ask the question if he didn't want to hear the answer? She dug through the wooden chest, looking for a pencil, mumbling, "In some animal societies, they abandon males at birth."

"Pardon?"

She grabbed the pencil then faced him. "Your society is delightful because of your mirth."

He widened those striking green eyes. "I might have deserved that."

She laughed and then realized it was her first laughter of the day.

"But you must forgive me," he said. "I truly am excited about starting."

Actually, with all of the preparations and tension that normally came with making the arrangements for a flight, this was the first time she had laughed all week. "I'm sorry. I too am excited to begin. Now stand over there by the harness. That way I will have enough room to release the birds, and you will be in a good position to help me observe their flight. After they are released, I will write our observations down in the *Results* book. Ready?"

He stepped to his assigned position. Two seconds later, he returned to her side and mimicked her every move. "This is so thrilling. We could make a big discovery too, right?"

"Yes, any trip may find an important discovery. Our results today may even advance our understanding of many of nature's secrets." She elbowed him out of her way. The wind had died a little within the last fifteen minutes, making it imperative that she do her experiments before the day's fine weather changed. She examined the barometer and calculated they had lost one hundred feet, so she released some ballast to gain altitude. The madman, to his credit, did not speak, but he continued to shadow her every move. All she had to do to complete her tasks was ignore him. Once her pencil and the *Results* book were at the ready on a small bench, she grabbed the cage with a large, black crow. "This fellow was hard to capture, believe me. I am going to remove him now. Are you in position?"

"Right ho!" He jumped to his place by the harness, and the sway created by his vigorous movement caused them both to clutch the side of the basket.

She fought to restrain the large wings of the black bird and not fall overboard. "Ow."

He rushed to her side. "You need my assistance. Let me help."

The bird had pecked—rather hard—on her arm, leaving her all too pleased to hand over the struggling crow into his capable grip. His height also gave him an advantage with the troublesome bird, and she was secretly glad of his assistance. "I think, under the circumstances, it would be best if you release all of the animals, while I record the results." She sat on the bench, opened the *Results* book, and clasped her pencil. "Ready?"

"Yes, yes." He tossed the crow up in the air.

The bird immediately flapped his wings and flew about twenty feet before turning to fly in a large circle. After four leisurely circles, the crow dove and was quickly out of sight.

She started writing her observations in the *Results* book.

"Shall I tell you what I saw now?"

Glancing up from her entry, she noticed his knees, clad in butter-colored buckskins, directly in front of her. "Once I finish writing our observations of the crow's behavior, we need to continue these experiments while our altitude remains steady." She caught his fallen expression and soft sigh. "Very well, tell me what you saw."

"Bless your bonnet." He proceeded to eagerly describe the crow's descent using unscientific, emotional words like "bravery."

She duly wrote them down in the book.

When he finished, he took the next cage, reached in, and carefully grabbed a small sparrow. "Hallo, little brown bird. Come, come. Time to fly away home."

"Don't get too close to the edge. A Frenchman once tossed a goat overboard, lost his balance, and fell out of the balloon."

"That Frenchman got what he deserved. Goats cannot fly." He crouched, stiffened his gait, and slowly approached the side. "Are you watching?"

"Yes."

He tossed the sparrow out in front of him.

All she saw was a dark-colored streak against white clouds. "What did you see?"

Turning to face her, his happy countenance had disappeared. "I was too busy worrying about the edge of the basket. I'm sorry. Please forgive me." He dropped his head slightly. "Is there any way I can make amends?"

She smiled and recalculated her opinion of him. He did have a good heart. From now on, she'd try to think of him not like a fashionable Tulip or a fearless madman, but more like an attractive puppy named Parker—a creature too adorable for her to look away. "I think you are doing fine. The important thing is to note our mistakes in the *Results* book and continue forward. So next up is the pigeon."

He smiled in penitent gratitude. "Thank you. I must admit I am having fun." He carried the pigeon's cage over to the bench, opened the top, then grabbed the bird. "Coo coo."

Eve turned to a new page, then noted the time and altitude. "Ready."

"Watching me?"

"I'm watching the pigeon." However, if she was completely honest, a good part of the time was spent admiring his overall appearance. He had wide shoulders on top of a slim, straight figure. His woolen clothes appeared expensive, serviceable, and tailored to perfection. Even now, after a wild ascension and tussle for the draw line, his outfit remained spotless and in proper order.

He tossed the bird about a foot above his reach.

The pigeon flapped his wings and began to fly. The bird's wings beat furiously as it moved away, his altitude slowly sinking. Within a minute, the pigeon sunk below the bottom of the basket.

She noted this in the *Results* book. Then on the next page, she discovered her father had written specific questions in regard to each bird. Since birds made various types of sounds, he had made a reminder to describe the noises made after each bird's release. She hadn't heard anything remarkable, so she asked Parker. "My father has written a question here. Did the pigeon coo at all, or make any other noise?"

He spun to face her. "You jest! That bird was too busy trying to fly."

"I will note your observations."

"Miss Mountfloy?" He placed both hands on his hips. She looked up from her notes. "Yes."

"What happens to these birds? I mean we have crows on the estate, and they really are fine birds—smart too. Well, that pigeon was frightened, and I don't blame the fellow. I know our efforts will gather information to save humanity, but do these birds live after they are released from a balloon, or will we never know?"

He was obviously concerned, so she replied to the

best of her ability. "I don't have a definite answer to your question. But our theory, and the evidence so far, is that they regain the ability to fly once they leave the rarefied atmosphere, and the air becomes thick again."

He sighed in relief. "Thank heavens. Mr. Pigeon should be home by nightfall. Right, next up?"

"Next is our final bird, the duck."

"Never understood why my father loves to shoot God's flying creatures. I mean the man can shoot ducks all day long. When I was young, he invited me to keep him company. I didn't mind, really. Being the youngest of eight sons, it's nice to feel needed." He grabbed the duck, and the bird quacked in protest. "Right, little fellow. Thanks for saving humanity. Ready?"

The duck quacked his answer.

Eve was not ready. His physical charms, while substantive, were no match to the allure of his kind, open manners. So she forgave him for restraining her after their ascent. She also had no doubts that, in his father's presence, he'd rather serenade the ducks than shoot them. She chuckled softly but stopped after realizing she might have a pang of regret when she let out the gas to double-cross him. "I'm ready now."

In one smooth movement, he tossed the duck into the air, then leaned over the side.

Since she missed the duck in flight, the bird must have fallen. "Well?"

"Dropped like a stone." He shook his head.

She noted that fact in the *Results* book. "The duck precipitated to the ground."

"Huh? The duck was—*is*—a feeling animal, not a variable."

She ignored him. "My father has written here if the duck quacked with apparent satisfaction?"

"Apparent satisfaction?" he yelled. "No! He quacked in frustration. He quacked from the cold. He quacked his bill off. He quacked, 'Help, I'm falling!'"

She wagged her finger at him. "That is not logical. You don't speak duck. I will make a note that he quacked."

He stomped up to her, causing them both to clutch the sides of the swinging basket. "Do you speak duck?"

"No. Do you?"

"Yes, and the duck quacked emotionally, not logically. So I repeated exactly what the duck said." He pointed his finger at the book. "Now write that down."

"Very well." Eve finished a notation about his belief in the duck's feelings. When finished with her entry, she noticed him leaning over the edge of the basket, perhaps looking for the duck. "Ready for the next one?"

He turned to face her. "What? The duck was the last birdcage."

She pointed to several small tightly woven baskets near the boxes. "In those small cages, you will find a bee, and in the other, a butterfly. Once we test those, we have completed this batch of experiments. Later we can perform tests that include taking air samples and tasting spices. Once in the laboratory, we will compare the animals' ability to fly with the amount of oxygen in the atmosphere at various elevations." While she waited for him to collect the cages, she checked the hygrometer, both the wet and dry thermometer, and the barometer. She then noted several observations about the clouds at their present elevation and temperature.

After moving the larger boxes aside, he pulled out the two little baskets. He peeked inside one and turned to face her. "This is the bee. Ready?"

"Ready." He lifted the top, and the bee flew upward out of the basket only to quickly disappear into the thin air.

He continued to scan the heavens for several minutes before addressing her. "Did you hear him? He definitely hummed, but I don't speak bee, so write down what you will."

"Thank you." She made a notation about the bee's audible hum. "We're almost finished. I'm ready for the butterfly now."

He found the last small basket and held it close to the edge. Then leaning over until his lips almost touched it, he spoke to the butterfly. "I've watched you in wonderment many times floating through the air, wishing I too had the freedom to fly. Now that I have joined you moving on a breeze, it's even better than I had dreamed. Safe travel, my friend." He opened the lid, and the butterfly rose into the air.

The animal must have decided to remain with his new friend, because it flew down close to the floor of the balloon. The butterfly then circled a few times before landing on an empty cage.

"I don't blame you," he said. "You just sit tight, and before you know it, we'll be in France. I'm sure you will like France, little one."

She gasped. The pigeon had somehow returned and

was perched on the edge of the basket. "Look!" She pointed to the bird.

Once he caught sight of the pigeon, he slapped his knee and laughed.

Somewhere deep inside her, floodgates opened, and she laughed like a madman too. Couldn't stop it if she tried. His pure gaiety brought out the longest laugh she could remember.

He stepped close and put one arm around her shoulder. "We really must capture the fellow so he'll be safe."

She waved her hand. "The pigeon's fine right where he is."

His laughter stopped, and he stepped away, pointing to the bird. "But he might be like the duck and fall."

"Let the pigeon choose. Why don't you leave the cage open? Maybe he will return by himself."

He piled the cages into a row and opened all of the doors, giving the bird every opportunity to find shelter. "Now that we have completed these experiments, you must agree to be my witness. My assistance with the birds surely meets the definition of Service to a Lady. I know Lady Sarah will appreciate my efforts. Not to mention my father will be impressed."

The catch in his voice when he spoke of his father surprised her. "I'm sure your father is impressed with you. How could he not be?"

"Thank you." He flashed a wry grin. "Got all the prizes at school, never spent my evenings foxed or in the arms of a housemaid. Some of my other brothers were experts in that regard. But when Richard returned from America a big hero, my father now speaks of no one else. Richard is the favorite son, and he ignores the seven remaining sons. Especially me, on account of…"

Her throat seized, and she bit her lower lip. How could she possibly bludgeon him now or even tie him up for that matter? She had waited too long and had grown fond of him. No longer could she even consider double-crossing him. It appeared that her best option was to land the balloon now. Otherwise, she'd have to accept the risk, try to ignore any thoughts of glory, and continue onward to France.

After checking her instruments, she calculated their elevation, estimated their speed, and examined the status of the shimmering balloon above them. While she did her work, he stood with his gaze fixed on the pigeon and waving an arm toward the cage, obviously inviting the bird to return.

"Parker, as captain, I must tell you that this is a good time for us to land. I hope you have reconsidered your journey to France today."

He dropped his jaw. "No! Of course not. I bet we are almost there, right?"

She paused and decided she needed more current data to evaluate the dangers of attempting to reach the shores of France. She then took measurements and discovered that they were over the plains of Kent and would be reaching the coast soon. The sun hung low in the sky, and the light wind would probably propel them to France before darkness fell. Since the temperature was tolerable at their current elevation, if she gained altitude, they would reach France sooner. Except higher elevations meant colder temperatures, so she calculated the possible temperatures at various elevations using one degree per four thousand feet—not exact calculations, but adequate to make a decision. She then chose the highest elevation that matched an acceptable temperature. Aeronauts routinely huddled to retain warmth, and she wondered if Parker could efficiently huddle. Huddle with a Tulip…

Stop. Do not attempt dangerous calculations.

She made sure she did not glance his way, so her decision did not suffer bias by his warmhearted personality or his attractive person. She then asked herself for an honest evaluation of their chances of success. Unfortunately, she had enough experience to easily answer her own question. History proved anything could happen. In the worst case, the wind could die or change directions, the balloon could rent, and the weather, which had been exceptional up to this point, might change into a violent storm.

Upon further evaluation of the serious dangers ahead, if the wind died during the night, they might never reach the shores of France alive. The gas would condense in the cold night air, causing the balloon to lose altitude and crash into the ocean. Once they were in cold water, their survival would be measured in minutes, unless they could be rescued by a boat. What were the chances of a boat about at night, much less witnessing their crash in the dark?

However, on the bright side, after Major Money's rescue in 1785, cutters that normally rescued mariners now followed balloons out to sea. The major's balloon lost its lift, and he spent hours in the North Sea. A cutter that headed in the direction of his flight, followed him, and saved his life. She glanced up. Her balloon still had plenty of lift, the light wind remained steady, and the day continued to be an unusually warm one. Considering all of these facts, she gained the conviction they would eventually succeed and reach France.

Parker, her all-too-handsome passenger, stood in front of the pigeon and cooed softly.

She chuckled to herself. *A coo really is a lovely sound.* If he could speak duck, maybe he could speak pigeon as well. The thought of disappointing him now seemed unbearable. Besides, there was every indication his resolve to reach France had remained steadfast, so he'd probably tie *her* up if she tried to descend. Nevertheless, she explained the hazards of their current situation. "Knowing we may perish in the cold ocean, do you still want to continue?"

After an examination of the heavens and the balloon, he hesitated, a soft empathy filling his emerald eyes. "Yes, I acknowledge your concerns and the dangers ahead. I take full responsibility for our journey, but I just have this feeling that we will reach the shores of France safely."

The pigeon took two hops down into its old cage.

"Ha," he said, closing the cage door. "You were right, my smart miss. I have every confidence your abilities will guarantee our success. So what do we do now?"

Eve stared at the golden tips on the gray clouds ahead. "Pray the wind holds."

Four

BOYCE MOVED THE PIGEON TO THE END OF THE BAL-
loon's basket and stacked several boxes in front of the
bird's cage. This would provide a shield from the cold
wind after they gained altitude. He wondered how
much higher she intended to go. "What elevation are
you aiming for?"

She cut a bag of sand and straightened to face him.
"I estimate six thousand feet. That elevation should be
high enough to clear the Channel at our current trajectory. Unfortunately, the wind might alter direction
or fall off completely. Even with blue skies, a troublesome storm can brew within an hour. Success will
also depend upon where we cross. A crossing further
north is considerably wider and will take longer than
if we cross near Dover. Still, my calculations indicate
we have plenty of ballast for our descent, unless the
conditions become steadily worse."

Boyce wondered why females had such an uncom-
mon affinity with drama. Last week, one young miss
had sought his opinion upon a new puce ribbon
trimming her best bonnet. Now any gentleman alive

would naturally condemn a puce ribbon, but seconds after his judgment escaped, the young lady indulged in a fit of hand waving, palpitations, and some disorder involving the nerves. He quickly admitted he must have been mistaken—the light insufficient—and the drama ended. In the future, he vowed to be more circumspect on the subject of ribbons.

Now he watched the pretty female standing before him warning of the dangers ahead, but her emphatic life-or-death concerns sounded like another example of drama. So far, their balloon adventure had provided the most exciting moments of his life, the trip easier than planned. Nothing about the balloon seemed amiss. The glorious sky remained mostly cloudless, and the wind continued to propel them in the right direction. He harbored not the slightest apprehension of their fate. They would likely reach France in a few hours, perhaps just after the sun set.

Still, this female was vastly different from the usual young miss of his acquaintance. So were her warnings wise words or another example of feminine drama? But then how many females of his acquaintance used words like *estimate* and *calculations*? Come to think of it, he was not sure *he* had ever used them. "Eh, why do we need ballast? I thought releasing sand made you go up."

She turned to face him, the alluring apple–pout hanging on her lips. "When the air cools after sunset, the gas compresses, and we lose lift. So imagine you are in a rapid descent. Below is the ocean..." She crossed both arms. "No, for our piece of mind, let's say a village next to a lake. The basket lands safe enough on a street, but since the balloon is not yet fully deflated, the wind catches it and propels it forward. Now with the speed of a team of four at full gallop, you are being dragged toward the lake, beaten and bruised along the way. Don't you think it would be quite nice to drop some ballast and gain altitude to make it over the water, then travel whatever distance is necessary to find an open field to safely land?"

"Now that you mention it, I would indeed prefer avoiding that fate. This is a fine coat, and I'd hate to see it ruined."

She kneeled to take readings from her instruments. Boyce noticed her frown, take measurements, frown, glance at him, and frown again. To deserve so many frowns, you would think he had kicked a doe-eyed puppy. He leaned over to watch the sand dribble out of the cut ballast sack.

"Oh, look," she shouted. "Parhelia. Wonderful!"

He straightened to face the brilliant sunlight from just above the horizon. Before him three suns beamed in radiant splendor. One big sun and two smaller suns, but the two side suns shone like suns, nevertheless. The two little ones had luminous arcs of light beaming from the top and bottom. "I've never seen these other suns before. Yes, yes, how wonderful. Is this some sun secret people of science know all about, but have not informed the public? I'll wager it is. Imagine the romance of three sunsets. I must come up with a song to celebrate three suns. Let me think…"

Miss Mountfloy looked up at the extraordinary sight before them. Grabbing the sextant, she held it up to her eye before starting to scribble in the *Results* book. Then more instruments were pointed at the suns and mumbled over. "Three degrees…twenty-two degrees, I thought so."

"I wonder if a fellow can get three shadows from three suns?" It seemed an exciting idea, so he spun around to examine the side of the basket. A hint of his shadow appeared upon the rough wicker, but he could not determine if they were three separate shadows. "My soul is warmed by the glorious sun, sun, sun—"

"Enough. Do you always sing with the least provocation?"

"I'm sorry, but this is big, happy provocation, if you ask me. Have you ever seen this before? Isn't this a beautiful sight?"

She wagged a finger. "Each sun on the side is officially called a *parhelion*. Two are usually seen and the plural term is *parhelia*. Most people call them a mock sun or sun dog. They are rare and believed to be caused by the sunlight refracted by ice crystals in the atmosphere. The crystal shape—"

"Wait! That Shakespeare fellow saw multiple suns. In one of those Henry plays—there really are *too* many Henry plays, don't you think?—Shakespeare said, 'Dazzle mine eyes, or do I see three suns?' Maybe I got that wrong? Even so, I bet this is an important discovery."

She smiled and almost reached the point of laughter. "Yes, you are right. Parhelia are a rare phenomenon. Moreover, I seem to remember there is some disagreement about the distance from the sun, the lengths of the arcs, and the exact colors observed. I can't wait to present my observations in a letter to the Royal Society."

"You present data to people—aloud?"

"No, not me." She shrugged her shoulders. "My father and I will present our observations first in a letter to the Royal Society, or perhaps a journal like *Newton's Journal of Arts and Sciences*. With any luck, our letter will be published. I cannot present my observations in person, because women rarely address scientific institutions."

His heartbeat escalated. "Will they invite me to speak? My father will be impressed if I give a scientific speech before a learned institution." He could even visualize himself standing on a dais, his audience hanging upon his every word, an unseen laurel crown held high above his head. "If I give the speech, you can tell me the important scientific bits, and I can give the speech for you. All with your approval, of course."

"I don't know what my father will say about that."

"He must agree. I have seen the sun dogs in person, and he hasn't."

"Firsthand observation is an important point."

"This calls for a celebration." He took both of her hands and pulled her forward to dance a little jig.

She watched him perform a few steps, then she too joined in with a couple of hesitant steps.

The balloon swayed more dramatically than ever before, so they immediately stopped dancing. "We'll dance a jig when we land," he said. "Or maybe now, but not so vigorously?"

She grinned before returning to her instruments. "Please excuse me from further celebrations. I must immediately record the conditions when the suns were observed." After she finished jotting down her notes in the *Results* book, she reached into her coat pocket and withdrew a few feathers. These were tossed into the air, then studied as they sailed up and over the edge of the balloon. The wind had dropped off, so she made a note. When finished, she moved to stand beside him.

His spirits became uncommonly light, and together they watched the two extra suns shrink and fade, their tails of light fading with the approach of sunset. The day's end gave him a new sense of joyous calm. All was right with the world, and tomorrow could only be better. He slipped his arm around her shoulder and was mildly surprised when she did not pull away.

They stood and witnessed the sky change from blue, to orange, and finally to gray. They remained side by side until nightfall, when the stars began to reveal their presence.

He sighed. For one of the few times in his life, a song would only interrupt his feeling of calm bliss. "Have you ever seen anything so fine? The stars are like living sparks tossed upon an inky vault."

Her nose gained a few wrinkles on the top. "Stars appear a bright white in rarefied air, and the atmosphere appears a darker black."

"White, black? No, no, you're wrong." He swung his free arm in a wide arc. "Living sparks floating upward to heaven through the abyss of an inky vault."

"I believe my statement contained factual information—white stars, black sky."

He gave her a one-arm hug. "You need to learn how to sing."

"I can sing, thank you." Pulling free from his

embrace, she rummaged in one of the wooden boxes, and lifted out a patent safety lamp and a thick oilcloth lined with wool. She tossed him the oilcloth, then lit the lamp.

"Really," he said, "I am not cold. Well, I am cold, but dash it all, the blanket goes to the lady."

She sat and the finger-pointing returned. "Listen. Our chances of survival improve if we keep warm. If your hands get cold, you will not be able to hold on to a rope thrown by your rescuers. And if your whole body gets too cold, you will expire."

"Expire." He exhaled. "Right, but I still refuse. The blanket goes to the lady first."

This time she let out a loud and protracted sigh. "Do you know how to huddle?"

After their shared experience of that lovely sunset, he had become so fond of his plucky miss, he would enjoy the chance to embrace her in a huddle. "Yes, yes, I can huddle, snuggle, cuddle, and nuzzle. Indeed, I am particularly good at all of those."

"I don't need you to do all of those—especially nuzzle. Just a simple huddle will be satisfactory." She sat on the floor of the basket and arranged the oilcloth around her shoulders.

He pulled a wool hunting cap from his sack, covered his head, and sat next to her. "What exactly is the nature of huddling? I mean scientific huddling, of course."

She cleared her throat. "Sorry. Hoarse. It's the altitude, you understand."

"Yes, my throat is dry too. Not to mention my nose. Funny thing noses. I know a song—"

"No songs, please. If we reach France safely, even I will sing with you."

"We would make such a pretty duet—"

"This is important. To huddle effectively, people must maximize bodily contact and minimize the air spaces between them. Also, it is best if your limbs are brought in close to your chest or under you. In other words, sit in the smallest ball possible next to me, our shoulders touching."

"But wouldn't one big ball of us both be better?" Nothing would have made him happier now than holding her in a warm, friendly hug.

Her blue eyes resembled large, dark orbs. "Yes, but—"

"Come sit in front of me, and I'll wrap my arms around you." He'd hold her and have a chance to physically demonstrate his fondness and gratitude.

She gulped. "It would not be proper to—"

He whispered into her ear. "I can confirm, my pretty miss, that pigeons do not tittle-tattle and can keep secrets. Besides, unlike the language of duck, no human can speak pigeon. So it would be difficult for the pigeon to start a scandalous *on dit*."

She bit her upper lip to stifle a laugh, but then she gave him a brilliant smile.

Her restrained gaiety filled his heart with affection. Her nose and ears were red, so she must have been very cold, but she had not complained. And now with her vibrant smile, he noticed a dimple for the first time. Nothing more alluring than dimples, even a cold one. He leaned over and kissed her cheek.

She gasped. "I realize, under the circumstances,

proper behavior is difficult, but let us try to observe the proprieties. Call me Miss Mountfloy, please. I'll call you…Parker. Is that acceptable?"

"My friends call me…" He gulped. His friends called him "Whip." An obscure joke made by schoolboys, but he did not want her lovely—now pale—lips to call him that nickname. He certainly was not going to tell her that London's newspapers had once called him "Piglet Parker."

Her head was cocked to the side, waiting for his answer.

"You are the captain, so you choose. Parker, Boyce, Madman—I will answer to them all." He stood and looked down at her. "I must get the pigeon. He will want to huddle too." He moved to the far side of the basket and reached for the pigeon's cage. Then he noticed the butterfly. It was no longer resting on one of the boxes, but lay lifeless on the floor. Its pale yellow wings were folded on top of each another. Boyce carefully picked up the little creature. Now he felt very low. If he had not insisted upon this journey to France, this little fellow would be settling in for the night on top of some big, shiny, green leaf. He tapped a wing gently to see if it would move, but it remained still. He sighed and carried the butterfly to the edge of the basket. "Farewell." The breeze caught the little creature and lifted it from his palm. The butterfly disappeared into the night.

"What are you doing?" she asked.

After grabbing the pigeon's cage, he returned to her side. "The butterfly is dead." He couldn't help but wonder how their journey would end. His ambition had brought them up here, and there would be consequences to his decision. Hopefully, their future would be nothing like the butterfly's. He sat next to her and patted the floor in front of him.

Following a second of hesitation, she moved to sit in the space between his legs and twisted to arrange the oilcloth around both shoulders. Then she settled back upon his chest. "Remind me to record the animal's death tomorrow."

He pulled the pigeon close. "My fault the butterfly died." He draped a corner of the oilcloth over the pigeon's cage and took a deep breath. "Miss Mountfloy, I owe you an apology. In my excitement to succeed, I clearly was not thinking properly. I should never have attempted this tomfool plan. Without a doubt, you were right. We should have landed after the experiments were finished." He stared up at the dark shadow of the balloon overhead. "If your warnings come to pass and something happens, I will become a famous Lord Parker, but once again, for all of the wrong reasons. You have to believe me. I meant you no harm. Please forgive me."

She twisted to face him. "After we lifted off the ground, I suppose neither one of us contemplated our actions very deeply. Or if we did, we were blinded by the allure of success. I agreed to the journey too, remember? I guess being the first female to cross the English Channel appealed to me. You know…bask in the fame. Perhaps that fame would earn us wealthy supporters to fund our research. All those ambitions seem silly now." She bit her lower lip.

He nodded, unable to say anything more. Regrets

tasted like a sour lozenge that refused to dissolve. He
should have been wiser and never have attempted this
havey-cavey scheme in the first place. "Can we let out
the gas and still land on solid ground?"

She pulled the oilcloth tighter around them. "I
don't think so. Not on English soil anyway. We are
too high. If we descend immediately, by the time
enough gas escapes to land, we will be over the
Channel. That is if the valve works and is not frozen
shut. Our chances of survival are better if we keep our
altitude as long as possible—at least until we are well
over France. Right now our biggest threat is from the
cold and the rarefied air. Aeronauts can lose consciousness in thin air. This has never happened to me, but
we will be at a high altitude for a long time. My advice
is to do your best not to fall asleep and huddle to
conserve heat. We should keep up the conversation,
as well, to keep each other awake."

"How about a hymn for the butterfly?"

"Let's try and be positive, start with normal conversation first. Later we will reevaluate our circumstances.
Of course, if it gets too cold, we'll dance our jig."

After the butterfly's death, he had felt like a rud-
derless ship, but her calm, optimistic words banished
his doldrums. He squeezed her affectionately. "Thank
you. I promise to stay awake. In order to do so, tell
me about yourself, your father, your friends"—he
hugged her again—"any suitors vying to claim your
pretty hand?"

He expected her to blush, but her features remained
ghostly white. She was probably too cold to blush.

"No, my responsibilities are to my father and our

research, so I am not seeking suitors. Mostly, except for ascension days, I live a quiet life, reading scientific journals, a cat upon my lap."

"Tell me about your father. How did he become an aeronaut?"

She looked up at the swaying, dark balloon. "He wasn't, not at first, but after my brother died…" She placed her head on his shoulder. "Warmer just here." She swallowed audibly. "His name was Thomas, like our father. When Tom died, my mother fell into a decline. Normal low spirits from her grief, we thought, but she faded a little every day. Six months after Tom's death, she died."

He tightened his arms around her.

"My father studied aerostation then. He once worked for Parliament and had previous dealings with the Royal Society, so he knew everyone there. After training with other aeronauts, he started his own research. Now he rarely mentions either my mother or brother. Sometimes though, I see him examining my face. I've been told I resemble my mother, so perhaps he is remembering her. I'd like to think so."

"I'm the very likeness of my mother too. Whenever I meet one of her old acquaintances, their first words are about her. I think we are lucky in that regard."

A minute or two passed in silence.

"Funny thing, ballooning," he said. "Up here in this glorious firmament, I feel happy. For the first time I can remember, there is no one to please. My journey is in the hands of God, and even I cannot influence that."

She nodded under his chin. "Up here I'm happy too. I work with the hope that women can be more than…more than our established roles in society—more than a daughter, governess, or our husband's housekeeper—and that we too can contribute new knowledge to the world. I always lose that optimism once on the ground. Then my duties as a daughter return." She became silent.

Her head rested heavily upon his chest, so he figured she was probably asleep, poor lamb. A quick glance revealed her eyes were open. He kissed the top of her head and expected her to pull away, but she remained. Now guilt and self-recrimination overwhelmed him. If she were to die by his actions, what would he say to her father? From this moment on, his goal must change. As a gentleman, he had to right the situation he had created. He needed to do everything within his power to restore her to her father. This objective became his first priority.

After all, he had a whole month to reach Paris, so he could easily see to her welfare first, then return to the race. Looking at wisps of her hair dancing in the slight breeze, he remembered her warning about losing consciousness. Her eyes were now shut, but her breaths continued to be strong. He just could not bring himself to shake her awake—too uncaring and violent—so he first tried to waken her by murmuring, "If you asked me before now, I'd say nighttime in a balloon would be quiet as a cathedral, but it's not. The soft whistle of the air, the basket creaking as it sways, and the sounds traveling up from below… that racket I did not expect. Cowbells, dogs barking, the entire countryside is alive every minute, and all that noise travels to heaven. And *look* at that heaven.

I never thought anything could be as remarkable as the sunset today, but this inky vault overwhelms me. Heaven is magnificent."

She murmured something incoherent before lifting her head off his chest. "I have an idea," she said. "Hold your gloves out."

His spirits lifted with the knowledge she was awake and well. If her request would make her happy, then why not? The gloves were not his best pair, but old ones still decent enough to be worn by a gentleman with his sartorial reputation. He had chosen them for the journey because they were warm and soft like kitten fur. Pulling out his gloved hands, he held them before her nose for approval.

She grabbed a hand and pulled it down close to hers. Then she took off her gloves and slipped her bare palm on top of his. "My hands are cold. I believe if we put our hands in the same glove, they will become warmer." Her frozen little fingers slid smoothly between his, but there was not enough room for them to reach the fingertips. She attempted to slide her other hand into the other glove, but the second was tighter than the first.

He whispered into her ear. "Push."

She pushed.

Electricity shot through him, and his breathing quickened. For heavens sake, he might as well be running.

She wiggled her fingers as far as they would go.

Her touch felt unbearably intimate. They spent the next several minutes with their joined hands resting on her belly, both breathing loudly.

He closed his eyes. An inescapable urge made him

slide his right hand out an inch and shove it back in. To his surprise, his hand felt warmer, and his body felt warmer too. He continued this pleasing gesture. His fingers encircled hers. Then he pulled out and slid in again. He quickened the pace and felt warmer, much warmer. *Rub. Rub. Rub.*

"What are you doing?"

The sweet sound of her voice called him back to his sense of decorum. "Ah." Boyce tried to come up with a scientific explanation to please her. "It's my idea. I call it chafing. It makes you warmer, right?"

She twisted to face him, her eyes wide. "I do feel warmer—strangely so. Continue." She kept both hands steady, allowing him to thrust again with his hand.

Within minutes, the warm air from her rapid breaths on the underside of his chin proved unbelievably arousing. If he closed his eyes, her steamy breath felt like numerous little kisses. Taking a peek at her face, her parted lips only increased his discomfort. He scooted slightly away from her, since his forward behavior might shock a naive young lady. Time to focus on something else. "Are you having trouble breathing?"

"Altitude," she said a little too quickly. "The pulse rate of the human heart increases with altitude. It is scientific fact. My panting is not…is due to the rarefied air. An aeronaut's heartbeat can escalate to over eighty beats per minute. This is quite normal, I can assure you."

Her raspy voice sounded like London's most beautiful high-flyer beckoning him to a night of passion. He pushed her forward an inch. "Your voice changed. Promise me you are well?"

"I promise. The moisture content of the air is very low at high altitude, so my throat is dry. It's perfectly normal, like the extreme cold. Although it is colder than I expected. I must have miscalculated. With the heat from the lamp being insufficient, we'll just have to maximize contact."

"So my chafing idea was a good one?"

"Yes, it was, but let's continue the friction."

He hesitated, unsure how to explain why friction might be a bad idea. Perhaps she possessed some additional knowledge about the cold atmosphere that he lacked. However, a first mate must follow his captain's orders. Cupping their joined palms under her breasts, he pulled her higher on his chest. Now he observed her lips were no longer apple red but bloodless enough to match her skin. "Put your lips on my neck. Your lips are very pale, and my neck is warm."

"That won't be necessary."

"I'm worried about you. Do you want me to do it first?" He rocked her sideways in fun. "I promise I won't call it a kiss."

She trembled a little, perhaps from the cold. "No, I'm not sure this is necessary under the circumstances. Since friction is not involved, I doubt the gesture will go far in making either of us warmer."

"Please," he whispered.

She hesitated. "If you insist, we can do the experiment. But remember, it's not a kiss." She then placed her lips just under his ear.

The coldness of her lips caused a shiver to run from his ear to his toes. Best to concentrate on the friction, instead of kissing her witless. With their joined hands still in the gloves, he vigorously rubbed every inch of their bodies within reach. Both of their thighs, her stomach, and under her breasts were chafed.

While he rubbed, her lips remained under his ear, and they began to feel warm and wet.

"Ah, yes, a positive reaction," she whispered.

Deciding it would be safer for all concerned to return to the finger-stroking scheme, Boyce pulled his hand almost out of the glove and shoved it back in. With each arousing push, he grunted softly. Gradually, the chafing slowed until he stopped altogether. Then he heard a sound that wasn't his galloping heartbeat, something outside of the basket. He listened carefully for several minutes. The pulsing noise began to sound like crashing waves. "Listen."

He lost consciousness.

Five

EVE HAD NO CONCEPT OF THE POWER BEHIND REPEATED, rhythmic touch when applied by an attractive male specimen. Everyone heard stories about the successes of London's rakes and libertines, and she had always wondered why women would fall for that sort of charm. Now, sitting here, undergoing a thorough petting, she developed a better understanding of the power behind masculine wiles. Her rapid heartbeat became too fast to distinguish individual beats, and every inch of her skin falling under his touch tingled. Nevertheless, logic dismissed her reactions as a natural female response to…the rubbing started again, and her world swirled in a dizzying haze.

He repeatedly rubbed her torso under her breasts with their hands encased in soft fur. Within seconds, she felt a pleasant ease she had never experienced before. When he first had started this "chafing" routine, she blamed her response on the altitude, but it did not take long before doubts rose in her mind. Now those doubts had decidedly flown. She had never studied passion, but she was no fool. Passion was whispered about, and every good student of science naturally observed the details of everyday life. She, of course, had paid attention, but even she was awed by the intensity of her physical response to his touch—a response she mistrusted, because her intellect had no control over it. Therefore, she could be led astray and into difficulties where she possessed no skills to extract herself.

Parker continued to play her like a fiddle.

Was he aware of her body's response to his immediate touch? She let out a small chuckle. *Of course he knew*. The chafing stopped, and their joined hands rested on her belly. She waited, then lifted her head a little and noticed his eyes were closed, probably in sleep. The sight of his whisker growth visibly darkening his cheeks lured her to reach out and pass several fingers over the roughness. She forced herself to glance away. Why did Parker engage her passions? Or were his actions an innocent way of ensuring warmth? Either way, she *did* feel warmer.

Parker slowly collapsed to his right, pulling the oilcloth away.

A gush of icy air cooled her left side. "Parker, are you asleep?"

No response.

He appeared to be in a rather uncomfortable position, so she concluded he had fainted from the rarefied air. Examining him, she found a regular heartbeat and steady breaths. *Thank heavens*. She tucked the blanket under him to keep him warm. Then she checked her instruments and recorded their altitude, temperature, and humidity. They had climbed higher than she had expected, which explained his lack of consciousness.

They were currently losing altitude, so she didn't think releasing gas was necessary. He would likely wake soon.

She decided to take scientific advantage of the rarified air and retrieved a bottle of water from one of the boxes on the floor. The bottle was designed to evaluate the chemical composition of the atmosphere. She stood carefully, so as not to disturb the blanket, grabbed the bottle, and pulled the cork to empty the water over the side of the balloon. This would ensure that only air from their current altitude would enter the bottle. Then she capped the bottle, labeled it with the current altitude, and wedged it back into the basket for transport. Once the bottle was received at the laboratory, it would be opened underwater and the air trapped in the inverted glass measured for the amounts of oxygen, nitrogen, and carbon.

Before she returned to the warmth of the oilcloth, she also examined the terrain below, but it was too dark to distinguish any distinct features. She had heard crashing waves earlier and now only a few lights were visible in the distance, so more than likely, they were well over the Channel but had not yet reached the shores of France. She listened closely for any noise that would betray a dangerous loss of elevation, like the sound of waves, but all she heard was the soft rush of the wind over her head. This observation, the cold air, and her fast heartbeat convinced her that her altitude calculations were correct. They had not lost altitude significant enough to be in any immediate danger.

She examined the balloon above her and observed additional evidence that they were indeed very high.

The silk balloon had taken on a silver sheen from a thin coating of frost. The frost also coated the rigging, making the ropes resemble waterfalls of liquid silver.

Pushing Parker into a more comfortable upright position, so he'd have fewer pains when he woke, she shook his shoulders until he moved slightly. She then sat and pulled his arm over her shoulders. "Are you well?"

He nodded sleepily. "Tired."

Then she wrapped them both tightly with the wool-lined oilcloth. She snuggled her face into his firm chest and soon fell asleep.

She woke when Parker suddenly sat board straight. "I'm leaking," he exclaimed. "Look at me."

After a moment to gather her wits, she rubbed her eyes and made a quick assessment of their circumstances. She found him holding his nose with his handkerchief. Gently pulling his hand away, she found fresh blood staining the snowy linen.

"Tell me. Have I stuck my spoon in the wall?"

"No, you haven't." She rose to her knees and grabbed his handkerchief. "You are bleeding from the altitude, nothing more." She dabbed the balled linen on his nose and discovered the bleeding had ceased. "There, the bleeding has already stopped."

He looked skeptical. "Look at my coat. It's ruined. We're both disheveled."

She bit her upper lip and reached for his hand. "Honest, you are well. Why don't you get up and see? I hoped we might catch a magnificent sunrise this morning, but we must have missed it because we are shrouded within bright clouds at the moment. Although, I bet you have never been inside a cloud before."

With a quick glance at the wall of gray surrounding the basket, he dismissed any interest in viewing the inside of a cloud. Instead, he stood to survey his attire. Then he brushed his trousers, coat, and waistcoat. "Don't suppose you have a looking glass on board?"

She had never heard that question before in a balloon. "No, remember weight is at a premium. We usually don't carry such frivolous items."

He swirled his tongue over the front of his lower teeth. "What I wouldn't give for a little tooth powder too. I suppose no powder?"

She shook her head, smiled, and glanced up at the balloon. They had broken through the clouds, and the morning sunlight began to warm the balloon. As the gas heated, the balloon swelled rapidly, causing the great pleats of silk to unfold with a sound similar to ripping canvas.

She busied herself with a current reading of her instruments and calculated their present elevation. They were much lower than expected, so she consulted the *Results* book to determine if their current height would be sufficient to complete the next experiment. Previous explorers had observed spices lose their taste on high mountains, like the peak of Tenerife. So this experiment would test the previous observations to determine if the taste of various spices became insipid in rarefied air. "If you wouldn't mind, I'd like you to assist me in our final experiment."

He spun to face her, a glint in his eyes. "Ho, ho, would I." He surveyed the small space of the basket. "But what's left? No more animals I hope. Got some surprise over there in that small box?"

She chuckled and removed several small snuff-boxes from the chest. "These contain spices. I would appreciate if you would describe how they taste. For example, does the pepper taste like pepper as you know it? Perhaps it tastes weaker or even more intense than your previous experience on the ground."

He sat on the small bench at one end. "Come sit on my knee."

She took a single step before logic prevailed. Touching him had proven dangerous in the past. "This is serious. I see no reason to sit on your knee. Just take a box and place one pinch of the spice on your tongue. Then describe the sensations you get from that spice."

"I love sensations." He winked. "Now be a good lady of science and sit on my knee. I will close my eyes and open my mouth. You can then add the appropriate pinch of spice. But don't tell me the identity of the spice. I want to give you an unbiased response." He spread his knees outward and patted his large, firm thigh. "Come."

Blast. Why couldn't the man trapped in her balloon have been a gentleman whose company was calm and comforting? Why, instead, was the man sitting before her one of the most handsome gentlemen under God's blue skies? Trapped in a basket, she could not run or ignore him. The only thing she could do was to keep her mind strictly focused on the task before her.

But just look at him—what a specimen.

She cataloged his most alluring features. The dark brown hair escaping his cap was unruly and fetching. She knew his locks were soft to the touch, and his embrace was as warm as a fire in a cottage hearth. His bloodstained cream breeches were soft and outlined every muscle in his legs. He would be a good model for scientific study on muscle development... Her heartbeat raced, so she stopped her unsuccessful attempt to describe him dispassionately. Fetching? Cottage fires? Something was wrong with her. She vowed to stifle all future wayward thoughts of feelings and focus on facts.

He had a wry smile on his lips, evidence he knew *exactly* the type of emotions he created.

It took a great deal of discipline to drag her gaze up to the balloon.

A chuckle escaped him, and he patted his thigh again. "Come, come. Do not delay. We need to complete the experiments first before we land. That was my agreement with your father, and I have every intention of holding up my part of the bargain."

She stared at his broad thigh again then gulped. *Focus. You can do this one simple task.* As soon as she took her place on his thigh, she had second thoughts about this scheme. Her impulse at the moment was to lean in and wrap herself within his arms and then wiggle in an unspoken desire for another thorough rubbing. "Oh!" *How could she even think that?*

"Something amiss?"

With her cheeks warming every second, she chastised herself for her wayward thoughts. Happily, she found a suitable excuse. "The altitude has given me the headache."

He smiled, no doubt aware of her shocking fib.

She removed her gloves, opened the first

snuffbox, and took a pinch of the ginger. "Right, open your mouth."

Leaning slightly forward, he opened his mouth.

That very second, the only experiment she wanted to do was brush her hands over his whisker growth, run her fingers through his forelocks, and kiss his full lips. It took every ounce of any intelligence she possessed to place the pinch of ginger on his tongue with a steady hand. The instant she felt the wet warmth of his tongue, she jerked her hand away.

If Boyce closed his eyes, he might get himself through this experiment without getting himself into the type of trouble unique to gentlemen. Then his physical response to the sight of her fetching blush, hesitant naïveté, and prominent, lusty pout would disappear. They would complete the last experiment, land in a field, and he could restore her to her father. He shut his eyes, vowed to think only of the spice, and clicked his tongue on the roof of his mouth to taste it properly. "*Tsk, tsk.*"

"Well?"

He kept his eyes closed. "Have you ever licked... no, steady on." He took a deep breath and forced himself to forget about licking. "Bland, like week-old rice pudding. You try it." Proper manners dictated he open his eyes, so he did so unwillingly, unsure of his physical response.

She placed a regulated pinch upon her tongue and closed her lips. Her cheek distended slightly, so she was probably rubbing the ginger all over the inside of

her mouth. This unknowingly seductive action necessitated he clear his throat—numerous times.

Slightly parting her lips, she inhaled sharply. Perhaps
to determine if the rush of air would intensify the flavor.

"*Ah, hem.*" He squirmed on his seat, his discomfort
growing.

Without paying any particular attention to him, she
rose and scribbled notes in the *Results* book. When
finished, she stared at him in an odd, unsettled countenance. "Ready for the salt? Oh, I forgot—"

"Salt, that should do the trick." The tang of salt
should dampen his desires. He exhaled in relief; his
composure returned to normal. In a matter-of-fact
manner, she took her seat once more on his lap, and
his ease instantly vanished.

Taking a measured pinch, she dropped the salt upon
his tongue.

"You must have taken the wrong snuffbox," he
said. "This tastes sweet to me. It has none of the
piquant sting I normally associate with salt."

She examined the label upon the lid of the box.
"No, it says salt." She placed a pinch upon her own
palate and moved her tongue around.

"What I wouldn't give," he whispered, his body
stiffening. *Damnation.*

"Pardon?"

He closed his eyes and resolved not to fantasize
over her agile tongue. Unfortunately, his mind was
capable of imagining without any input from his eyes.
Thank heavens she retreated to the opposite side of the
balloon to record her observations. "What next?" he
inquired in a somewhat choked voice.

"Pepper."

He straightened his back. "Ha! That should be a refreshing, much-needed slap in the face."

"Pardon?" Her angry, apple, amorous pout returned.

For some reason, she repeatedly returned to sit upon his knee, curious that. He was wondering what excuse he could use to ask her to politely rise when she wiggled slightly. Now he was in trouble; his breathing quickened.

A frown crossed her pretty face, and he knew she was completely innocent of his impending situation. The frown vanished, and she blithely continued with her observations. "At this elevation, I think we can confirm that the tongue becomes insipid, don't you agree?"

He moaned and stared at her placid face. *I must not think of the word* elevation. He bit his tongue.

"Granted, we are not very high," she said. "Still, I believe we have made progress toward establishing the altitude limits where we begin to lose taste."

He inhaled as deeply as possible to slow his obvious panting. "Let's get this over with. I am very eager to land." He stared up at the balloon and focused on the lovely blue color—the same hue as her eyes. He focused on the rigging.

"Just one more." She fiddled with the box and, in doing so, rocked upon his knee.

This time his moan could have awakened the dead. "What next?"

"Sugar."

"Get on with it," he said, his tone sounding like a growl. His sight fixed upon her lips.

She placed the sugar in his mouth and started to do the same for herself.

The second the pinch of sugar neared her tongue, he jerked forward, knocking the majority of the sugar upon her lower lip and chin. He moved his hands to cup the back of her head, pulling her forward until he could see only her beautiful sapphire eyes. "Miss Mountfloy, have you ever been kissed? As a scientist you must be curious. You must want to gather facts and learn what it feels like?"

Oh, Eve wanted to know all right. Give a thousand pounds, if she had the money. His warm breath was having a devastating effect upon her, so she searched deep within herself for the control she had mustered earlier, but she could not summon it. She gulped, fixed by the intensity of those frolicking green eyes. "No…I don't think so," she whispered, realizing the possible dangers of newly acquired knowledge.

"No, you've never been kissed?" He moved forward, their lips lightly touched. "Or, no, you are not curious?"

She prayed her voice sounded firm. "Both."

He trailed his lips in a feather-like movement across hers before he lifted his lips to whisper, "If I were to use logic, I'd say you lacked knowledge then." He hesitated. Their lips made contact again; he repeated the light brush then paused. "Service to a lady for me." The soft touch of his mouth returned before he lifted his head. "Knowledge for you."

Perhaps she gave a barely perceptible nod.

His lips closed upon hers while his hands moved to her back and pulled her close. He kissed her with a light touch, then after she made a tentative response in kind, he opened his mouth and fully kissed her.

She had a brief moment of coherence—*This isn't bad, shockingly invasive but, on the whole, quite pleasant.* Then he kissed her deeply, and her analysis ended. She reflexively grabbed his shoulders to steady herself. A newfound type of joy overcame her, and she wanted to discover the full extent of this happiness. He used his tongue to tease and stimulate, so she returned the favor. In the back of her mind, she wondered if he was feeling a similar joy. Her heartbeat sounded in her ears, and an unfamiliar urgency grew inside her. The minute her arms wrapped around his shoulders, he pushed her forward to hold her at arm's length.

He was breathing hard and wore a somewhat startled expression. "I suppose all ladies of science learn quickly."

She ignored his comment and wondered if he found her forward behavior inexcusable or abhorrent. Doubt seized her, and she blushed for what seemed like forever. She escaped with quick steps to the edge of the basket and then leaned over to place her burning face in the bracing wind.

He began to sing, "'Then turning around we parted, she speechless went her way, Because I could do nothing, but kiss the Queen of May.'"

"You know the oddest songs. Did you just make that one up?"

"No, it's an old favorite. I even included it in a songbook I published."

She was not going to make herself miserable thinking about his kisses. She needed to calm down, focus on the job before her, and make the final notes of the tasting experiment in the *Results* book. Once completed, she would ignore him and concentrate on landing the balloon today. Five minutes passed before her breathing returned to normal. In the early morning light, she watched the patches of green fields and dense woodland scoot by below them.

He joined her at the side of the basket, apparently composed. "I really think we should head in that direction." He pointed to a flat patch of green next to a village only partially hidden by low clouds. "How do we get over there?"

"As you may have observed by now, you cannot direct a balloon. We are dependent upon the prevailing wind."

He huffed. "Before we lifted off, I had planned to invest in balloons—a good idea for hauling cargo, you know—but now I see balloons have no use." He lowered his eyes for a brief second. "No practical uses other than science—um—but besides atmospheric studies, what good are balloons?"

She grinned, knowing this was her chance to explain her love of science. "What's the use of a baby?"

He gave her a hard stare. "Right. A baby might become Newton."

"Or Newton's mother. If you consider history, once man dug out the first canoe, did he build a ship of the line the next day? You should consider the process of scientific discovery like building an Egyptian pyramid. With each result we obtain, we add a stone.

But we do not know where our stones will be in the final structure. One person will have the honor to put the last stone on the top and gain all of the fame over his great accomplishment. But all of the other stones are needed in place before he can set the final stone."

"So today we are piling stones on a pyramid?"

"In a way, yes."

"Sounds like not enough glory if you cannot be the fellow who puts the final stone on top." He scratched his head. "You have convinced me balloons are really like canoes, so it is too early to invest in them." Something caught his eye, and he leaned way over the edge of the basket. "Look! That man below is waving at us. Good morning!" He leaned over and waved both arms. "Forgive me, I mean *bonjour, bonjour.*" He pointed below him. "Look at that old man. What a grump. He's shaking is fist at us. What did we do?"

"He is probably worried we will land in his field. Many farmers get violent when balloons land in their fields and ruin their crops. In the past, we have had to pay farmers on several occasions just for the chance to recover our balloon. I hope we don't have any unpleasantness today."

"Are we going to land in his field? What are the French words for, 'Sorry I damaged your vegetables'?"

"We have a speaking trumpet in the box if you wish to carry out a conversation. But I recommend you observe the trees. Do you notice anything amiss?"

He leaned over to examine the terrain below them. "No."

"We are not in France."

He spun to face her. "We must be. A minute ago,

I saw the French flag. With all that turmoil overseas now, I'm not quite positive what the flag looks like these days. Perhaps blue or maybe white with those little gold French *fleurs*. Well, I just saw a blue flag with gold spots, so we must be in France."

"I recommend you examine the tree shadows *carefully*. You will notice the shadows are falling in the direction we are traveling. Since it is still morning and the sun is in the East, we must be traveling westward."

Within a minute, they glided over a single tree in the middle of a large field. "What?! We are not in France? Dash it all. Where are we?"

Six

"I'M AFRAID IT MEANS WHAT YOU THINK," EVE SAID. From the life-or-death urgency in his tone, she had underestimated the seriousness behind his goal to reach France.

He ran to the opposite side and stumbled on a wicker birdcage, causing the balloon to sway violently. They grabbed the sides so as not to be hurled overboard. When the basket stopped swinging, he finished scanning the countryside and stood in place, his mouth open.

"Since we are traveling in the same direction as the shadows, we must be heading west over England. We could've been well over France in the night, and then as the gas cooled, we descended into a westward air current. Layers of air currents blowing in different directions simultaneously, or even changing directions, is one of the many interesting discoveries made by aeronauts. My best estimate is that we lost altitude during the night, then moved into a prevailing wind blowing back toward England. By the description of your blue flag, we are probably in Sussex."

"Sussex! Pleasant place and all, but dash it, I need to be in France." He paced three steps forward and three steps back. This caused the basket to sway again, so he stopped pacing and glared at the balloon above him.

She stood beside him. "It's not that bad. Once we land, you can return to the coast, cross over to France on the packet, and then renew your journey on horseback. When you recount your tale to the earl, you can describe your courageous flight to the English coast in a balloon, and it will be true. You can leave the second leg of your journey to France out of the story. I'll wager no one else thought of traveling across England by balloon."

"Ha! You are right." Lifting her off the floor, he carefully swung her around. "This calls for a song." He hesitated and tilted his head to the side, perhaps waiting for her remonstrance.

She put her hands on his shoulders to steady herself and tried to ignore the press of his strong fingers around her waist. "I've learned your singing is like the duck's quack—a noise natural to you. So you sing, and I'll prepare for the landing. Now please put me down."

"Noise?" He frowned for a second. "Right, I teased you, so I deserved that. Yes, yes, you're a fine and clever girl." He put her down and leaned over the side to serenade the fields below. "'Tis glory, proud glory enraptures the mind, and strengthens the hero in flight. Roll de roll dee."

As she went about making her preparations to land, she found herself tapping her foot to the tune. He had an excellent voice that could only be described as a deep harmonious rumble. She carefully pulled open the valve and began to monitor their descent.

"Then fame let thy trumpet, thy trumpet resound, and echo the strain to the skies! Roll de roll do."

She tied off the valve line, leaned over the side, and visibly inspected the burlap bags holding the sand ballast. They were ten pounds each, and she could either cut the bags to let out approximately half of that weight, or untie the rope and release the full ten pounds. After counting the number of sand bags, she concluded they had plenty of ballast for any contingency they might face. In her final preparation for landing, she untied the rope holding the grapnel onto the basket. Looking at the ground below, she figured they were at approximately a thousand feet. Thankfully, the terrain appeared to be mainly cultivated fields separated by hedgerows, but scattered between every five or six fields stood thick woods, probably remnants of the Weald's primeval forests. There was nothing more she could do now but wait for the balloon to lose altitude.

"The aeronaut in flight more valiant is found, when glory, bright glory's the prize! Roll de roll di."

At the moment, she did not want to think about the word *di*. Landing a balloon was always difficult and fraught with many unforeseen types of danger— not to mention it would be her first time landing by herself without expert assistance. Experience in handling the grapnel and ballast bags was crucial to a successful landing. She then explained Parker's duties during their upcoming landing and was grateful that he appeared to understand her instructions.

Glancing again at the rapidly approaching ground, her palms dampened. She needed to draw deep from within her stores of courage. When her brother's ship had flailed upon the rocks, Tom had rescued six people before he had been taken by the sea. If Tom had had the courage to save other lives before himself, logically as his sister, she too must possess similar courage.

"I am going to miss this balloon." Parker grabbed the harness and leaned forward over the green English countryside. "Cradled in its rope and wicker embrace, I have never felt so free. Although we are dependent on where the wind blows us, even that fact gives us independence. We cannot change the wind." He turned to face her and winked. "We cannot change the wind—*yet*." Clutching the edge of the basket, he held one arm outward. "We cannot choose our direction or our fate. We have to pluck up and move forward—accept what comes."

"I disagree," she said. "Life is full of choices, and we can—to a certain extent—control our fate by our decisions. The same situation occurs up here in the balloon. We can control our fate with the valve, the ballast, and perhaps the guide rope. But—"

"You don't feel the freedom?" He turned to face her. His fetching brown locks whipped around his face in a teasing dance that framed his emerald eyes.

She gathered her wits and avoided looking into those seductive eyes. "I don't understand you. Perhaps freedom is not a concept I consider, since I'm bound by duty in so many ways."

He moved to the center of the basket, raising both arms skyward. "No, freedom is absolute. It is all around us. Come, come. Give me your hand." He held his palm out. "Let me show you freedom."

Those damnable locks danced and muddied her brain again. How could he show her freedom? Was he going to point at the clouds and make some metaphor about freedom? What could freedom mean to a Tulip? Were kisses involved? Eve decided not to pursue these questions. "Look! We are about to land." She turned to focus on the rapidly approaching ground.

"We are?" He joined her at the side of the basket. "Doesn't look like we are descending very fast. Any way to speed it up?"

"We could rend the balloon. The problem with this option is that we will descend with the approximate speed of the duck."

"I have no intention of meeting the duck's fate," he said. "Though I'm sure the fellow is all right. Just a nasty scare."

In silence, they watched the balloon lose altitude.

She repeated the normal procedure to ground a balloon, including ways to prevent several of the possible mishaps that might cause a violent landing. They were within yards of the green field below, but a thousand feet to the West, she noticed a small stand of woods. Within the next sixty seconds, she would have to decide whether to keep her course or release some ballast to fly over the trees. She bit her lower lip, glanced at Parker, and examined their situation again. She made a decision and prayed it was the right one. By her current estimate, the gas should escape fast enough to land in the cultivated field growing rapidly larger directly below them.

"Here we go." He jumped up and down several times, causing the basket to sway and the ballast bags to bang against the side of the basket.

The noise and the sway jangled her nerves. "Listen, madman, a safe landing is serious business."

"Yes, yes, of course."

"Now would be a good time to take the grapnel and ready yourself." They were a couple of hundred feet over the ground, and the balloon had lost over half of its gas.

"Yes, yes." His face brightened, and he almost leaped to the side. Grabbing the rope, he held the grapnel in the ready position. He then stared at the ground, crouched like a cat ready to spring into action.

She held up her hand, waited, and yelled, "Now."

"Right, here goes." He threw out the grapnel, and they watched it fall until it dug into the dirt below.

"Job well done," she said, bracing herself for the jolt she expected when the basket reached the end of the grapnel's line.

A second later, a strong breeze kicked up.

The wind quickly lifted the basket over fifty feet into the air. She looked up at the shimmering balloon and realized her worst fears had come true. Even though the silver balloon was less than a quarter inflated, the wind pushed the remaining gas in a flattened arc, kept in place by the rigging. As a result, the balloon now looked and behaved like a giant parachute.

The grapnel ran out of line and violently tipped the basket sideways. The balloon seemed to be pulled by an unseen hand determined to drag it into the woods.

She made a hasty decision and shouted for Parker to release the grapnel line.

The basket tilted violently, but through his sheer strength, he managed to pull himself up using the rope. "But won't the grapnel stop us eventually?"

The wind stopped as suddenly as it arrived, and they were now losing altitude fast.

"Look," she yelled, pointing to the grapnel dragging a trench through the field of Spanish turnips. Seconds later, the basket crashed to the ground. The balloon flared out in front of them and dragged the basket over on its side. "Release the grapnel or we will be dashed to bits," she shouted over the explosion of wicker, rigging, turnips, and dirt as they were propelled toward the woods at the speed of a runaway horse. "We are too close to the trees. Release the grapnel. I'll release ballast." She managed to pull her entire body weight to the edge of the basket and free a bag of ballast.

Parker untied the grapnel line, and the basket flew upward, both of them landing in a heap on the floor facing each other, each breathing hard. "Eve, I need to tell you—"

"Untie more ballast." She managed to stand and discovered they were mere feet away from the dense woods and gaining altitude. At their current trajectory, they were about to hit a large tree dead center. She screamed, "Drop a bag! Drop a bag!"

Seconds after Parker released a ballast bag, they hit the first tree.

She instinctively threw her arm over her face to protect herself, but leaves and branches hit her almost everywhere.

Parker embraced her fully and turned. His back took the brunt force of the whipping branches, and he winced once or twice.

The balloon above them appeared to be unhampered, so it continued to pull them through the trees. They could not gain altitude because the basket and rigging were caught amongst the branches. Pieces of wicker from the basket groaned and snapped.

In a brief moment of calm, he attempted to release more ballast. Then the basket hit another large trunk, the deep, bell-like sound reverberated through the woods. Around them, startled birds flew up into the blue skies.

After impact with the giant tree, the ensnared basket tipped ninety degrees.

Eve fell to the floor again and began to tumble toward the edge. Directly in front of her, the green underbrush loomed, like a green sea waiting for her to dive in. As she attempted to grab onto the side of the basket, she noticed her father's *Results* book slide down alongside her. She reached under some falling cages to clasp the book, but a strong hand around her calf stopped her forward progress.

The book slid beyond her reach and bounced around in a jumbled mixture of cages and instruments.

Her stocking started to bunch, and the grip slipped down to her ankle. "No, no, save the book, save the book. Let me go. Save the book, not me."

His grip tightened. "Don't be foolish. Your life is worth more than a book."

"Nooo."

"Certainly." With a loud grunt, he pulled her

upward until she lay about a foot from the edge. "Worth." His other hand clasped her other leg. "More." Even with slippery stockings in his hands, his significant strength pulled her several feet up and away from the edge. "To me."

She watched in horror as the book slid over the side and disappeared into the deep underbrush.

Next, the cage with the pigeon fell end over end down the length of the basket. The door opened and the pigeon flew up and out of harm's way. The wicker cage plummeted into the green underbrush.

"Thank God," Parker uttered.

They hit the third tree hard. In a rare second where the basket ceased to travel, they both managed to right themselves. They reached for each other and hugged. Parker gave her a swift kiss on the top of the head. "Right, release more ballast."

Seconds later, they hit the branches of another large tree just as Parker managed to release a ballast bag. The basket then rose violently, hit a large branch, twisted over on its side, and Parker fell on his back, resting on the very edge. One more hit, and he'd likely roll off. They exchanged glances. Neither could look away.

He had saved her life; now he could lose his.

She moved toward him, but before she could reach him, she watched in horror as the basket hit another tree. Parker flipped out of the balloon like a rag doll. She screamed. A flash of light off the sole of his boot was the last thing she saw before the dark undergrowth swallowed him.

Seven

THE BALLOON FINALLY LIFTED ABOVE THE TREETOPS, and Eve grabbed the rough wicker edge to catch her breath. In the middle of the crash, her mind had been fixed upon the book, but now there was only one matter of importance—Parker. If he were to die, her vaulting ambition to be the first female to cross the Channel would be to blame. Her stomach churned, and she almost cast up her morning biscuit. Despite Parker's expressed fears that he had lost his father's respect, the marquess's actions revealed he may not have been pleased but in no way had forsaken his youngest. He didn't cut him out of his living, for example. How could she explain Parker's loss to his father? How could she find Parker quickly? How could she ever forgive herself? She wished she had used her wits to note their location or elevation at the moment he fell from the basket. Now she had no data to determine where to start her search or if his fall could be a survivable one.

Below her, at least a hundred feet of woods remained, and beyond, she could see another broad stretch of cultivated fields. She would have to wait until she reached the safety of open ground before she could release any more gas. Turning back to examine the spot where Parker had likely fallen, she memorized every detail in the hopes that an odd tree or unusual landscape feature would help her find him in the future. She noticed a dead tree with a completely brown canopy amongst the green trees. Parker must have landed within yards of that tree, so she'd use it later as a marker to find him.

Once over the cultivated field, she was pleased to find it was a very broad one. A stand of woods loomed in the distance, but she would land before she reached the trees, barring any more freak winds.

This time she managed a rapid and controlled descent. No sudden gusts caught the balloon. The shimmering silk above her merely undulated in the breeze. Thankfully, the plowed rows of turnips below her would provide a relativity soft landing. Within twenty feet of the ground, she noticed a man in his wagon heading in the direction of her landing. She had no idea whether he rushed to assist her or attack the balloon as some giant monster.

In readiness to land, she widened her stance and held on to the side.

The basket hit the field with a soft thump. At first it remained upright, but after the silk balloon landed on the ground, it spread out upon the field and still retained enough power to pull the basket onto its side.

There was nothing for her to do at that point except continue to hold on and pray. If she fell out, the basket might run over her, grinding her into the dirt. All she could do was wait until the remaining gas escaped.

After several minutes, the silk balloon collapsed enough so that the basket dragged through the turnips at a fast walking pace. She managed to exit the basket and pull the edge in an effort to stop its forward momentum.

The farmer sat upon his wagon pointing out the balloon to a young boy. "Ah, well, would you look at dat, Jem. A young miss."

She tugged on the basket again, but her efforts produced very little effect.

All of a sudden, she noticed the boy on the other side of the basket doing his best to help her. The slim lad was around twelve years, but she knew every little bit of opposing force helped.

"Come away, Jem," the farmer shouted. "Don't want yo' getting hurt. Let de lady handle her own problems."

The boy smiled at her and pulled the basket with greater effort, grunting in the process.

She returned his smile. "On the count of three, let's give one big tug. Ready?"

The boy nodded. "Ready."

"One, two, three." They tugged hard and their efforts proved successful as the basket slowed.

A minute later, the farmer strode forward, grabbed the basket, and widened his stance. Then with one mighty jerk, he pulled the basket to a complete stop.

She hugged the boy. "Thank you." She then ran forward to gather up the harness and fold the balloon as best she could so it would remain stationary.

The boy emulated her movements in earnest, his tan face focused on rapidly folding the silk.

"Never dought I live to see ladies flying about in balloons," the farmer remarked, removing his cap to scratch his scalp. "And it may be all right for you, miss. But what about da turnips? You've damaged half an acre, maybe more. Missus won't be too happy neither." Dressed in corduroy breeches tied at the knee and an open waistcoat, his slow manner of movement announced a hardworking man unlikely to be unsettled by any event. He had probably handled a multitude of disasters before, so no mishap could ruffle his feathers now. "Now, my lady, do you have recomp…" He rolled his limp felt hat in his hands. "The funds for turnips spoilt?"

She glanced around at the destruction of the turnip rows. She even had quite a few leaves, not to mention dirt, on her person. "Yes, I apologize, Mister…"

"Ah, my name is Mr. Muckles. Missus calls me Frank. She puts good store into my judgment too. So I expect payment for damages."

"Of course, Mr. Muckles. But you see my passenger, Lord Boyce Parker, fell out of the balloon into the trees, so you must help me find him immediately. He might be injured or—"

"Now don't you go running off, payment first. Den we can search for this lord o' yours."

"But the circumstances of my lift-off were unusual, so you must understand the fact that I have no immediate funds on board to compensate you for your turnips."

Mr. Muckles headed toward the basket, straddling

each row of turnips with a single stride. "Jem, let us see what we can take from dat basket—"

She followed but struggled to keep pace. "Mr. Muckles, please. My father and I will pay you for your turnips. When I get back to London—"

"Look for a good find, Jem. Some instrument or another, I suppose."

"Mr. Muckles! We must search for his lordship." The blank face that greeted this statement urged her to emphasize the logic of the situation. "If we find him now, I am sure he will pay you twice what your turnips are worth."

Mr. Muckles ignored her and dragged the big chest out of the basket.

Why did he ignore the gravity of the situation? "Please, Mr. Muckles, a man's life is at stake."

He looked up and brushed his hands upon his loose plaid waistcoat but showed no signs of movement toward the woods.

"Please, I insist you call for help. He could be hurt or in pain." The thought unsettled her, and she forced it out of her mind. "Sir, Lord Boyce is an important young gentlemen. I am sure his father will be very pleased if every effort is made for his recovery."

He continued to pull items out of the wicker chest.

She restrained herself from kicking him in the shins, turned, and marched toward the woods.

Once she reached the beginning of the trees, her heart sank with the discovery of a thick undergrowth of bracken, gorse, ferns, and brambles. She ran up and down the edge, looking for a footpath, stopping only to cup her hands and yell, "Lord Boyce." No response. "Parker." She repeated her call again and again only louder. "Parker."

Mr. Muckles and Jem reached the edge of the woods and waited until she moved closer. "Well, miss, we have a machine labeled 'barrowmeter' from de box of instruments in da wagon. Dat should satisfy missus until you can get your funds you be talking about. So come with us back to the priory, and we can set out a proper search party for the lord o' yours."

"Please, Mr. Muckles, he could be bleeding. Time might be of the essence. Is there any pathway through this wood?"

"The only pathway drew the woods is up by de stables. Jem, fetch de wagon and we'll be off."

She couldn't abandon Parker; she just couldn't. "You don't understand. His lordship is a fine young gentleman, much more…caring than most." Her words seem to land on deaf ears. "He likes birds; he even sings. Please, Mr. Muckles, I need to know the direction of the pathway."

"If you won't come with Jem and me, we'll return to the priory now. You see, missus won't be happy if we spend de day playing with balloons, missing gentleman, and de like."

"Now, now, my good man. Can you give me some assistance?" shouted a deep voice resonating from within the woods.

Eve's heart almost leaped out of her chest at the sound of Parker's voice. She ran into the fern underbrush, but her gown became hopelessly stuck on a bramble after about twenty feet.

Mr. Muckles frowned in the direction of the

speaker and without hesitation waded into the verdant undergrowth, swatting thorny branches with his bare hands. He soon disappeared out of her sight.

She waited and waited and waited. Then she saw Parker, supported by Mr. Muckles, slowly making their way through the underbrush. As they neared, she noticed Parker had lost one boot and sported a torn coat sleeve, revealing a bulge of bare muscle on his upper arm. When clothed, he appeared to be very much the fashionable Tulip, but now she understood the source of the strength he had used to restrain her during the ascension and later when he helped with the cages.

"Careful now, your lordship. Not too fast. We will get dere soon enough."

She had never, never been so glad to see someone in her life. She started running toward him, twisted her ankle in the soft dirt, but continued, albeit with a decided limp. As she got close, in unison, they both foolishly grinned and started to laugh. Now even she felt like singing.

Parker opened his arms, and she practically jumped into them. A long, rocking hug ensued. "I'm so glad, so glad," she said. No other words came to mind.

He grunted. "Careful, bit bruised. Now what is the problem here? Mr. Muckles says you are being uncooperative."

"Mr. Muckles wants me to pay for the damages to his turnips, but I have no money, so he took our barometer. I expected to land immediately, remember." She took his other arm and helped Mr. Muckles escort him back to the open field.

"Careful, my child, I'm a bit sore. Had a tangle with a boot-grabbing tree." He moved stiffly; with each step a strained expression flitted across his handsome face.

Mr. Muckles must have noticed his condition too, because he adjusted his arm around his lordship's waist to support him better.

"Now, my good fellow," Parker said. "Miss Mountfloy here has crashed her balloon. I know you have a good heart, so you understand she is feeling lost, injured, and stranded. We must help her, sir, a lady in distress. As Englishmen, it is our duty. So I plead for your assistance on her behalf. Please do not worry about compensation for your most excellent turnips. I will personally see the situation is set to rights to your satisfaction."

Mr. Muckles must have believed the promises from a young man who could only be described as the remains of a fine gentleman—rather than listening to a young miss with a common, soiled, and torn gown. He stopped complaining about his turnips. "I believe you, your lordship. But since you are feeling so poorly, I will take you up to de house, so as a doctor be called right and proper."

Parker uttered an involuntary sigh. "Thank you, Mr. Muckles. The girl too."

"Aye," said the farmer as he gently helped Parker up into the back of the wagon.

She gathered what remaining instruments she could easily carry, so as not to leave them in a field, and returned to the wagon.

"Now Jem and I will fetch all of your possessions.

You don't need to worry on dat score, and I'll get de stable hand to help with de balloon."

Over Mr. Muckles shoulder, she noticed a lady in an elegant gig approach. Her coach was unsuitable for a plowed field and violently bounced over each row of turnips. By her equipage and dress, Eve could tell she was probably the lady of some nearby country estate.

The lady pulled up, and Jem ran to steady her horse. With great effort of arranging her gown so it would not be spoiled, she carefully stepped out.

Eve had seen women like this one before. Her great-aunt Elizabeth was a fine lady. This beautiful female straightened her shawl in an uncanny awareness that a part of her raiment had become out of place. Even a simple head toss was quickly met with a hand to check no curl became disturbed.

Knowing she probably looked as proper as an overturned turnip, Eve adjusted her cap, brushed several wayward curls behind her ears, and glanced at her gown. Dirt streaks and deep creases marred every inch. She quickly brushed the front with her hand and then sighed when her efforts produced no notable change. Even wearing her best gown, she would never be considered beautiful. She straightened her shoulders and held her head high.

As the lady neared, she came to the conclusion that if the finest French confectioners made a sugar cake, this lady was the embodiment of that cake. Statuesque, not a single gold ringlet out of place—she gave the appearance of floating when she moved.

Hesitant to put her white kid gloves on the dirty boards of the wagon, this female confection gingerly approached to examine the wagon's contents. "What do we have here, Frank?" She leaned over the side of the wagon and took a long look at Parker. "Well, well, my prayers have been answered. It's Piglet Parker."

Boyce frowned.

She giggled. "Oh, I beg your pardon. I mean the remains of the charming Lord Boyce Parker. I am very, very cross with you."

Eight

THE CONFECTION GIGGLED.

Eve thought the sound remarkable. Her childhood friends had giggled, but this sound involved the throat, so the notes were deeper. Yet somehow it still gave the impression of lightness and the promise of fun. Since her mother's death, Eve had rarely found herself in female company. She spent her days with her father, his assistant, or other gentlemen of science.

The confection widened her eyes, and Eve noticed glances exchanged between her and Parker. His expression appeared rather odd, sleepy, and heavy lidded. The giggle, decidedly for his sake, was a mature female sound meant to gain male attention.

Parker made an effort to sit up, failed, and then closed his eyes. He waved his hand in a giant arc. "Mrs. Lydia Buxton, it is with great delight that I introduce you to Miss Eve Mountfloy, the dedicated lady of science. Miss Mountfloy, Mrs. Buxton, the late widow of Mr. Gill. Recently married, if I remember rightly, so felicitations are in order. While we have never met formally, I've heard quite a few stories about you too. And I see no reason why you should be cross with me."

Eve dropped her best curtsy, an ironic gesture wearing such a filthy gown. "Mrs. Buxton, a pleasure."

The confection gave Eve a brief nod and, by the swift movement of her eyes, a complete and thorough analysis. "That gown is the very color of the dirty turnips, is it not?" She did not wait for an answer. Instead, she placed her glove tenderly on the Parker's boot. "Where are you hurt, dear…may I call you Boyce? You must call me—indeed—you both must call me Lydia. There, isn't this nice. I already feel like we are old friends. So imagine my distress to find my friends in this regrettable state. It does make me worry so."

Parker remained lying down. "Yes, yes, but please do not worry on my account. A day's rest, and I'll be pluck in no time." He tried to lift his head again, grimaced, and laid back on the wagon's boards. "I'd be honored to call you Lydia, since we have many friends in common. So, Lydia, I'd like to request the assistance of your fine fellow, Mr. Muckles here, to take Miss Mountfloy and myself to a nearby inn. Perhaps tomorrow, with your permission, he could assist the lady with the recovery of her balloon."

Lydia giggled again, a little softer, probably a sound in affirmation. "Why, both of you will reside at Duddleswell Priory with us, of course. Dear Buxton is in temporary residence in London these days. All of which is the fault of your friend George, but we will speak about that and why I'm so cross with you later. So there is only dear Buxton's mother and myself at the priory now. I know Lady Buxton will be pleased to have your company." She made a few small claps. "We'll have a regular house party." She turned to address Mr. Muckles. "Do what you can to help the young lady, won't you, Frank? I don't know what is involved with all of this ballooning equipment, but surely Burwell can find space in the stables."

Mr. Muckles doffed his hat. "Yes, missus. Me and Jem will take de young man to de house, and we will return to pick up his machine." With those words, he nodded and waved to Jem. The two climbed up onto the wagon's seat then urged the horse forward.

"Wait," Eve called, expecting to ride in the back of the wagon with Parker.

Lydia turned to Eve and repeated her head-to-toe perusal. "I'd be delighted to have your company in my gig, Miss Mountfloy. I'm sure you don't want to sit in the back of a wagon and spoil the remains of that gown."

Eve dropped a slight curtsy this time. "Thank you, ma'am. You are very kind. I can't tell you how grateful we are for your rescue, but I wish to accompany his lordship back to the house. He was my passenger and therefore my responsibility." She climbed into the wagon and the two conveyances set off for the priory. "What happened?" She reached over to loosen Parker's neckcloth. "Do you need a surgeon immediately? How badly are you injured?"

"Injured but survivable." With the first bump over a row of turnips, he moaned. "Ended up flat on my back on some sort of shrubbery, with berries—red berries. Then I heard a strange sound and decided to follow it. The sound turned out to be your pretty voice. Definitely hurt everywhere, but nothing broken. Might be stiff for a week though. Still, I made a solemn promise to return you, and your balloon, to your father. He must be anxious about your whereabouts."

"Thank you, but what about the earl's race to France?"

Despite his physical injury, soiled garments, and dirty face, he smiled. "Some luck there. It's a month-long race, so I have over twenty days left to reach Paris. My stay in Sussex must be short though." The wagon bumped over endless rows of turnips. "Ow. After I leave this place, I will never eat turnips again—painful vegetables, turnips."

Once they arrived at Duddleswell Priory, Parker fell under the butler's care. Mr. Tut had reigned over the priory for fifty years, and he efficiently saw that Parker was taken upstairs to a guest room, undressed, and the surgeon called. Later, when Eve and Mrs. Buxton were allowed to enter the room, Tut instructed a housemaid to fetch a glass of barley water for the patient.

Eve entered the room, recognized an unfamiliar urge to grasp Parker's hand, and dismissed it.

Lydia performed that office first. "Dear Boyce." She reached out with her other hand to pull back the soft, blue coverlet. "Where does it hurt?"

He seized her wrist before she could adjust his coverlet.

"Nothing to see, ladies. I am not gravely injured, just a little sore here and there."

The door flew open and a tall matron stood on the threshold, dressed from head to toe in black, except for a striking gold quizzing glass hanging from her neck. Within seconds, the older woman's sharp gaze took in the details of everyone in the room. She then addressed the confection standing at the bedside. "What is this all about, Lydia?" The matron marched over toward the bed but stopped in front of Eve.

"Lord Boyce Parker fell out of his balloon, Mama. And this young lady does something with balloons." She frowned. "Why were you in the balloon, Miss…?"

"Mountfloy," Eve answered, dropping a curtsy to the older woman.

"Oh, yes." Lydia smiled broadly, revealing noticeably white teeth. "Miss Mountfloy, this is my mother-in-law, Lady Buxton."

The matron surveyed Eve for one second. "Tut!"

The butler appeared in the doorway. "Yes, my lady."

Lady Buxton clutched the gold chain of her quizzing glass. "See that the surgeon is called for. And make sure you call Mr. Hulbart and not Mr. Young— his breath kills his patients long before he has the chance to cure them."

"I have already sent Henry to fetch the surgeon, my lady."

"Of course. I should have known." Lady Buxton approached the bedside and held her quizzing glass up to briefly examine Lord Parker. "You must be the youngest. Rumors are you are an out-and-out frivolous buck. Is that true, young man?"

He widened his eyes. "Well! I wouldn't say—"

"You look just like your mother," the matron stated, followed by a sigh. "She was a childhood friend, you know."

"No, I did not—"

"It's the green eyes, of course. Quite rare. But

you have her hair, her chin—in fact, the resemblance is remarkable." She exhaled a long and deep sigh. "Young man, you have made me sad. I liked your mother and haven't thought of her in years. Despondent when she died. As children, we used to play cat and mouse at her uncle's house. Your mother always lost the game because her laughter gave her away. Lovely woman, lovely." Lady Buxton pulled up a cane chair and sat. "Since your mother and I were such close friends, I will naturally treat you as my son during your stay here at the priory. If there is anything you need, let me know. I'll be sure to inform Tut of the importance of your comfort. Now tell me all about this ballooning adventure."

"Mama, I—"

"Have more chairs brought in, Lydia," Lady Buxton said, nodding at Eve. "I'm sure our guest would like to sit."

Lydia glanced once at Parker before she dropped his hand and left the room.

This time Eve boldly strode forward and took Parker's hand. Decidedly cooler than normal, she wanted to chafe it vigorously, like their warming game, but she didn't want to explain this to the others. So she moved to block Lady Buxton's view of their joined hands, then slowly and softly rubbed his palm.

He squeezed her hand and smiled up at her. "Is my face presentable enough to be viewed by ladies?"

"You have two bruises, one of them quite alarming in size, but you are certainly presentable." She caught his glance, smiled, and squeezed his palm in return.

Lydia returned followed by Tut and a footman carrying several turned oak chairs with thick cushions.

Tut pointed to locations around the bed, and the footman placed each chair on the exact spot.

By the time everyone was comfortably seated, Parker attempted to sit up but soon became restless. "Ladies, if you will excuse me, my ribs are paining me. At the moment, I'm in no condition to chat."

To spare him physical discomfort or difficult explanations, Eve offered to describe their accident. "If you would pardon me, Lady Buxton. Perhaps you will let me relate the nature of our adventure, since his lordship is injured."

Lady Buxton raised a brow; the madman grinned.

Eve smiled at both of them in turn. "You see, your ladyship, Lord Parker has an interest in aerostation and wished to invest in balloons. His primary interest, however, was a race to Paris sponsored by the Earl of Stainthorpe. For that purpose, he joined a flight planned by my father and myself. We planned to perform our experiments and then cross the Channel to France. During the night, the wind changed directions and blew us back over England. I must compliment Lord Boyce because his help was invaluable in completing the experiments on board—"

Lady Buxton huffed. "I find your father's actions hard to believe, Miss Mountfloy. I do not approve of two young people engaging in a dangerous adventure alone."

"He meant to join us after we briefly touched down, but landing became impossible and my father was unable to board. At the time I was...held up."

Parker groaned then lifted the coverlet over his mouth.

"So together, his lordship and I soldiered on. This is by no means an unusual event, as we frequently have only two on board. I want to assure you that my father did give his lordship some sage advice before we left. I don't remember exactly what he said—"

"Hang on," Parker said, followed by a chuckle. "I have great respect for this young lady. The goal of our journey was to save humanity. We only thought about experiments to understand our weather and save lives." He stared at the ceiling and smiled broadly. "Miss Mountfloy needed my presence to assist with these scientific experiments too. I also landed the balloon under difficult circumstances and saved her life when we were caught in the trees. I also—"

"I agree," Eve said, "that you saved my life, but you don't deserve all of the credit for the landing. The two of us worked together to land the balloon the first time, remember?"

"Yes, yes, I stand corrected. The first attempt at landing was a team effort, but I did save your life."

She turned to Lady Buxton. "It was after the first attempt to land that the freak gust of wind caught us and blew us into the woods. His lordship is very strong and kept me from suffering his fate and falling out of the basket. So, yes, I'm grateful he saved my life."

"I repeat," Lady Buxton said, "your flight sounds dangerous and not up to conventional standards of behavior."

"It was only dangerous at the end," he said. "Also, concern over the propriety of our flight is unnecessary. Besides, at thousands of feet in the air, no one could see…"

Lydia gasped. "Thousands! Oh, I just realized how high that must be. How frightening."

Lady Buxton lowered her chin, indicating she questioned the veracity of their story, but she did not pursue it further.

"Oh, but you are a gentlewoman, my dear," Lydia said. "I have no intention of being vulgar, but one does wonder. I mean there are no airborne privies. How exactly do you…?"

In less than a second, Eve determined the nature of her question, since it was a common one. "Over the side, ma'am. The other aeronaut faces the opposite direction for privacy and does not turn around. Under the circumstances, it is a matter of honor."

"No!" Lydia slapped her palms together and held them in front of her chest. "I couldn't. I'd rather die first. Oh, Miss Mountfloy, I don't see how a lady could exist under the unpleasant conditions you describe. It is just not natural."

Lady Buxton appeared to be made of sterner stuff than her daughter-in-law. "You are a remarkable young woman, Miss—"

"Actually, that bit is quite natural," Parker said, another chuckle simmering in his throat.

"I see you enjoy the same outrageous levity as your mother," Lady Buxton admonished. "Without a doubt."

He whipped his head around to peer at the matron. "Really? How wonderful."

"Lady Buxton," Eve said, "in the crash, I lost my

father's *Results* book. Perhaps you could lend me the assistance of your servants and a horse, so I might retrieve it?"

Parker instantly sat up. "Yes, you must help her. You see, I funded the flight to win the earl's race, so if anything happens to Miss Mountfloy's research, I'll be the one to blame."

Before the matron could answer, Tut entered the room and announced the arrival of Dr. Hulbart.

The surgeon bowed. "Lady Buxton, ladies. I understand the young gentleman fell out of a balloon. This is my first patient from a ballooning accident, and I am quite excited about it." He moved to the bedside. "You must be the young Lord Boyce Parker I've heard about. Very pleased to meet you, sir." He turned to face Lady Buxton. "I prefer to examine his lordship alone, if you don't mind. Once I have finished my examination, I will inform Tut, so you ladies can return." The surgeon held his arm out. "No arguments, please."

The women exited the room.

During their wait in the drawing room, Eve wrote her father, explaining their whereabouts. Once the letter was handed to Tut for the post, she joined the two women, and consumed four pots of tea and a great deal of yellow almond cake. Lady Buxton mostly remained silent and watched Eve with great attention, while Lydia inquired ceaselessly about the hardships of balloon travel, putting great emphasis on the effect of wind upon one's hair. She then offered Eve several recommendations of various bonnets found to be reliable in wind storms before the surgeon called them back into the sickroom.

"A week or two of bed rest and you'll be well enough to charm all the ladies in the house again," Mr. Hulbart said as the women took their seats. "I've also given him a draught of laudanum, so he should sleep like an infant tonight."

Eve strode to the bedside. "What is the prognosis, sir?"

Parker winked at her. "Seems my ribs took great umbrage from bouncing off a tree trunk into shrubbery. But I heal fast. Tomorrow I'll help you recover your book and then the day after escort you back to London."

The surgeon snapped his leather case shut. "No, your lordship. You will do as I instructed and spend the next week or two in bed. If your ribs become inflamed, the consequences could be severe."

Eve's mind raced after hearing the word "severe." She certainly did not want to associate severe with Parker's injuries. She must insist he follow the doctor's orders and remain in bed. She even vowed to sit on him, to make him obey. "What can I do, sir?"

The surgeon turned to answer, his spectacles resting on the end of his nose. "See he gets bed rest and barley water. Any brand of restorative jelly is acceptable too. In my experience, there is nothing like restorative jelly to improve a patient's spirits. I will return tomorrow and check up on his progress." Mr. Hulbart spoke softly to Lady Buxton for a minute or two.

Lydia stood to show the surgeon to his carriage. "I promise to nurse you later, dear Boyce." The two of them left the room.

"Boyce, my dear," Lady Buxton pronounced, "due to my advanced age, I have a great deal of experience with people. I can easily recognize a person thinking of noncompliance from across the room. Tomorrow, I will see that a nurse is engaged to enforce your bed rest."

Parker opened his mouth in probable protest. "But—"

"Behave," Lady Buxton admonished, pointing a finger.

He gave her a radiant smile. "My dear Lady Buxton, since I have given my word as a gentleman, I have an obligation to see our lady of science here returns to her father. My wounds are not serious enough to stop me in that endeavor, I can assure you."

Lady Buxton glanced over to Eve, and to her astonishment, the older woman *winked*. "You will do as I say. I claim acquaintance with your father too, and I have confidence he will approve of my actions. We can all discuss this balloon and what's to be done tomorrow. Tonight, I insist you sleep. I will, of course, nurse you myself this evening. Tomorrow, our housemaid will do the job until a proper nurse arrives."

Eve devised a logical plan so her hostess would leave him under her care, but there was something about the elder woman's air that spoke of resistance. The stubborn set of her jaw combined with the manner in which she stabbed her needlework indicated to her that England's most powerful steam engine could not move Lady Buxton if she did not wish it. "With your permission, I will stay with—"

"Cats," Lady Buxton said.

"Pardon?"

"Do you like cats, Miss Mountfloy?"

"Why, yes, I have a ginger I am very fond of."

Lady Buxton smiled, and the twinkling firelight reflecting in her eyes made her appear younger than her somber dress and gray hair suggested. "I love cats. Don't always know the mischief they are going to get into, of course. But sometimes you can predict their behavior. I have seven cats altogether and the prettiest is a white fluffy one with long fur. Her name is Annabel, and she is my favorite. A completely selfish, frivolous creature whose only talent is her fur. Three of my other cats are excellent mousers. I really have nothing against mice, you understand. Although they can ruin the walls in a shocking manner. Joe—my best mouser—once brought me three mice in one day. What a fine fellow. Nothing so worthy as a good mouser, is there, Miss Mountfloy?"

"Well, I—"

"But for some reason, I prefer the silly, useless Annabel. I spoil her shamelessly and have been known to give her sweets. I cannot help it, because she is happiest sitting upon my lap, and I value her affection. With such a true heart, I can easily forgive her faults." She laughed. "She is beautiful too. Do you enjoy beauty, Miss Mountfloy?"

Parker's slow but steady breathing indicated he must be asleep.

Eve rose to check on him, and when she turned to answer the older woman, that lady watched her with a soft light in her eyes. "I think my balloon is beautiful. You should see it ascend into the air. No sight in the world is more magnificent than a balloon climbing into the heavens." After Eve described her hopes for ballooning to assist mankind, the two women lapsed into silence. Finally, the excitement and toil of the day overwhelmed Eve, and she fell asleep in her chair. She woke upon hearing voices.

"Yes, my dear," Lady Buxton pronounced, "his lordship's ribs are still in his body."

Lydia giggled. "But, Mama, I worry so about his ribs. I just had to see if they were inflamed. I am not sure what inflamed ribs looks like, but for his own safety, I had to check."

Eve straightened in her chair, rubbed her eyes, and found Lydia had pulled Parker's coverlet down to his waist, her hand rested upon his bare chest.

Likely still under the effects of the laudanum, he remained asleep.

"While I had never actually met his lordship previously," Lydia said, "I find we have many acquaintances in common, so I consider him a most excellent friend. There is no gentleman in London who is said to be more amusing. And I do worry so."

"I can imagine how amusing he is, my dear. Poor puss sacrificed all your London friends when you married Buxton, and now you're stuck way down here with only an old lady to amuse you." The older woman took her daughter-in-law's hand. "You have a good heart to be concerned over his lordship's welfare. Now come away, and let's see if, between the two of us, we can find a room and some more suitable gowns for Miss Mountfloy to wear during her stay." She tucked Lydia's arm under hers and addressed Eve. "I insist you sleep tonight in the room we have prepared for you. Tut will ensure you have everything you

need. I will also arrange for Christine to be your maid
while you are here at the priory. You cannot be an
effective nurse for his lordship, you know, without a
meal and a little rest."

"Thank you," Eve said.

"So wait here, and we will return when everything
is ready." Lady Buxton followed Lydia out of the room.

Eve concentrated on her plans to search for the
Results book tomorrow. She had no worries about
Parker's care, since tomorrow the ladies of the house
would probably go out of their way to spoil him. But
she could imagine numerous variables that might cause
the book's destruction. Rain could damage the pages
or animals might shred it to pieces for nesting material.
She gulped. They could lose a year's worth of data in
an instant. By the end of the day, she fell asleep only
when she pictured herself holding the book.

❧

The next morning, Eve attempted to open the
casement window and discovered every muscle in
her body announced its displeasure from yesterday's
adventure. With her mind not fully awake, she yanked
the leaded window open and flung it to the side. A
soft wind refreshed her spirits, and she delighted in
the promise of fine weather for the day ahead. With
her mind now as clear as the pale blue sky above, she
refocused on important matters. First was an assessment of Parker's condition, followed by the necessity
of finding her father's *Results* book.

Upon entering Parker's room, she discovered him
fast asleep. If he remained unable to move for a week,

she must find another accomplice to help her search. Since her father would suffer financially from the book's loss, she hoped he and his assistant, Charles Henry, would arrive soon and join in the search. However, Charles Henry could not identify the terrain in the approximate area where the book was lost, while Parker could. She placed a finger on his neck to confirm his heartbeat.

Upon her soft touch, he opened his eyes. He stared fixedly at the ceiling and blinked several times. He turned his head and smiled after he recognized her. "Feel like I've gone ten rounds with Gentleman Jackson and lost. How long have I been here?"

"You have probably slept since yesterday evening." She examined his face to determine if the bruises were healing normally. The hours he had spent without a shave had altered his normal boyish appeal. Now his dark lashes, uncombed locks, and whisker growth framed the brilliance of his grass-green eyes. She fought another overwhelming urge to place her hand on his cheek. This new desire to touch him must be an inherent female urge to provide comfort, she decided. At least, the hypothesis sounded logical.

"And you?" he asked. "I must say you look quite anxious. With all that crashing about, hitting trees, and dirty landings, I don't see how any person can travel by balloon and maintain acceptable standards of dress. Have they taken good care of you? Call Tut and let me have a word with him."

"I'm well." Eve lifted her fingers off his neck. "You will be pleased to hear that the ladies of the house have given me a half-dozen gowns to wear until mine can be cleaned and mended."

"You gave quite a fine story for Lady B. Maybe you should write a book for me to edit and publish."

"Listen, I expect to be out of the house within the hour. But I'm disappointed that you will be unable to join me."

"Out of the house? Join you?"

"If I don't find my father's *Results* book, our research will be lost. I hoped together we could find the field I crashed in by locating the damaged turnips, and then you might be able to retrace your steps into the woods. If we discover the location of your fall, we can begin our search for the book from there."

With a short groan, he managed to sit upright. "Not as bad as expected, although not quite as pluck as anticipated. Yes, yes, well enough to drive you to the woods. Afterward, when I return you to your father, all will be set to rights—daughter, balloon, book, minus a few birds with a tale to tell. You know once we reach the woods, maybe we'll see our friend the pigeon." Crossing one arm over his lap to adjust the coverlet to a greater degree of modesty, he moaned in heart-wrenching pain.

She stood, looking at his neck and upper chest. "You are in no condition to drive me anywhere." He sported several bruises on his chest; the dark red marks stood out in contrast to his fair skin and light brown chest hair.

He imprisoned her hand. "Miss Mountfloy, I want to…" A serious expression settled upon his face, and it was quite unlike anything she had seen before.

Unsure of the feelings that now took hold of him,

she worried he might be blaming himself again for her predicament. Both of them agreed to the journey. And while at the time she yelled at him to rescue the book, not her, she now realized how ridiculous it was to value a book over human life. "You want to sing, is that it?"

He grinned. "I am so pleased you want to hear me sing, but not now. I just want to make everything right for you. Unfortunately, I am unable to do so at present. Maybe tomorrow will be different. Can you postpone your search until tomorrow? I'm sure I can help you after another day of rest."

Waiting was not an option. She could not risk the book being damaged. "Don't worry. I'll drive out and survey the area. Tomorrow we will see how you feel. I know you have every reason to get well soon and resume your pursuit of Lady Sarah."

His lovely eyes widened and shone bright green. "Yes, yes, indeed, but your concerns are my first priority. It was my ambition that led to the loss—temporary, I'm sure—of your book. I'll write to my brother, Richard. He will help us." He pulled her hand to his lips, then kissed it.

It took all of her control to keep her eyes open. She also fought the urge to caress his cheeks or run a finger along the length of his lips. But most unlike her—silly goose she had become—the hollow in his throat pleaded for a soft caress. She stared at it and could not look away.

He gracefully kissed her hand again. This time his lips lingered on her skin.

Her breathing stopped, and she felt her knees go weak.

After a swift knock, the door opened.

Nine

EVE DROPPED HIS HAND LIKE A HOT COAL, ELICITING a short laugh from him. Obviously, she must analyze her remarkable defect in breathing at a more convenient time.

Lady Buxton entered, followed by Lydia. Lady Buxton hesitated, evaluated the situation, and then strolled into the room. "Is our guest feeling better today?"

This morning, Lydia wore a yellow muslin gown covered with a lace overlay that appeared to float in obvious disregard to the forces of gravity. The fabric's lightness would even befuddle Newton. She stood by Parker's bed and adjusted her sleeve. "Oh, feeling better today, dear Boyce? You must get well, you know, for all our sakes."

He grinned. "That is very sweet of you, Lydia, but I must impose upon your hospitality for a little while longer. Not quite up to my normal sangfroid at the moment. But I hope you will assist my friend here finding her father's *Results* book in the woods. It fell out of the balloon, you see, and she must recover it."

"Don't fret over the boy, Lydia. Sit down." Lady

Buxton turned to face Eve. "How can we be of service, Miss Mountfloy?"

"Thank you, ma'am. Perhaps I may borrow a cart today? I would like to visit the crash site and retrieve anything that might have been lost."

"What is this book Lord Parker mentioned?" Lady Buxton smoothed her stiff bombazine skirt around her.

His lordship eagerly answered her question. "The book contains her scientific results that I must recover. Indeed, I must ensure Miss Mountfloy, together with her book, is returned to her father. The book fell from the balloon just before I suffered my mishap, so I am the only person who can find it. I'd hate to think scientific progress could be lost because of me." He moved his arm to pull back the coverlet but stopped and groaned. "Perhaps not today though."

"So once you find this book," Mrs. Buxton inquired, her mouth slightly open, "you will leave us?"

Lady Buxton stared at her daughter-in-law before turning to Eve. "Then the book must be found immediately. Tut!"

Parker nodded. "She should have a chaperone for her own safety too, Lady B."

"Of course, son, you are not to worry."

"I cannot spare my servants today. They are all busy," Lydia said. "But Christine is free to assist dear Eve—"

"Thank you. I'll begin my search this instant."

Everyone let out words of protest at the same time, but the assembled company eventually acquiesced.

After donning a serviceable flax-colored dimity gown, Eve headed to the stables first to check up on her balloon. She found it neatly folded in the corner, next to the basket. Upon examination of the pile of instruments by its side, she discovered many of them missing. They likely fell out of the basket like Parker. A knot in her stomach formed when she considered her father's disappointment at the loss of his instruments, so she must do her best to recover all of them when she searched the woods.

Soon traveling in the same elegant gig Lydia had driven the day before, she and Christine headed for the turnip fields. They passed the home farm and then came to a fork in the road.

Unsure of exactly which road to take, Eve stood to survey the entire area. Off in the distance to her right, she observed a line of the priory's servants headed in the direction of the trees where the woods began. To her left, Spanish turnips grew in a field that might be the one she was looking for, so she urged the horse left, down the lane to the fields.

After ten minutes, they met Mr. Muckles and Jem, each carrying a hoe. Mr. Muckles touched his hat and greeted her.

"Are you weeding turnips today?" Eve inquired.

"No." Mr. Muckles spat over his shoulder. "Missus has special work for Jem and me off in de woods o'er dere." He pointed off to her right.

Eve twisted around and noticed he chose the same stand of woods the servants had entered. "What kind of job?"

"A sort of fetch'n job, miss." He put his hand on Jem's back and pushed him forward. "Now you enjoy your ride. Maggie dere is a fine beast. She'll lead you into no harm, dat one."

She watched him disappear before heading the gig further down the lane. "Do you know what this fetching job is, Christine?"

"No, miss." Christine pulled the brim of her bonnet lower to shield her face from the sun—or Eve's scrutiny.

She had no reason not to believe Christine, since she appeared a forthright, honest housemaid. Still, it seemed strange the housemaid possessed no idea of the other servants' assignments, since Lydia had claimed they were all busy today. She suspected the servants had been ordered to search the woods to find the book.

Urging Maggie forward, they came upon the first evidence of disturbed turnips. She left Christine and the gig at the edge of the woods and gingerly walked into the turnip field. A long swath of disturbed earth cut across numerous, perfectly manicured rows. The dirt gash ended in a fifty-foot area completely leveled by the wagons used to rescue its occupants and remove the balloon.

Upon careful examination of every square inch surrounding the spot where the balloon had rested, Eve could not find her lost instruments or anything of value left behind. The area contained a few pieces of rope and the remains of a ballast bag.

Returning to the gig just under a cool canopy of the woodland's trees, Eve bid Christine to stay where she was while Eve searched the woods. She began by inspecting the light undergrowth for a path but found none. Heading directly toward the estimated spot of the brown tree, she stepped into the undergrowth.

The fern and bracken shrubbery soon became thick. The foliage reached her waist, and she had trouble wading ten feet, much less the thousand or so feet she estimated was needed to reach the brown tree.

After what seemed like hours of gradually moving toward the center of the wood, carefully searching under every bush, she sat against the trunk of a hornbeam tree to catch her breath. By her calculations, she should have been near the spot of the brown tree, but she had kept her eyes on the canopy above her and failed to see any such tree. She concluded all future searches would be laborious and require a large number of people.

When rested, she started her search again. A long time passed and ended in failure to find the book. Somehow, the woods appeared even denser. Pushing sharp bushes aside, she cut her hands until they bled and began to pain her. Feeling tired and cold, she sat at the base of a sweet chestnut tree, dumbfounded over her predicament. From the air, the stand of woods appeared a mere island amongst the fields, but now, deep within it, the thick clump of trees seemed as though they must have been over a mile in diameter. A person could easily get lost in woods a couple of miles wide.

She needed to remain calm and not panic. Logic recommended she retrace her steps in the direction she had taken to find her way out. She kicked herself for not making a mental map of the landmarks, like trees, during her journey.

How could she be such an idiot to get lost?

Furious at herself for inadequate planning, she stood

and wiped off the collection of leaves now ornamenting her dirty gown. The question became: which direction had she left Christine and the gig? Taking the blame for failing to bring a compass, she tried to locate the sun's position through the treetops. Her theory was that if she could determine the direction of the sunlight, she could use that as a fixed point to head in one direction without going in a circle. This worked for several yards, but she found herself in spots where the thick canopy of trees hid the sunlight falling on the treetops. This made it difficult to determine the correct orientation of the sunlight and thus the appropriate direction to escape the woods and return to the gig.

Blast. A quick search of the ground for evidence of her previous tracks revealed that they too became easily lost within feet, so retracing her steps would be difficult to almost impossible.

Her next theory was to walk in the direction of a light breeze. If she could feel a breeze on her cheeks, it might be coming from the direction of open fields. So she struggled forward, wading through the shrubbery. At least an hour later, she came upon the same sweet chestnut where she had rested earlier. Now truly exhausted, she collapsed on a large root and caught her breath.

She had made a terrible mistake, but self-recrimination would not help. Cold and hungry, she felt like taking a small nap before she resumed her efforts to escape, but warning bells went off in her brain. Similar to high altitudes, sleep preceded unconsciousness, and she had no desire to expire beneath this lovely tree.

Blast. She stood. The day had lengthened into afternoon, and she could no longer think about the book or search for it. Her strength failed her completely and even a single step became difficult. Her only choice at this point was to wait for help, counting on the fact that Christine knew her last location and would return to the priory to tell them of her disappearance. She sighed and forced herself to concentrate. What else could she do to free herself? Mr. Muckles and Jem came to mind, weeding the fields. Perhaps if she yelled, they might hear her. "Mr. Muckles, help! Help, somebody, help!" She yelled in this matter for at least ten minutes, stopping each time to listen for a reply. Finally, her voice became hoarse, so she put her fingers to her mouth and whistled. Startled birds rising from the canopy of trees provided the only results of her whistling experiment.

With her strength exhausted, all she could do now was wait—wait and pray someone would find her. Indeed, she resolved to remain in one spot, so if a rescuer searched for her, they wouldn't miss each other. She made herself comfortable on a bed of leaves in a slight clearing under a large ash tree.

Approximately an hour later, the sunlight began to fade with the coming dusk. She wondered when Christine would return to the priory and summon help, and about the difficulty of any rescue party actually finding her before the light faded altogether. Finally, her thoughts turned to Parker. What did he mean in the balloon when he asked to show her freedom? Now she might never have the chance to discover the meaning of his words.

A tear gathered—surely one of exhaustion, that's all. She glanced up at the last gleam of sunlight dancing on the treetops. She closed her eyes and remembered him singing a lovely song about clouds. "Roll de roll de. Roll de roll di."

If she was never found, would Parker feel sad at her eventual death from the cold nights? Would he miss her? Would he continue his race without giving her demise a second thought? She knew that if the tables were turned, she'd be heartbroken. A tear fell as she thought about him: his laughter during the ascension, his silly songs, and his love of nature. Her heart actually began to pain her.

If Parker stood before her now, what would she do? Seek happiness and reach out for him? She vowed that if she ever saw him again, she would run into his arms and kiss him senseless.

Like Tom in his final moments, she would act upon the emotions filling her heart and not the logic of her head. Tom had had a sweetheart when his ship had foundered—something to live for. He had recognized that same reason to live in others, so he had risked his life to save them. His efforts had saved many men wanting to return safely to their loved ones and sweethearts too.

Upon hearing of Tom's sacrifice, her father, in his grief, had mocked Tom as weak and sentimental. Now she realized her father's reaction had stopped her from opening her heart to find her own sweetheart, and had led to her single-minded pursuit of knowledge for the betterment of mankind.

Her chest constricted, giving her the feeling of

being caged and unable to breathe. She remembered the butterfly. Her efforts to gently catch it while the animal rested on a tall gladiolus in her garden; then, carefully placing the butterfly in a small, dark cage with only enough space between the wicker strands to receive air. Rapidly blinking to clear her vision from unshed tears, she recalled Parker's tender words to the animal to travel safely. Then she remembered her last sight of the little creature, its wings folded in death, resting in Parker's palm as he lifted it into the breeze.

Hot tears gathered and fell. She would never contribute to the world's knowledge or find the happiness of a wife and mother. Here, in the cold, against this tree, in a day or two, she would die within walking distance from her bed at the priory.

Ten

"WHAT, IS SHE LOST?" BOYCE FOUND HIMSELF THINK-ing about variables, a concept Eve used to make deci-sions but one he had never fully appreciated before. What if she had fallen out of her gig and lay injured? What if highwaymen were in the vicinity? What if the silly girl had entered the woods by herself and fell victim to a brethren of the boot-grabbing tree? Boyce inhaled to fill every inch of his lungs. "Tut!" He grabbed the blue coverlet to cover his nakedness, but Nurse Hadley objected to his attempts to rise.

She snatched the other corner of the coverlet and vigorously engaged in a tug-of-war. Her brooch hung with silver scissors and whatnots swayed and jingled. "Please, your lordship."

"I can stand. Just watch me." After a swift tug side-ways, he claimed his prize and wrapped the scratchy blue coverlet around his torso. He swung his feet to the floor, then with slow, purposeful movements, he managed to stand. Once upright, some unseen, irk-some fellow shoved red-hot needles into his ribs and right knee.

Nurse Hadley widened her eyes after an accidental glimpse of his tender bits, then fled the room, passing Tut in the doorway. "Feverish, that one is."

Tut's eyebrows rose for a fraction of a second before the mask of the discriminating butler descended over his countenance. "Yes, my lord."

"I understand from Nurse that Miss Mountfloy has not returned. Is that true?"

Tut calmly addressed him, seemingly oblivious to Boyce's inadequate attire. "Yes, my lord, the young lady has not returned to the priory."

"Bring me my breeches, shirt, and coat. Immediately, if you would be so kind. Oh, and can you acquire a pair of boots for my use?"

"I will see what I can do, your lordship. May I make a suggestion?"

"Yes, yes."

"We have arranged for John to be your valet while you are here at the priory, but he is currently out with the other servants performing an errand for Mrs. Buxton. Perhaps I may be of service."

"Of course. I shall try not to be too much trouble. But I really insist my clothes are fetched this instant. If Miss Mountfloy has not returned, I am quite sure she is in need of me." He stepped over to the oak washstand and groaned at the sight of whisker growth shading his checks. "I say, Tut, what's this errand that called the servants out of the house?"

The butler turned in the doorway. "A matter of business, my lord. However, that business is unknown to me. With your permission, I will retrieve a suitable pair of boots."

One of those pesky variables troubled Boyce's brain again. If she were injured, how would he get Eve home to the priory? "Yes, yes, and, Tut."

"Yes, my lord."

"I need a horse." He pictured her trampled by her own cart and lying on the ground, writhing in pain. His heartbeat raced. "Can you obtain a suitable hack for my use?"

"I will see what I can do." Tut left the room and returned soon after. His arms were full of Boyce's clean clothes and a pair of borrowed black boots polished to a pier-glass shine.

"You're a magician, Tut, thank you." Boyce grabbed his clothes and moved behind a Chinese screen. With some difficulty and a few audible winces, he stepped into his breeches, threw his shirt over his head, tucked the tails of his shirt between his legs, and then buttoned his breeches. He had just finished with the three buttons on the top of his white linen shirt when Lydia entered his room unannounced.

"Oh, let me help you dress." She giggled, rushing forward.

He stepped from behind the screen and held up his palm. "Stay where you are. Thank you, I don't need help. Where is Buxton, by the way?"

Lydia pouted and walked over to the window. "Buxton is away in London on business. He wants to be Chancellor of the Exchequer, you know. Evidently, our money or currency or something needs to be changed. *Decimal* is the word he uses. It has something to do with ten fingers and toes. It means nothing to me, but it is ever *so* important.

That's the reason you only have me to amuse you during your stay at the priory, and I would like to amuse you, dear Boyce."

"You were married what—two, three, eight months ago? I'd expect Buxton down here with his pretty new bride, not in London messing about with old coins."

"That is all your fault. Buxton is rather put out with me at the moment, but I truly love him. I do."

"My son finds it necessary to be in London." Lady Buxton expostulated from the doorway. "He feels time apart to reflect upon the solemn state of matrimony would be beneficial to his wife and to himself. So he has left her with me for the time being. I can truly say that I am grateful for her company and assistance. At sixty years of age, my mind is not as it used to be. A few months ago in the spring, I instructed the gardeners to cut the roses by the front door. I meant to say grass, not roses, so now you understand why bare stumps greeted you upon your arrival. I cannot express my gratitude enough to my daughter-in-law for taking over the responsibilities of running the household." She stepped forward to enter the room but halted after a couple of steps. "I see you are dressing. Come, Lydia, let his lordship dress in peace."

"Boyce doesn't really mind if I stay, do you?" Lydia waved her hand. Her fluttering lace sleeve resembled a kaleidoscope of butterflies.

A transitory frown crossed Lady Buxton's face, replaced by a serene countenance and a tender grin.

"Delighted you are here, your ladyship," he said. "Have you heard news of Miss Mountfloy?" He reached for his cravat and wrapped it several times around his neck. Fear for Eve's welfare knotted his stomach, but he needed to hide his distress, to spare the ladies concern.

"Oh!" Lydia clapped her hands "I hope you are going to tie the mathematical. That knot is the kick of fashion. And it makes a gentleman ever so handsome—irresistible, in fact."

Lady Buxton exhaled audibly and sat next to her daughter-in-law. "No, Miss Mountfloy has not returned. Nor have the servants. Christine is with her, so no harm will come to her, I'm sure."

"I'm sure they will be back soon, Mama," Lydia said, adjusting her yellow muslin skirt into smooth, perfect folds across her lap.

Boyce stilled while Tut stepped forward to correct the hash he made of his neckcloth. "A simple knot, please. Since I will be riding."

"Yes, my lord."

"Where are you off too?" Another pout crossed Lydia's perfect lips.

"I plan to search for Miss Mountfloy," he said. "It is growing dark, and I fear for her safety. She is my responsibility, and I must see that she is restored to her father."

"Young man," Lady Buxton pleaded, "you are not well enough to ride. When the stable boys return, I will send them to hunt for Miss Mountfloy. You are not fit to undertake such strenuous exercise. Inflamed ribs can be lethal."

While he slipped into the sleeves of his coat, biting his tongue to suppress a grimace, the nurse reentered the room. Clearly she was one of those uncanny females with a second sense to indicate when her patients were fully dressed.

Lady Buxton turned awkwardly in her chair to face the nurse, an indication of possible stiffness in her hip. "Nurse Hadley agrees with me that you should rest. Don't you?"

The nurse nodded and approached the bed. "Of course, your ladyship. The surgeon indicated the young man should stay abed for at least a week before any attempts at perambulation."

Boyce wiped away the new smudge he made on his borrowed top boots before taking his first step with care. "Yes, yes, Mrs. Hadley, I like you. You are doing a fine job. Indeed, I cannot thank all of you ladies enough. Now, if you will excuse me, I will borrow one of your fine horses and hunt for Miss Mountfloy. Tut, I lost my hat when the balloon lifted off. Can you procure something suitable for the time being? Preferably the brim not too wide, mind you."

"I will endeavor to find something satisfactory, my lord." The butler exited the room.

Lady Buxton clicked her tongue. "Just like your mother, all reckless emotion and no common sense. I suppose there is no stopping you? If your ribs become inflamed, I plan to scold you to the devil."

Boyce tentatively strolled over and kissed Lady Buxton on the cheek. "I like you too. I couldn't be more pleased to know I resemble my mother. And to show my gratitude, I plan to enjoy your scolding—"

The older woman slapped him on the cheek. "You young rapscallion. Anyone can see how important Miss Mountfloy is to you, so off with you."

"Where's my kiss?" Lydia turned her cheek to Boyce. "I feel ever so slighted."

"Of course you do." Boyce gave her a kiss on the cheek with a loud smack and then turned to Nurse Hadley. "You're the one who actually deserves a kiss. Do you want one too?"

Nurse Hadley's wide eyes appeared genuinely horrified, while the other ladies laughed in unison.

Pleased with his success in hiding his anxiety over Miss Mountfloy's fate, he used the interruption to escape outside. There in the courtyard, he found a groom holding a real Sussex horse. Not as heavy as a shire or fat as a Suffolk, the good-sized beast sported a dun-brown coat and matching flaxen-colored tail and mane.

"If yo' have to go in yon woodlands," the groom said, "this animal is better than the missus's fine stepper and will get yo' through the bracken without a fuss."

Boyce took the reins and accepted a hand up. Within minutes, he found himself galloping down the lane next to the turnip field. The smell of dirt mixed with sour turnips warmed by the hot sun filled the air. The horse's strides sent more burning pins into his chest and leg. Because the approaching dusk dimmed the sunlight, he almost missed the disturbance in the rows of turnips where the wagons hauled the balloon out of the field. He didn't bother entering the field to inspect the site. Instead, he wheeled the horse toward the woodlands. Nearing the edge of the timber, a horse and gig came into view, a young lady standing by the front wheel. After a brief discussion with Christine, the variable he considered the worst of the bunch became real. Eve must be lost in the stand of trees and unable to find her way back to the gig. "Miss Mountfloy!" His voice echoed back, but the only other response was a sudden flight of startled birds.

No response.

His jaw tightened. "Christine, you head back to the priory and summon help. Explain that I have entered the woodland to rescue Miss Mountfloy." Without waiting for her reply, he carefully urged the snorting, hesitant Sussex dun toward the low spots of foliage and bracken. Once they reached the thick undergrowth, the large beast stopped and flipped his head up. "Miss Mountfloy!" He called her name until his throat felt raw. "Miss Mountfloy!"

He spent an hour urging the reluctant horse forward, around, and through a combination of ferns and unknown, intensely green shrubs. The deeper he entered into the stand of trees, the more the reduced sunlight stunted the undergrowth, so the horse had an easier time. However, this new ease contrasted with Boyce's inability to determine his direction of travel. For all he knew, he could be moving in a giant circle. Finally, he heard a muffled sound from his right, so he headed in that direction. "Miss Mountfloy."

"I'm here, over here."

The sound was faint, but he heard it nevertheless. In what seemed like a decade later, he reached her trembling figure.

She held on to an oak tree trunk, and from the tenacity of her grip, the tree was probably all that kept her upright. The bottom half of her gown was torn and stained, while her face appeared downright filthy.

Renowned for his high standards of dress, it seemed odd to him that she appeared the prettiest woman he had ever seen.

"Eve, Eve." Dropping the reins, he jumped off the horse, winced in pain, swore, and leaped over shrubs regardless. When near, he noticed tears streaking down her pale cheeks. He grabbed her up in his arms and held her tight. For some reason, he could not think of a good reason to let her go.

Her tears only intensified. "Thank you. Thank you. I was so frightened. I did not think anyone would find me before dark." Her sobbing grew louder.

"Shh, you're safe." The second after speaking these words, Boyce tried to decide which one of them felt more relieved. Her violent sobs against his chest and her sorrowful state of dress indicated she had had a rough time. She must have struggled in vain for hours to find her way out of the woodland. By contrast, his desperation only swirled about in his head in relative physical comfort, so she must have suffered the most.

When he released his grip, she kissed him full on the lips.

She must have been in more distress than he had initially realized. He held her at arm's length to examine her fully. Perhaps he missed an injury. He found her dirty but well. "Yes, yes, good to see you're not hurt." Now he felt emboldened enough to aim for those apple lips. Upon the touch of her lips, his physical awareness became lost in a fog of joy. Since his lips were otherwise engaged, his heart sang a happy tune. He kissed her cheek. Upon the touch of her skin, his every care for the last several days melted. For him, his kiss was no general peck of good wishes or even the beginnings of seduction; it was an unspoken expression of "I'm overjoyed you're well." Actually, he liked kissing her, so he continued to do so. Soon, he covered every inch of her pretty person with a kiss— well, every inch that could be kissed. So he kissed her ear—she grinned—he kissed her neck, long and slow. "Yes, yes, so pleased you're safe."

She sagged in his arms. "Ah."

"Seems to me I should record that you just uttered a sound of apparent satisfaction."

"Enough," she said, chuckling softly. Her cheeks were as apple red as her lips. "Listen, madman, how do we get out of here?" She punched his chest.

"Ow!" He clutched his upper arm.

"Oh, sorry, sorry, I am so sorry. Please forgive me. I forgot about your injury." She paused. "What are you doing here? You should be in bed. I apologize, I really do, but numerous kisses will not assist us in finding our way out of the woods."

He ignored her and smiled. "Perhaps not, but kisses are too much fun." Recalling her earlier desperation, he realized his selfishness. "Right, out of the woods it is."

"We'll need a clear and well-thought plan."

"I devised a plan this morning and soon discovered it would not work. I thought hounds would be just the ticket. Find you by smell—beg pardon—in no time. So I asked Lydia where to find a dog, but it seems the only one available for miles is a greyhound. A sight hound is no use in a forest where you cannot see. So a well-thought plan was not responsible for your rescue. You owe your recovery to emotional fortitude and pure strength, my desire to find you and the shrub-crushing physical strength of this Sussex beast here, not logic and planning."

He mounted the dun then helped her up to sit in front of him.

While she adjusted her skirt and he held her tight to stop her from falling off, the horse started forward in a direction of its own choosing, the loose reins trailing through the shrubbery.

She settled sideways in his arms, to address him directly. "It sounds as though, when you chose this strong animal, you planned to forge through the bracken."

He hesitated, staring at the sable waves of her tousled hair. She was right, of course. Only he had not chosen the animal; the groom's brains were responsible for the choice of beast. But since he belonged to the society of males, he had no intention of voluntarily admitting his failings.

The horse turned right to avoid a large guelder rose shrub covered in red berries.

She searched his expression, then chuckled. "I see. You did not choose the horse. The groom must have suspected the type of animal needed for woods and used logic to make *his* choice."

He withheld a reply, needing to think carefully to win the argument that greater success was achieved by using emotion instead of logic.

The horse continued to plod forward.

He glanced ahead, formulating the words for his defense and avoiding the beckoning, luscious pout. "Ahem. Maybe the groom had a tragic, emotional experience with painful shrubs and, as a consequence, used his heart to choose the beast." Flawless reasoning, without a doubt. He then realized the irony of using reason to bolster his side—the emotional side—of the argument. *Best not to mention the irony.* "Old Brutus here will use his giant heart to lead us out in no time."

"The horse will use feelings to lead us out of the woods?"

"Of course. Trust him. He is such a great hulking brute. He'll use his emotions to propel his mighty strength forward. With that fortitude, he'll lead us out of here and into the clear blue sky."

"That sounds more like logic than emotion to me. Except it will be night soon, and we'll not be able to see the broken branches to retrace Brutus's path. I really do not relish spending the night curled up next to a tree trunk."

"Don't be so daft. I'm nothing like a tree trunk." He rocked her within his arms.

She laughed and shook her head.

"Much better, my pretty miss. I love to hear your laugh. How about a song? I don't know any 'Help, I'm lost in the woodlands' songs, but a nice fireside song should make us feel warmer. Yes, yes, let me sing—"

"Shh. Do you hear that? We must be getting close. Can you see anything?" She pointed to the right, her arm level with his shoulder. "Look."

On his right, a small oval of a gold field, framed by dark trees, shone in the distance. Minutes later, the brush and trees began to thin. He could see the top half of two men apparently walking along a path.

"See?" he said. "Brutus used his big heart to bring us to safety."

"No, you're wrong. Now that I think about it, Brutus used logic—the location of his feed bag—to bring us out of the trees."

He caught her glance and held it. In unison, they broke out in laughter. However, he still needed to hold up the male side of the argument. "It's a universal truth that males consider hunger one of the primary emotions."

Hearing their laughter, the men stopped and peered into the woods. As the giant Sussex stepped from the undergrowth onto the path along the field, the men doffed their hats.

"Hallo. Hallo," Boyce called. It suddenly hit him that Eve's rescue would count as a service to a lady. He couldn't wait to tell everyone at the priory of this achievement, but then guilt assaulted his conscience. He patted Brutus's neck. "Good boy." The horse had provided the service to them both.

The servants approached, and Eve and Boyce learned the two men were from the priory, one an under-gardener and the other a groom. After pleasantries were exchanged, followed by a description of their ordeal, Boyce discovered they were part of the group sent out by Lydia to search the woodland. Before he headed Brutus in the direction of the priory, he casually attempted to confirm his suspicions. "Did you find anything of value, fellows?"

Both men just smiled.

Eleven

MIDMORNING THE NEXT DAY, BOYCE HEADED INTO the stables to inspect the balloon. The brown wicker basket rested off to the side in the main stables, next to the tack wall. Humming an upbeat tune, he watched as a shaft of sunlight illuminated the folded silk balloon, causing it to shimmer silver and blue. It seemed unbelievable that the beautiful pile of cloth in front of him had taken him halfway across Britain.

"You are not hiding from me, are you, dear Boyce?" Lydia gingerly stepped into the stables. "I expected you to remain in bed."

"I've had enough rest. Pluck to the backbone this morning."

Lifting her dainty, pointed shoes an inch off the dirt floor, she slowly moved forward, the placement of each step carefully planned. "Oh, I am glad to hear you are well."

Boyce smiled at her delicate dance as she approached. Her repeated desire for his company endeared her instantly. "Come, look at this pretty balloon. I'm sure you will admire it too." Lydia and his best friend, George Drexel, had discreetly shared a bed for a year after her first husband died. She had tired of Drexel's company after he had made it known that he would not be formally giving her his addresses. Searching for her next great love, she found solace in the arms of another beau. Boyce had been genuinely happy when he learned she had married Buxton, an honorable man and a favorite school friend of one of his older brothers.

She stared at the straw beneath her feet. "Oh, I forgot how dirty it is in the stables." Holding her skirt up ever so slightly, she gingerly took another wide step forward. "I forgot the repulsive smells too. Almost as foul as the streets of London."

After catching a glimpse of her well-shaped ankles, he remembered Drexel extolling her prettiest parts—not surprising since his engineering friend had a habit of remembering his females to the inch, like every structural detail in his iron bridges. Boyce swallowed and forced himself to look up at her pretty face instead. "Now, what is a fine lady like you doing out here amongst all this muck?"

"Searching for you."

"I suppose you want to hear my story. I mean the story of my adventures in the balloon, don't you? Let me tell you about the scientific experiments I helped to complete. Did you hear about the great discovery I made? I mean, well, Miss—"

"Dear Boyce, in this short time we have known each other, I have learned to enjoy your company so—so humorous, so lively." After another dainty step forward, she laid her hand softly upon his chest.

He covered her small hand with his to lift both off his chest. "I have not had a chance to properly congratulate you on your marriage. What has it been, three months? I wish you both happy. Nice fellow, Buxton, by the way. You could not have chosen a better man for a husband."

"Dearest Buxton, I love him so much that I sacrificed everything, you understand. It is a great injustice he sent me down here to rusticate with his mother. I'm to be punished, and it is not as if I was ever unfaithful to him. Once we met, I never thought of anyone else. We were so happy. Then he made all sorts of wild accusations after he found my name—I mean, my initials—in dear George's field guide. Such an ungentlemanly act for our mutual friend to pen a book like that."

Boyce lowered his head to gaze directly into her eyes, and pursed his lips in a friendly smile. "To find your wife's initials between the pages might have been a shock to a newly married husband, now you must admit."

She paused, a dainty scowl spoiling her flawless features. "I had always been honest with dear Buxton before our marriage, about everything too. Perhaps he didn't believe me and thought I exaggerated. Anyhow, for some reason, he took the presence of my initials under the column 'Happy Goers' rather badly."

"I can understand his reaction entirely. What I can't understand is the number of women pleading with Drexel to elevate their status *to* 'Happy Goers.'"

She gave him a sideways glance. "I can." Then a sigh escaped. "Seeing my initials made dear Buxton so cross."

"Is that why he sent you, the toast of London, down here to rusticate in an old priory? He does not mean to abandon you here, does he?"

"He must be." Glancing up and around the stables, she shuddered. Then her eyes widened, revealing a flash of blue eyes between dark lashes. "You published Drexel's field guide, that's why I'm cross with you. I'm going to hold you partially responsible for my woes. You owe me then, dear Boyce." After a giggle and toss of perfect curls, she regained her smile.

"Yes, yes, but if you are not happy here, why don't you return to your many friends in London?"

"Because he has forbidden me. And as his wife, I truly desire to make dear Buxton a good one. After all, I gave up everything for him. Oh, the injustice. Evidently, he needs privacy or calm or something to write legislation. He says he cannot write and worry about me at the same time. It is very sweet of him to worry about me, don't you think so?"

"I am sure many a gentleman worries about you, Lydia."

"Ha, ha, so sweet. All gentlemen are so very kind. I…" She paused at the sound of an approaching horse.

A footman led a chestnut gelding into the stables a mere thirty feet away.

Once the footman disappeared deep into the far stalls, Boyce stepped forward and offered his arm to lead her back toward the priory. "Yes, I understand why Buxton worries. Let's go inside, shall we? Someone might come to the wrong conclusion if they find us alone together in the stables."

"Oh, but I've sent all of the stable hands, except

that one—my most trusted servant—to help refurbish Lady Buxton's favorite carriage. I can assure you, we will not be disturbed."

"We will not be disturbed because we are returning to the priory. Miss Mountfloy must be awake and ready to discuss her plans to recover her father's *Results* book."

"This book is important to you, isn't it?"

The slight rise in the intonation of her voice, coupled with her reticent servants the previous day, deepened his suspicion that she knew the whereabouts of the book. "Sweetheart, tell me: Have you found it? If so, you must return it immediately to its rightful owner, Miss Mountfloy. You're right, the book is important, and she is distressed by its loss."

She uttered a halfhearted titter. "Oh, I am just merely testing your dedication to leaving us. I mean, if I did have this book, would your gratitude include staying here to keep dear Lady Buxton and me amused awhile longer?"

His suspicion grew to the point where he could not leave the stables without knowing the truth. "You must not play games with me."

"Naughty, naughty." She stepped closer, her smile coy. "You haven't said anything about my new gown." Grabbing the ends of her shawl, she held them out to expose quite an impressive décolletage covered by an ivory silk bodice held together by two buttons in the center.

He involuntarily made a sound, something between a gulp and a choke.

Still holding her shawl out, she stepped forward

until his waistcoat came in contact with her—chest. Then she did the most remarkable thing. Lydia caught his glance before slowly looking down at her own bosom. She even arched her back, which seemed to shove her chest upward.

Two buttons—did that surprise him? No. Two buttons were irresistible to all men with a pulse, because of their ease in popping them open. Ten buttons could be a problem, but one or two buttons only begged to be released. Moreover, it was common knowledge that men, even the most pure gentlemen, had a hard time turning their gaze away when presented with such a womanly feast, so it came as no surprise that his throat dried. "Yes, yes, my apologies. It's a pretty gown, but not nearly as pretty as your smile." He stepped backward a foot.

"Ha, ha, you always say the most charming things." Yet she made no movement to restore the shawl.

"It's a fine gown, and the lady in it delightful too. But that lady is married, and there are rules."

After a fleeting purse of her lips, she began to stroke his cheek. "It thrills me when you are so direct, so forceful, so good. But you have broken the rules with other ladies before."

"Now, Lydia…" He imprisoned her hand within his own. "Your husband is a friend. As far as I am concerned, married ladies are forbidden."

She pulled her hand free and slid both arms around his waist, just under his jacket. "Dear George and I had such fun. Did he ever tell you about me? We could have fun too."

All he seemed capable of at the moment was to stare

at the roof's heavy beams. He then managed to grab her forearms and pull them away from his backside. "I do not wish to be a scoundrel of the worst sort. Buxton is—"

"Dear Boyce." She maneuvered her hands until she held his palms in a firm grasp. Then she placed his hands directly upon her hips.

He gasped. "Lydia, I—"

"Dear, dear Boyce."

He removed his hands, grabbed the ends of her shawl, and wrapped it over her gown. "Sweetheart, tell me the truth: you would never be unfaithful to Buxton, admit it."

She paused, eyes wide. "At least, I never believed that I could do something like that before he abandoned me." A sound escaped her that could only be described as a soft moan. "Now I don't know. Do you believe dear Buxton would do the same and be faithful to me? He's been away for such a long time, months and months, leaving me alone down here in the wilderness."

"Buxton is not the type of gentleman who would ever be unfaithful. You know that in your heart." He put his arm around her shoulders and pulled her close. "Courage, sweetheart. When he returns, he'll realize his mistake in leaving you alone and without company. Believe me, all will be well."

"Lord Boyce Parker," Eve said.

He stepped away from Lydia and turned to discover his aeronaut, her father, and the young man with the drab coat standing before him.

Eve's flushed cheeks revealed she must have witnessed the last minute or two. Mr. Mountfloy narrowed his eyes while the slim man couldn't tear his glance away from Lydia.

Eve cleared her throat, seemingly hesitant to speak. "Lord Boyce Parker, you have previously met my father at the ascension, but let me introduce my father's assistant, Mr. Charles Henry."

"Yes, yes, a pleasure, sir." He stepped forward to shake Mr. Henry's hand, then he provided introductions all around.

"Mrs. Buxton," Eve said, formally addressing their hostess. "Please, from what little I overheard, I must know. Do you have my father's *Results* book? If so—"

"What's this?" Mr. Mountfloy turned to face the two ladies. "Mrs. Buxton, is this true? Please hand it over immediately. I cannot stress enough the importance of its recovery."

Lydia appeared unconcerned, intent only upon a thorough perusal of Mr. Henry. A few long seconds later, she turned to Mr. Mountfloy and sighed. "Seems I need to look for this book then. Now please, everyone, follow me to the priory. Tut will see to refreshments for us, I'm sure."

Mr. Mountfloy stood fixed and failed to join the others as they started back. "Mrs. Buxton," he said with a raised voice, "you must—"

"Father, perhaps another time," Eve said, smiling at Lydia.

Lydia ignored him and ran forward to slide her arm into the crook of Eve's.

Boyce decided the two women shared confidences or some secret, since they whispered as they strolled out of the stables.

❧

Since Lydia had requested a private conversation, Eve stepped into her sunny, large bedroom on the priory's first floor. A broadside of duck's egg–blue satin, trimmed with gold tassels, festooned the walls and curtains. In contrast, each item of furniture—chair, mirror, and bed—gleamed from the rich, dark brown of the finest mahogany.

While the room could only be described as the pinnacle of femininity, Eve considered it unsettling. All of the furniture, several lamps, and the wash basin were ornamented with a medallion of Wedgwood's blue-and-white jasperware. Everywhere you looked, the blue room seemed crowded with little white cherubs, like a tiny built-in audience.

"There you are," Mrs. Buxton said, waving to the housemaid to place several jewel-colored gowns on the bed. "Dear Eve, aren't these lovely? I went to great trouble to choose gowns that would complement that lovely dark hair you have."

Years ago, Eve's mother had said almost the exact words. As the dutiful parent of a daughter, she had trained Eve in all of the skills necessary for a young lady to make an advantageous match, hiring tutors for singing, pianoforte, and watercolor, since the expected future any gentleman's daughter had a right to expect was wedlock. Then after Tom died, Eve volunteered to help her father. He accepted her assistance but warned her against any ambition relating to scientific discovery. He told her that women lacked the rigor of mind necessary for science.

Once those words had escaped his lips, Eve vowed

to prove her father wrong. She'd learned from his example and strove to make a great discovery for the betterment of mankind. Now, after her fright in the woods, she was beginning to have doubts about the wisdom of that pledge. If she did not change, her future would become like that stone lodged deep inside a pyramid—not a lady in a jewel-colored gown admiring the pyramid in the company of her loving husband. She wondered if someday in the future, women could fulfill both dreams. "I want to thank you again for your hospitality, Mrs. Buxton. I—"

"My dear, please call me Lydia, remember? We'll become the best of friends, I can tell." She stepped forward and clasped both of Eve's hands. "I cannot describe the joy of having another female in the house. Oh, Lady Buxton is pleasant enough, of course, but she is old. I don't think we have ever discussed a gown once. Imagine that. Last week, I joined Mama in a whist party at our neighbor's, and not one woman took the bother to dress impressively. Not a single lady wore a tiara or a trembler."

"Lydia, please, I must know. Did your servants find the *Results* book?"

Lydia dropped her hands and went to stare out the small, leaded window.

Her silence surprised Eve, since she had never seen her hostess reticent and still. "His lordship mentioned you might have the book. And we saw your servants searching the woods." Eve stopped speaking, unsure if Lydia heard a single word. While she waited for the other woman to speak, she let herself stroke the fine fabric of an emerald silk gown.

The mantel clock with two Blanc de Chine cherubs holding up the dial ticked away.

"I envy you," Lydia said, with a soft voice and possibly watery eyes. "While I'd be too frightened to meddle about in a balloon. You have a busy life, friends, good society composed of successful people. Everyone listens to you." She stopped speaking to focus on arranging her Indian shawl. "I will be very appreciative if you could use your influence to sway dear Boyce to stay at the priory, a month at the very least. You are young and cannot understand the comforting presence of having a gentleman in the house—not only for protection, but for the lively conversation and generous praise unique to gentlemen."

Lydia's voice remained steady, but Eve heard something else too—a tiny plea for acceptance or perhaps the fear of loneliness that caused her forward behavior in the stables. Eve knew Parker was a seductive gentleman, and he had mentioned several women of his acquaintance before, so she understood why Lydia desired his company. She strode over to her hostess, still standing by the window, and took both of her hands. "Ma'am, I cannot thank you enough for your kindness to me. Your servants handled my balloon with great care, and I know they have done their best to recover my instruments as well. I admire you and will do all I can to please you, but I have no influence over his lordship—"

"Yes, this is the very gown." Lydia pulled her hands away and swooped up a glorious amethyst silk gown with a sheer overdress. Holding it up to Eve's shoulders, she urged her to look in the tall looking glass. "This bright color will do wonders for your skin. So attractive. I've noticed dear Boyce look at you too, my dear. I know that with a little effort, you'll find it rather easy to persuade him to stay. He feels such terrible guilt about the crash of your balloon, I am positive he will agree to any of your requests."

Eve blushed and couldn't find the right words. Could she influence Parker?

"Moreover," Lydia continued, "I really do not believe he intends to complete this race. What do you think? He must be in his late twenties and has not succumbed to any lures cast by the young ladies of his acquaintance, so he must not want to marry this Lady Sarah, not really—not in his heart."

Eve considered Parker's motives as she never had before. Was marriage to the earl's daughter or his father's forgiveness his goal in the race? During their flight, she recalled that he had rarely mentioned Lady Sarah, an odd incident. Winning the race, both the intelligence and courage challenges, seemed foremost in his mind.

Eve smothered a sigh. Standing in front of the looking glass, she saw a lady she did not recognize. She chuckled and turned to take in her side view. "Perhaps marriage is not his goal, but whatever his reasons, I know he wants to complete this race. He is quite determined to win these challenges." Since hearing Lydia call him Piglet Parker, Eve hoped to learn from her the story behind his unfortunate nickname. "Fame and public recognition is the only way he believes he can wipe away any memories of *Piglet Parker*."

"Oh, what nonsense. Everyone has forgotten that youthful escapade."

"I've never heard that name until you said it. What happened? Why is he called that terrible nickname?"

"It could be worse. Consider Poodle Byng."

Eve bit her lower lip. "Imagine the horror of having to choose between Piglet and Poodle."

"The word *piglet* is such an injustice. Dear Boyce is so amusing, so kind, not nasty and full of squeals at all. From what I understand from my friend Fanny, he planned a piglet race in the park to amuse several of his favorite lady friends. Quite a few, if I heard rightly. All those brothers of his and their wives attending—it must have been a happy crowd. I'm sorry I missed it. My friend dear George was there. I wonder why he didn't ask me to join him. He must have known I would have enjoyed it so."

"How can a piglet race go amiss?"

"It was years ago, so I don't know the details, but it was very bad. The talk of the town even." Lydia widened her eyes, her pupils dark. "Dear Boyce's father, you know, the Marquess of Sutcliffe, the politician? He was not pleased about his youngest making a mockery of the family name. Then all the other fellows in his club started calling him Piglet Parker—in front of his female friends too, poor boy. Gentlemen can be so cruel, don't you think so? Surely everyone has forgotten that incident by now."

Eve laid the purple gown on the coverlet, then casually stroked the lovely skirt. "I do not think his lordship has forgotten it. In some ways, perhaps men take mockery more to heart than women do. An embarrassing nickname does stay in one's mind and—"

"Oh, poop." Lydia moved to stand in front of

the looking glass. "I am quite familiar with Boyce's reputation, my dear, and I can say not a lady in London thinks the worse of him for a silly nickname. His charm has endeared him to many, and now I can include myself."

"But gentlemen need to appear successful in front of other gentlemen."

"Oh, yes, I truly believe that is the heart of the matter. The general tittle-tattle is that after the publication of *The Rake's Handbook: Including Field Guide*"—Lydia leaned close—"his father was so angry over his son publishing a scandalous book, he gave Boyce the cut direct. In front of everyone too. Shocked all of London." She clapped her hands. "Let's try the rose-colored satin, shall we?"

Eve nodded, not really wanting to refuse. When would she ever get the chance to even dream of gowns like these? "I still believe he is earnest about joining the race and will not stay just because I request it."

"He'll stay if you ask him in the appropriate manner. Look at all the effort he made to find that book. And he has not rejoined the earl's race now, has he?" Lydia caught Eve's glance in the looking glass. "You must try to make him stay." The brightest of smiles shone from her face. "I am sure once dear Boyce announces he will stay a month, your book will likely be recovered. Women know ways to make a gentleman do what they want, don't they?"

Eve wanted to point out that Lydia had not been too successful herself in trying to make Parker stay, but if she mentioned that point, Lydia would realize Eve had been listening to the conversation in the stables.

"Female persuasion is harmless really," Lydia continued. "As a lady intent upon the study of science, you should understand that wearing this lovely gown, you will achieve results. Think about it, my dear."

Twelve

"YES, YES, I FOUND YOU." BOYCE HAD SEARCHED ALL afternoon for Eve, but she wasn't in the stables or down by the small stream. Even though she had promised to rest after her ordeal, he knew that intelligent brain of hers planned the next search of the woods. He found her in a large round room used as the priory's library. Tall oak bookcases stretched up to small windows set at least twenty feet off the floor. In this part of the priory, the Saxon stone walls and floor remained exposed, without plaster walls or fancy carpets. "What exactly are you doing?"

Eve sat at the center of the table, surrounded by books and an instrument with gleaming brass numbers set in white enamel. She seemed to search behind him. "Considering the possible loss of the book, I've spent my day trying to remember all of the details of the parhelia we observed. I think, with a little effort, even if the book remains lost, we still might be able to send a letter describing its discovery to a learned institution. So if you would forgive me, I escaped in here to hide…be alone."

"But you don't want to hide from me. I saw the sun dogs too and might be of help. Besides, I've searched for hours for you, even completed the walking circuit. Nice place this, don't you think? I mean it's Sussex and this county is universally recognized as pretty close to heaven." His boots clicked on the stone floor as he strode over to sit beside her. "Who are you hiding from?"

She frowned, and wrinkles appeared on the top of her nose. "Earlier, my father and Charles Henry headed in this direction, so I ducked into the nearest room and found this delightful library. I-I was not quite prepared to meet with either of them this morning. I have no new plans to find the whereabouts of the book, and for today at least, I left the recovery efforts in their hands. Besides, I'm tired and a little unsettled today. I really do wish for some privacy."

This information did not surprise him. Her father appeared to have a talent for suppressing her good spirits. "Yes, yes, I'll just stay for a minute or two." Boyce sat close and laid his arm over her shoulders, on top of the pretty purple gown she must have borrowed from Lydia. "I hope your father has not blamed you for the loss of the book. If so, tell him it's my fault."

"No, the loss was just an accident, but that is only part of my troubles."

"Tell me your troubles. I can help. I hope it has nothing to do with Lydia's, well"—he cleared his throat—"friendly behavior."

She let his warm arm remain comfortably draped over her shoulders and pushed an open book in his direction. "Have you seen Mr. Howard's book on the modification of clouds? It's one of my favorites. He gave definitive names to each type of cloud—"

"Eve, Lydia can't help but flirt. She enjoys it. She is used to being surrounded by gentlemen who adore her. It's a game—the suggestive speech, a stolen kiss or two. I'm surprised she gave it all up for Buxton. Must be true love then. These days, her attentions are harmless, like a kitten rubbing against your leg."

With their faces just a foot away, she surprised him by looking directly into his eyes. "Are you a rake?"

"No, no." Lifting his arm off her shoulders, he straightened. "True rakes are vile creatures who prey on innocents or women without protection. However, it's not unusual for a gentleman to receive that title for behavior that is nothing more than public flirtation. I'm merely a young man in my twenties… and a few consenting widows have given me the honor of being my…" He failed to think of a suitable word to describe his amorous widows. Now he was in trouble.

Boyce turned away from her wide-eyed astonishment and cleared his throat again—twice. What word could he use that would not offend a young lady but would clearly allude to the nature of his friendship with the widows? Also, a term that a young virgin might not consider vulgar. "Hmm." She waited patiently, so he flashed her a smile.

She raised a brow. "Of being your…?"

Like a dog with a beef bone. He reviewed several words commonly used by his friends to describe an amorous female who is by no means a prostitute that might be suitable. The *purest-pure*? No, too ironic, and the term *dirtiest-dirt* came to mind first. Right, how about his father's old slang *frigot well rigged*, hmm? That phrase didn't quite explain the, ah, friendship. Besides, it might make Eve think of boats or ropes—both unsuitable.

She tilted her head in inquiry, like a small bird.

Right, he had written numerous songs, several stories; he was good with words, so he should be able to find one. *Ladybird*? No, no, that word included some very unladylike ladies, indeed. *Rum Doxy*? No, no, that expression had two meanings, too confusing.

She knit her brows.

Right, he must find a word. *Ace of Spades*? Did Eve play cards? Doubtful, so that phrase was out. *Conveniency*? No, no, even when his friends used that word he thought of privies.

She laughed indelicately enough to cover those plump, apple lips with her hands. Clearly, she enjoyed watching him struggle.

"Mistress," he said with a small sideways nod and a Sunday parson's soothing tone.

She rocked back in her chair, whoops of laughter filled the round room. "You should have seen your face. I'd love to know what you were thinking about. Oh. Maybe I do." She laughed again.

He threw his arms around her; they laughed until whoops became snickers.

Her gaiety abruptly ended; then she kissed him square on the lips.

"What did I do to deserve that?"

"How do you know I'm not just a kitten rubbing your leg?"

"Everyone likes kittens." He moved his lips within inches, hovering over those prized lips, anticipating his pleasure upon the touch of her soft flesh.

The door opened. "Oh, there you are."

He recognized Lydia's voice but tried to disguise the proximity of his and Eve's lips by merely turning his head, so he'd appear to be reading the book before him on the table. "Come see this amazing book on clouds Miss Mountfloy has just brought to my attention." Did he fool her?

Eve played along. "Yes, do come see this, Lydia. There are a number of cloud illustrations I think you will find very pretty."

"Naughty, naughty, both of you. Dear Eve, you look lovely in that gown. I'm delighted you're following my advice. However, it's time to dress for dinner, so I'll see both of you in thirty minutes." After a toss of curls, she swept out of the room.

"She's right. You do look very pretty in that gown."

"Do I?" She seemed to search his face.

"Yes, you are an extremely pretty woman. And since you are logical, you know that already."

She stroked the skirt of her gown. "Do you want to stay here awhile?"

"No, look at me." He glanced at his chest. "If I must dress for dinner, I'll have to borrow one of Buxton's coats. Is there a good reason for me to stay?"

"No, never mind."

He winked and headed out to dress for dinner.

Twenty minutes later, having borrowed what must have been one of Buxton's finest coats, shirts, and cravats, he checked himself in the giant pier mirror in the hallway. Never fond of a slight brocade, he thought it looked too old-fashioned, but he had to admit the discreet gold swirls suited his style. He checked his side view, nodded with approval, and then entered the drawing room.

"As it must be obvious to you ladies," Mr. Thomas Mountfloy was saying, standing before the fire in the drawing room. "Independently funded gentlemen in the pursuit of scientific facts are the most intelligent gentlemen in Britain today." Miss Mountfloy's father and his assistant had joined the ladies before dinner. The famous aeronaut had easily spotted a potential donor in Lady Buxton and now regaled her with stories of his discoveries. He had received permission to smoke, so the room smelled like heavy tobacco, and a white veil of acrid smoke hovered in the air.

Lady Buxton sat by the fire stroking a white cat with the longest fur Boyce had ever seen. He nodded to Eve, strode over to Lady Buxton, kissed her hand, and sat next to her.

"Yes," Mr. Mountfloy pontificated to the entire assembly, "most of our aristocrats own the land and lead our government, but it's men of science who will lead us into our future and the new age of steam machines."

"Perhaps one day, ladies of science will lead us into our future too," Eve said, a smile gracing her full lips.

Mr. Mountfloy scowled. "No, my dear, do not get above yourself in the presence of such elevated company. I've explained this before. It is a general fact that females lack the dedication and rigor of mind for such studies."

"What!" The room spun around Boyce's head.

"Your daughter, sir, is the most capable person I've ever met. Well, at least as capable as my brother, Richard. I mean she got us across Britain. She even landed the balloon all by herself." He glanced over to Lady Buxton. "I was wrestling with a boot-grabbing tree at the time, you understand."

The older woman's eyes gleamed.

With absolute conviction in his heart, Boyce said, "Yes, yes, I really must introduce her to my father, because she's capable enough to run the entire country. No doubts whatsoever on that score."

Eve startled to chuckle.

"Eve!" Mr. Mountfloy admonished. "Mind you, don't let his lordship's fustian go to your head."

Several times during their flight, Boyce had watched Eve struggle to contain her mirth. Now he knew exactly the reason why—or, more to the point, the identity of the suppressor.

"Mr. Mountfloy," Lady Buxton said with the vocal projection of a Roman senator, "I insist you end this discussion immediately. Your daughter is a remarkable woman. I am not alone in my belief that you should celebrate her achievements more than you have shown. A generosity of spirit is what is required here, sir."

Boyce nodded his head several times. *Hear, hear, Lady B.*

Tut opened the door and announced dinner was ready. The assembled company moved into the dining room, where they became overwhelmed and delighted with the smell of roast pheasant.

Once everyone was seated, Boyce struggled to

reclaim his good opinion of the aeronaut, similar to his first impression when he hired the balloon, but serious doubts arose that he would ever call Eve's father a friend. Earlier in the evening, he had treated his daughter like a female footman, bidding her to sit here and fetch that. Then he had reacted to her comments by ignoring her, giving her a set-down, or belittling her ideas. Decidedly, his patience for Mr. Mountfloy's company had worn thin.

Mr. Mountfloy became temporarily tongue-tied. "Your ladyship, I would like to clarify one point. Surely even you do not suggest that females have the capability to succeed in the sciences?"

"What a silly thing to say," Lady Buxton said, with a wave of her fork. "As a man of science, I suggest you recall the efforts of Miss Caroline Herschel, sir. You'd be a very fortunate man, indeed, if you were to rise to her level of accomplishments."

"Yes," Mr. Mountfloy said, a blush appearing above the line of his whiskers. "I am aware of the achievements of Miss Herschel, but we shall never fully understand how much of her success was dependent upon her brother."

Lady Buxton held her quizzing glass up in Mr. Mountfloy's direction, probably trying to discern if the aeronaut's insult of one of the world's greatest astronomers was said in earnest. "Stuff and nonsense," she said, her tone sharp.

Mr. Mountfloy stood, glaring at her ladyship. "I object."

Boyce stood, glaring at Mr. Mountfloy. "Apologize, sir."

Mr. Henry stood, glaring at Boyce. "You must apologize."

Lady Buxton dropped her quizzing glass on her ample bosom. "Gentlemen, please, you remind me of being in a room full of jack-in-the-boxes."

Boyce remained standing while the two other men took their seats, somewhat guilty expressions appearing on both of their faces.

Mr. Mountfloy seemed to recall the presence of a possible donor and started to apologize to his hostesses. He then included everyone—including his daughter—in a general apology, so Boyce sat down.

Minutes later, any good impression Mr. Mountfloy had made vanished when he—without the consent of the priory's ladies—planned to monopolize their staff for the next day's search party.

Mr. Henry leaned over to pat Eve's hand. "Do not worry. I'll find the book for you."

"Thank you."

Boyce failed to understand why she didn't pull her hand away. Moreover, he continued to struggle with a burning desire to give her father a facer, an unseemly and unusual thought for him. His stomach ached, and his legs felt restless. So when the meal ended, he took his leave, bowed to each lady, and strode out of the room.

After an hour of cooling off outside on the terrace, Boyce headed upstairs to his room for the night.

At the top of the stairs, his candlelight revealed Lady Buxton's elderly maid. The servant scurried down the hall in front of him and vanished behind the door at the end of the hallway.

Seconds later, when he grabbed the cool brass doorknob of his room, he heard a noise.

"Boyce, dear."

He turned to see Lady Buxton tiptoeing in his direction wearing a claret-colored velvet robe and lawn nightcap. "Shh, keep your voice low. Now follow me." She walked down to a double-oak door along the far side of the corridor and slipped inside the room.

He silently followed her, stealth the unspoken name of the game.

"We only have minutes," she said. "I have sent all the housemaids downstairs to tidy up, so we must bustle." They stepped into a large apartment decorated in blue satin. The occupant was clearly a female, since no man on earth would put up with the number of little white cupid thingamabobs decorating everything from the furniture to the oil lamps.

Lady Buxton pulled him into a corner of the room and spoke softly. "We both surmise that dear Lydia has possession of Miss Mountfloy's book, although she denies it. I learned about it myself from one of my servants. Seems Lydia associated her gratitude with their silence, followed by a few shillings, clever puss. We only have a few minutes to find the book before she returns. It must be here, because if she hid it elsewhere in the house, one of the maids might find it and not all of them are a party to her secret."

"I knew in my bones she had it," Boyce said, taking a careful glance around the room. "Where do women hide their most precious things? I know—locked away in her jewelry casket."

"No, too obvious. Thompson, her lady's maid,

must be in on her secret, so Lydia must have hidden it somewhere practical and easy to access. In her dressing room, under her stockings, I think." Lady Buxton rummaged through a large corner cupboard. "No bit of luck there." She turned to face Boyce. "Let's follow your suggestion, her jewelry casket."

Boyce nodded, and they moved to the overly large vanity. "I chose the casket because the servants must have instructions to leave it alone. The only difficulty is we do not have a key."

"You inherited your dear mother's intuition about people, my boy. Don't worry though. I know where she keeps the key."

"Where?"

"Under her stockings, of course." Lady Buxton went back to the carved mahogany cupboard and found the key. With a smile, she held up an ornate gilt key hanging on a long, red satin ribbon. "Let's give this a try."

Boyce maneuvered the mahogany chest out from behind a large collection of multicolored glass perfume bottles. "Fingers crossed."

Lady Buxton inserted the key and attempted to twist it to the left. "Need your help, dear."

"Yes, yes." He deftly turned the key until the brass lock emitted a loud clunk.

She opened the lid and pulled several trays containing sparkling jewelry out of the box.

Five shelves loaded with bobbles were placed into Boyce's arms before the discovery of the *Results* book wedged into the bottom of the casket. "Thank heavens," he said a little too loudly.

"Shh." Lady Buxton held up her finger to her lips.

He nodded. "Miss Mountfloy will be so pleased." His heart sang a silent tune. "I cannot wait to go downstairs and present it to her."

Lady Buxton took the shelves from his arms one by one and returned them to the casket. "I hate to disagree with you, dear boy. But I insist we wait until tomorrow before we inform everyone."

"Why?" His heartbeat stilled. He pleaded, "You do not seem to understand. Miss Mountfloy is distraught over the loss of her book. I do not want her to suffer any longer than necessary."

"I understand, believe me I do." She patted his back, a sly grin on her mouth. "But consider the consequences. The whole house will be put in an uproar and everyone will be roused from their slumbers. And most important of all, Lydia will be upset. All I ask is that you give me the chance to confront her with the news first, so she can retain her pride. I love my daughter-in-law, and I do not wish to see her embarrassed by an indelicate outburst. The earliest you can rejoin the race is tomorrow anyway, isn't it?"

Together they set the room to rights, then returned to the hall.

"I was not thinking of myself," he said. "I am concerned about Miss Mountfloy's comfort and needs."

Lady Buxton patted his arm. "Of course you are. We all are. Such a wonderful young woman, don't you think so?"

"Yes, yes, she..." It struck Boyce that once he restored the book to Eve, he would likely never see her again—a sobering thought. He bent down and kissed Lady Buxton on the cheek. "Thank you for the advice. I am pleased my mother had friends like you. She was a lucky woman."

Lady Buxton's eyes filled with tears, and she squeezed his upper arm. "My dear, I am grateful for the connection. People like your mother, who release the hidden mirth in those around them, can never be replaced. I am grateful that I knew her, and in the future, I'll cherish her memory more often now that I know her son." A winsome smile broke across her lined face. "I will see you in the morning. We can discuss the appropriate time to present the book to Miss Mountfloy then. Good night."

Boyce hugged her and planted another kiss on her cheek. "Good night."

"You! What a rascal." She gingerly stepped back to her apartment.

Once in his room, he contemplated the following day. What would Eve say about his restoration of the book? No, that would not be fair. He must give credit to Lydia and her servants, but then he remembered Lady Buxton's warning. Perhaps Lydia did not want it generally known that her servants had found the book and that she had withheld it from the Mountfloys. He then tried to conjure up the words of gratitude from every person, except Lydia, in an attempt to avoid one subject—he and Eve must separate. Now that she was restored to her father, she would leave for London, while he must rejoin the earl's race. He pulled on his nightcap and slid under the coverlet. His goal had always been to set her to rights, wasn't it? Why then did he feel trussed, gagged, and about to walk the plank?

Setting the leather *Results* book on the table by his bed, he watched the sparkling gold letters disappear into the darkness after he blew out his candle. *Maybe he should alter his promise to include his safe escort to London?* With this pleasant thought in mind, he fell asleep.

Boyce woke with a knock upon his door. He donned a jacquard banyan and let the housemaid in to build the morning fire. He looked outside and saw the beginnings of another beautiful summer day. With happy thoughts of Eve's delight upon the recovery of the book, he glanced over to the table by his bed.

The book was gone.

Panic seized him; his throat dried. He searched above, behind, and around every object in the room. Taking a few deep breaths, he tried putting himself in Eve's dainty half boots and use logic. This effort failed to discover who stole the book, but logic dictated it was in the priory somewhere and would eventually be returned to its rightful owner. So her fears of the book being destroyed would not come to pass. The first chance he had to speak with her, he'd ease her mind and reassure her of its eventual recovery.

Minutes later, while his temporary valet shaved him, he relaxed enough to imagine Eve's happiness when the book was returned to her. His heart lightened once more. "The sun shines over Sussex, the sky is as blue as…" Boyce wondered what word he could use to describe the blue sky in his new, altogether appropriate song. Sapphires were too dark, and the sea was too, well, watery. Eve had blue eyes, didn't she? He sang his new song while he tied the latest fashion in cravat knots. Then he asked the valet where he might find Lady Buxton. Boyce knew, like him, she was an early riser, and he needed to tell her first about the loss of the *Results* book. He hurried down to catch her in the breakfast parlor.

Upon opening the door, he was confronted with a large number of smiling faces. The two women of the house, Mr. Mountfloy, Mr. Charles, and Eve herself, looking very pretty indeed in one of Lydia's pink gowns.

Eve immediately stood and approached him. "Good morning. I wondered when you would wake. Have you heard the good news? Charles Henry found the *Results* book. Isn't that wonderful?"

The imaginary blow that hit him almost toppled him over.

Mr. Mountfloy parroted his daughter's praise. "Capital. I cannot express our gratitude enough." He nodded in the direction of Mr. Henry, who just sat beaming at everyone around him. "Saved the day, my boy."

Boyce stared at Mr. Henry. The unspeakable, dunghill, scaly cur could not even look him directly in the eye. Yes, yes, he would give him a piece of his mind. "Mr. Henry did not find the book. I found the book."

"Boyce dear," Lady Buxton said, "do please come and sit down. My nerves this morning cannot stand loud voices." She patted the back of the mahogany chair next to her. "I will explain to you Mr. Henry's astonishing story about the discovery later."

She must have known Mr. Henry stole the book. Why didn't she speak out and accuse the scoundrel too?

Eve approached him. "I don't understand."

He remained silent, unsure of what to say.

She glanced at Charles Henry. "Where did you find the book?"

Boyce spoke first. "I discovered the book last night, and it was stolen off of my bedside table." He pointed to Charles Henry. "He must have stolen it."

Eve turned to the other man. "How, then, did you come by it?"

"Passed a servant in the hallway carrying the book, so I naturally took it from her, since your father is the rightful owner," Charles Henry said, appearing unconcerned.

"No, I found it." Boyce could hardly believe the cur sat there smiling after speaking such a bold-faced lie. "I found it for you."

"Did you?" Eve questioned. "Did you go into the woods and retrieve it? Or are you claiming a false accomplishment?"

Boyce dropped his jaw and his mind spun until reality blurred.

She shook her head. "You initially claimed you landed the balloon by yourself too. Are you merely seeking undue attention and praise? Or must I now question your veracity?"

Boyce kept his silence, staring dumbfounded at Eve. He had found the book last night. Why didn't she believe him? How could she not trust him? He had done everything he could to help her. He had even saved her life. He realized for the first time that he cared deeply for her; she had become the most important woman in his life.

"I suggest we all calm down," Lady Buxton said, "before any more words are exchanged that someone may regret later. Clearly, the priory's servants found the book in the woods. The chain of ownership after that included his lordship and Mr. Henry. I suggest we thank all of them for their efforts. The important part of the story is that the book is in the hands of the proper owner. In the future, Boyce dear, I recommend you consider the efforts of others before you claim an accomplishment."

A simple nod was all he could manage.

"Eve, please come and sit down," Mr. Mountfloy said. "Now that Charles Henry here was the last man to put everything to rights, we can forgive his lordship for the book's initial loss and return to London. I am eager to resume my research."

Eve glanced his way, shaking her head in acknowledgment of the injustice of her father's accusation. "The book's loss was not his lordship's fault."

"Humph." Mr. Mountfloy dropped his utensils on the table with a bang.

"Cheer up, Father," Eve said. "Since we have the *Results* book in our hands, I can accurately describe our discovery of the angle of the mock suns."

Lydia dabbed her mouth with her napkin and then spoke without looking at anyone. "This whole affair has been unfortunate. I am quite put out." She glared at Mr. Henry. "Indeed, I insist the ballooning party, except for dear Boyce, leave the priory immediately. My servants are too much put-upon to deal with such a large party. And, Miss Mountfloy, you will no longer need the use of my third-best rose-colored gown. Your own gown will be restored to you within the hour."

Still heartbroken over Eve's admonishment, Boyce caught her glance. All he could do was mumble, "Such a shame. You are extremely pretty in that gown."

"Sir—" Mr. Mountfloy's voice seemed overloud for the small room.

"Yes, yes, I beg your pardon." Boyce lowered his head. It was too painful to look at Eve.

Lydia stood. "Oh, I fear I have the headache and so early in the morning too." A dainty hand almost obscured by her long lace sleeves rubbed her forehead.

"Lord Boyce," Mr. Mountfloy said, grinding his teeth, "my daughter's appearance is no concern of yours." His expression lightened as he faced Lydia. "Indeed, ma'am, I understand the difficulties of such a large party in residence, so we will take our leave of you ladies. Miss Mountfloy and I are grateful for your assistance in the recovery of our balloon. Eve, let us prepare to—"

"Yes, of course, right away."

Boyce desired to leave too. What had started out as a brilliant blue day was now poised to become hours of tedious civilities and eminent boredom. "If I might, Lady B., I'll rejoin the earl's race today."

"You can't leave..." Lydia instantly dropped her gaze to her toast.

Everyone in the room turned to stare at her.

Her probable sign of partiality lightened his mood just a little, but he couldn't imagine staying at the priory without Eve's friendly face—not to mention her father would likely forbid him to join their party on their return to London. "Now that I have kept my promise and have restored Miss Mountfloy back to rights, I see no reason to stay. Paris is still a long journey ahead." Also, one part of him eagerly wished to resume the race. Since he had traveled by balloon across England, he had already won at least two challenges, the intelligence and courage challenges—unless one of those rag-mannered coves fell into a touch of luck during their journey to Paris.

"No!" Lydia exclaimed. She stilled, her petite chin elevated. "I mean, I was hoping you would stay to entertain Mama and me." She turned to Lady Buxton. "Ask him to stay, please do."

"In this instance, I must agree with my daughter-in-law. Stay awhile until you have fully recovered, Boyce dear. I cannot tell you at present why it is important for you to stay."

Eve tore her glance away from her meal. She did not speak, but her steady stare bespoke an earnest plea for him not to leave immediately.

He owed Lady Buxton so much for everything, but he could not stay. "I cannot thank you ladies enough for the hospitality you have shown me during my stay at the priory. But in truth, I long to rejoin the race right away. I know the story of my journey to Paris will win at least one challenge. However, if you will permit me, I shall call upon the priory after my victory is complete, so I can show you my gold cup, perhaps even present you with my new bride, Lady Sarah."

Eve jumped to her feet and fled the room.

Thirteen

STUMBLING DOWN THE FRONT STEPS OF THE PRIORY, Eve's feet barely reached the gravel of the drive before Charles Henry caught up with her. Without slowing her pace, she continued to head directly toward the stables. Her emotions seemed to fly everywhere, from upset to anxious, to angry, and she didn't fully understand why. She did, however, recognize a sudden hostility toward Lady Sarah, a woman she had never met before. If Lady Sarah had not been so picky over the choice of a spouse, perhaps the events of the last week would never have happened.

Charles Henry cleared his throat several times to gain her attention. "Why did you leave the room in haste? You do not seem like yourself today."

Eve ignored him, suppressing a strange, overwhelming desire to run. "I am still tired from my ordeal in the woods, that's all." They reached the basket, and she gripped the edge, because it kept her from complete collapse. The stables had become stiflingly hot already and the smell of acrid straw filled the air. For no reason at all, she tugged on a twig of loose wicker and kept her back to him.

He gave an exasperated sigh. "We have always been the best of friends. Please turn around and speak to me."

Blast. He was right. He did not deserve her ill will. But this was one of those rare times when the presence of a friend made matters worse. If only she had pretended to be busy. Refold the balloon or inventory equipment, then she'd have an excuse to politely ask him to leave her alone.

Charles Henry stood with his hand on one hip. Dressed in baggy beige trousers and coat, he seemed indistinguishable from the straw and wood walls. The expression on his face resembled a wealthy, spoiled man who expected to be attended.

"Lord Boyce appeared upset this morning as well. Do you and his lordship share some secret? Or perhaps the trouble is more serious and there is an understanding between the two of you?"

An odd choke escaped her. "No, no, of course not. He is wealthy, titled, and one of London's most admired bachelors." She feigned a carefree chuckle. "Yes, I am a gentleman's daughter, but you heard him. His lordship is an aristocrat who expects to marry a woman named Lady Sarah. I'm sure he would never even consider a woman like me. What a silly notion."

"Yes, I forgot for a moment that he is an aristocrat from such a distinguished family. Gentlemen of his consequence would never consider you as a potential spouse." Charles Henry narrowed his eyes. "Also, his abhorrent behavior in the stables proved that he is not in the least serious in regard to women."

He was right, of course. Parker would never imagine her—someone not a member of the *ton*—as the woman he might eventually wed. Still Charles Henry's words hurt, a small stab in the heart. But his accusation over Parker's behavior in the stables, Eve firmly believed, was unjust. While she did not fully understand the scene they encountered, she believed it to be an innocent one, despite appearances. She knew him well enough to know that he always tried to provide comfort to any female who was worried, sad, or unhappy. "His behavior in the stables was innocent, like a kitten rubbing your leg."

"Unseemly creatures, cats, but his behavior is not the point. My concern is your odd behavior since we've arrived at the priory. My restoration of the book and our return to London does not seem to excite you."

"I am delighted about the book's recovery." She recalled how odd and unlikely Charles Henry's story had seemed that he merely noticed a servant holding the book. She gave him a hard stare. "Tell me, how did you really acquire the book? Everyone had been searching for days, so I think it is rather remarkable that you just stumbled upon a servant who willingly gave it to you."

He made no sound or movement, but the color drained from his face. "This morning I saw the book in the hands of a servant. Of course, he refused to hand it over, stating it belonged to his mistress. It took a great deal of persuasion and cunning to persuade him to place it in my care, believe me."

The color returned to his cheeks, but the halting cadence of his voice led her to believe he fabricated the story. She suspected the servants found the book and gave it into the hands of one of the ladies of the priory. She also started to give credit to Parker's story. Since both ladies were fond of him, they might have presented it to him first. But how did it end up in Charles Henry's hands? Her respect for the Buxton ladies convinced her that the wisest choice was to remain silent. However, she could no longer unreservedly trust Charles Henry.

"After I presented you with the *Results* book," he said, "I could tell you were pleased. So you must be grateful for my efforts to recover it, even though I have not, as yet, received a formal thank-you."

She spun to face him. "Of course I'm grateful. Indeed, I cannot thank you enough. Many of your efforts are written on its pages, so you understand the book's importance."

His chest swelled in recognition of her praise. "I am glad you are grateful for my efforts to recover the book. I think together we make a good team, don't you?"

The word *team* grabbed her full attention. She then noticed his expression assume even more gravity. *Oh no—he wouldn't—not now.*

"As you are undoubtedly aware, you and I have expectations about our future. Unspoken, since we have never discussed it, but you are an intelligent young woman, so you must have been aware of it. I have recently spoken to your father and asked for your hand. He approved my request, of course." His speech took on the speed of a runaway team of horses. "I therefore ask *you* for your hand in marriage. Your father anticipated our eventual marriage, and he approved of my suit." He picked up her hand and slapped his on top.

Eve stared at his hand. He seemed composed, but his clammy palm betrayed his anxiety. Her stomach began to churn, and she regretted the choice of bacon for breakfast.

Before this week, her opinion of Charles Henry had been positive. He worked diligently and possessed a mind of the first order. But now, for the first time, she thought of him in a physical sense. She found his wet palms and dark-ginger whisker growth not to her taste in gentlemen, making her feel guilty. No woman in her right mind ever expected a Greek god, like Parker, as her partner in life. However, a gentleman with a figure and features similar to Parker's would make a suitable spouse. She immediately recognized the irony and injustice of her thoughts. Perhaps Lady Sarah was picky, because she too preferred a gentleman that resembled someone she had once been fond of.

"I give you my assurances," he said, "that I will be the husband you need. Together we can proceed as we are. The three of us will surely continue to accomplish significant atmospheric discoveries. In the future, your assistance will prove crucial in helping me become England's most celebrated aeronaut."

Charles Henry's ambition troubled her. There seemed to be more involved than just helping others through atmospheric discoveries. "I don't understand—"

"It also goes without saying that our union might be blessed with children," he said. "I expect they will eventually join us and carry our work on into the future." He jerked her hand up to his lips for a brief kiss. "What do you say? Let's make this a formal agreement, shall we?" His tone changed with this last question. Now utter confidence crept into voice. He briefly hugged her. "Of course we will marry." He kept both hands on her shoulders, but held her at arm's length. "Eve?"

She felt like running, but her feet remain dutifully planted. All she could do at the moment was notice his odd gesture of holding her far from him. "You mentioned our work in the field of atmospheric science, yet you did not say anything about—you know—affection. Those words are normally expected when a gentleman proposes."

"Ha, ha. We have known each other for such a long time, we don't need to use those words, do we?" He still held her at arm's length.

She failed to reply, staring at his perfectly stiff arms.

He laughed again. "Yes, I understand." He nodded his head sideways back and forth. "Women and all that love faradiddle. You do realize, of course, that mutual respect and affection are common before marriage, but love is earned only many years after the vows."

Was he mad?

"Yes," he continued. "I have heard about those stories of passionate romance ladies love to read, but those tales are all just fiction, like the tales found in three-volume novels. They don't happen in real life, or at least, not to people like us—good, sober, hard-working people. I expect to be deeply in love after the birth of our first child. Most people are by then,

I'm told." He gave her another lightning-quick hug. "Come on, Eve, what do you say?"

She couldn't think of a single word that would be a suitable reply. Squinting at the overbright sunlight streaming in through the open stable doors, she realized she had the headache.

"Eve, we must marry. With our marriage, I can rightfully claim my place as your father's partner, and we can continue our research on the atmosphere. You do realize there is no alternative to my suit?"

The only alternative Eve could ever consider would be Parker. Mortified at Charles Henry's indifference to her as a potential love interest, she considered her feelings if Parker were to ask for her hand. She felt light-headed for a moment. If she married Parker, she would have to give up science and become the proper wife of an aristocrat—no "meddling" around in balloons. She supposed she would have to entertain his family and friends by holding endless parties, teas, routs, or whatever aristocrats actually did to fill up their days. Her spirits reached a new low.

Perhaps if she waited and did not compromise her dreams by marriage to Charles Henry, she might meet another gentleman who suited her taste, one who engendered similar feelings to those Parker had awakened. She might even forget about Parker with the passage of time, a distinct advantage to her future happiness.

"Eve?"

She craved a hug or a shower of kisses, but not from the man before her. Fighting the unshed tears starting to pool in her eyes, she said, "I plan to walk the short circuit down to the stream, so I hope you will excuse me." She started in the direction of the path, and her heart sank when he perfunctorily followed her.

"I think fresh air will do us both a bit of good."

Eve quickened her pace, resulting in a steady crunch of gravel.

He easily kept up with her longest strides.

She tried to affect a carefree tone. "Thank you for your offer, but please allow me the privacy to give it full consideration and time to speak to my father." Before she ran away, she gave him what she hoped was a smile. "I must say, Charles Henry, I find your knowledge of females and romance truly enlightening."

Later in the afternoon, Eve stood before a tall looking glass in her room, holding up the richly colored amethyst gown with the lovely overdress and collar of delicate gold vines. She had neither the time, money, nor guidance from a fashionable modiste to dress in the latest fashion. But looking at the soft fabric overdress, shimmering in the sunlight from the windows, gave her a sense of calm joy—the type of joy where you comprehend the very moment you are happy. She sighed and glanced over to another gown lent to her by Lydia, a satin gown of soft rose, accented with Honiton lace around the bodice and puffed sleeves. If a highwayman stopped her carriage and demanded one of these gowns, she could never choose.

Stifling her fanciful thoughts, she returned to her comfortable world of logic. She hung the lovely rose-colored gown next to the purple silk, and donned her brown flannel gown. It had been cleaned and pressed, but its milled surface showed a few smooth areas of wear. Once she pinned her hair, she put on her tight-fitting cap. She headed outside to search for her father and discover when they planned to leave for London.

Eve eventually found him, and Lady Buxton, in the priory's drawing room. Close by the fire were four overstuffed wing chairs. The two chairs next to the fire must have been favorites, since the heavy leather on their arms were almost worn through from use. Lady Buxton sat nearest the fire, while Eve's father stood by the windows.

"Ah, Eve, there you are. Lady Buxton here has expressed great interest in my endeavors at atmospheric research. She has even done me the honor of expressing a desire to observe my next ascension. Isn't that a generous offer?"

Lady Buxton slowly stroked a large cat. The ginger animal appeared to be kneading its claws into the chair's cushion, but her ladyship did not seem to mind. "Come in, my dear. I have heard a great deal this morning. It seems you have important news to share with your father." She looked rather guilty. "I mean your father already knows, of course. But perhaps you would like me to leave, so you can talk to him alone about your future?"

Blast. Her father must have revealed Charles Henry's proposal to her ladyship. "Please stay, Lady Buxton. You have been so kind to me during my stay at the priory that I now think of you as a relative. Besides, your ginger would be quite upset with me if you moved."

"Oh, you are very kind," Lady Buxton said, "and you're right. Old Arthur here would be quite put out if I got up. Now come here and tell us all about this engagement of yours."

Eve had no intention of relating any information about her lukewarm suitor. She took her seat in a wing chair and formulated the right words to draw out information before she had to reveal her own thoughts. "Tell me, sir. What exactly did Charles Henry say?"

Thomas Mountfloy rose to the bait like a hungry trout jumping out of the water to catch a false fly. "Why, yesterday Charles formally asked me for your hand." He leaned toward Lady Buxton. "Their engagement had been expected ever since Mr. Henry became my apprentice. It's only logical she would accept him. The young man will go far in this profession, and he'll need an understanding and supportive wife. Her efforts will allow him to concentrate on the science and not be held back by all the petty details of living that normally belong to women. Besides, Eve here likes him, and I am sure he likes her. What could be more natural?" He turned and extended his hand to his daughter.

Eve moved to take her father's hand, and he squeezed hers before letting go. After her mother's death, Eve had done everything in her power not to disappoint him. She was a dutiful daughter, and she obeyed him in all respects. "Lady Buxton, I am—"

"The young man has an adequate living," Mr. Mountfloy said to Lady Buxton. "But he is a gentleman's son who lacks sufficient connections in science.

I see no reason for Eve not to agree to his proposal. I personally wondered what they were waiting for."

"Yes," Lady Buxton said. "I can see how expectations of their union would become natural."

"He really is a fine man, your ladyship," he continued. "I could not be happier having him as a son-in-law."

The smile on Lady Buxton's face faded. She stroked the ginger with slower more measured strokes. "And what do you feel about your engagement, my dear?"

Eve inhaled a long, deep breath. "I am…I am considering the match, your ladyship. It is all so very strange and our lives topsy-turvy at the moment. I do not fully understand why Mr. Henry made his proposal here and now."

The soft smile returned to Lady Buxton's face. "Yes, Mr. Henry's timing does seem a bit odd—understandable under the circumstances but still odd."

"And what circumstances would that be?" Eve asked. She suspected Lady Buxton perhaps knew something she did not.

"Nothing odd about it," Mr. Mountfloy pronounced. "Once they are married, we can all go on as before. I see no real changes to our lives. Of course you will marry him. Take a day or two—it's important not to rush into these things. But once you agree, we all can continue our experiments for the good of the people of Britain." He nodded at Lady Buxton. "And I am positive her ladyship has no real objections to the match, do you?"

Lady Buxton stopped petting the cat and looked directly at Eve. "Miss Mountfloy has repeatedly impressed me with her good sense. I am positive she has the courage to recognize her heart's choice when it comes time to pick a spouse. Now, if you two will excuse me, I will leave you alone to discuss the matter."

The older woman started walking to the door, so Eve ran to open it for her.

"Thank you, my dear. Come along, Arthur."

The ginger disobeyed, sat on the floor, and groomed his nose.

Lady Buxton smiled. "Puss, you traitor. If you need someone to talk to, Miss Mountfloy, please don't hesitate to find me. Agreed?"

Eve nodded and the older woman swept from the room.

Mr. Mountfloy held out his palm again. "You have always been a very obedient child, so I am confident you'll do what I recommend. Won't you?"

Every woman knew the right time and the wrong time to pick a battle with a parent. Now was not the time. She sat in the chair her ladyship had recently vacated and the ginger jumped into her lap.

"You will do as I recommend?" Mr. Mountfloy repeated.

"I have always obeyed you."

Her father watched her steadily without speaking. "That is not a sufficient answer."

Normally, his gaze did not unsettle her as it did now. After all he was her father. The man she loved the most; the man who cared for her after her mother's death; and the man who tragically lost his family too, except for her. She wondered if she could please him some way other than agreeing to the match with Charles Henry.

The ginger circled her lap, sniffing.

"You have been a good girl. Now is not the time to make exceptions."

The frown on his face broke her heart. All she had ever desired was to make him happy. "Of course, sir." She decided her best strategy was to delay the marriage as long as possible, at least until she found someone to admire in a similar fashion to the way she admired Parker—or the thought of marriage to Charles Henry became more agreeable. Her father had some reason for pressing the match, and it must have something to do with Parker. He must consider Parker a threat to her future or to his.

Eve stroked the cat all the way to the tip of the animal's tail. The beast rewarded her by extending its claws into her thigh. She pushed the cat back, but the beast merely rose on all fours, stretched himself, and then attempted to place his paw on her lip. She turned her head to avoid it, then the purring beast circled her lap before it settled down in a tight ball. Not unusual behavior for a cat, but it did seem that all of Lady Buxton's cats had been trained to be lap-sitters. The only difficulty was the inability to get out of the chair easily.

Her father lit a clay pipe. "Just toss the animal on the floor. I don't want you distracted when I speak to you."

Eve lifted the ginger to the floor. The cat gave her a fulminating look that clearly expressed she was the ultimate of traitors and ambled off toward her father.

"You have always been a dutiful daughter and

have never given me trouble. I do not want you to get the idea that I don't appreciate you, because I do. Regardless of Charles Henry's assistance, I would never have accomplished as much as I have without your help."

Eve could think of a million things to say, but none of them seemed appropriate. "Thank you, Father." Her words sounded hollow, so she tried to lighten the situation by giving him a warm smile—except that did not turn out well either.

"Both Mrs. Buxton and Lady Buxton are women of consequence. Indeed, Mr. Buxton deals with a number of government committees that contribute to many of our scientific institutions. So we must be careful not to offend them. Do you understand?"

She nodded and smiled again, but he must have known both of these expressions were false. Happiness eluded her today. "I understand."

"For some reason, Lady Buxton has intervened and asked for our party to remain awhile longer, perhaps a week. She expressly wants you to compile your parhelia observations with the assistance of that undisciplined coxcomb, but I refused. Since she and her late husband were early subscribers to the Royal Institution of Great Britain, she desired the two of you pen a letter describing the phenomena and send it to the secretary. We don't wish to offend her, but I managed to convince her the task would be yours alone. It is for our combined future success that I ask you now to give me your word to wed Charles Henry."

Eve glanced at the cat lifting his head to determine if her father had a suitable lap.

Her father took a long draft on his pipe, crossed his legs to dissuade the animal, and exhaled slowly before he spoke again. "Women's minds are not as disciplined as the male mind, and I fear you are falling in love with that capricious rake. Do you love him?"

She looked directly at him but remained silent.

His countenance remained fixed like stone. "I suspect Lady Buxton must be aware of some partiality of his lordship's and wishes to forward some silly feminine idea of romance. Granted, the young man is handsome, but I firmly believe the two of you could never be happy. Considering his lack of seriousness, what would the two of you do all day?"

"Sing." The word escaped before she could check herself.

He slammed his pipe down on the table. "It is for that very reason—your partiality toward him—that I insist you must give me the assurances I seek. Lord Boyce could never be interested in you as a wife, so do not be a foolish female and harbor expectations in that quarter."

Eve had convinced herself of that fact some time ago. "Don't worry. I know his lordship could never have serious intentions in regard to me, but I do not love Charles Henry. Indeed, he has no concept of love."

The fight within her father vanished. He hung his head slightly and sighed. "I promised your mother…" He paused, staring at her. "She asked me to ensure that you wed a man of your own choosing." He pulled out a handkerchief and wiped his eyes. "However, the situation has changed. Indeed, I planned to keep this from you, because I don't know how to say this. But now you must be told."

"Father?" She started toward him, his distress palpable in his voice.

He dropped his head on his chest. "I am going blind." He held up his hand to stop her approach. "No, do not pity me. The condition is gradual, thank heavens. But now you know my full reasons for asking you to wed Charles Henry. In the future, I will require a great deal of assistance."

"Of course, I will help you." She hugged him anyway, her arms wrapped around his rough wool coat. "I didn't know about this. You should have told me earlier. What did your physician say?"

"Why?"

"I-I don't know precisely. Maybe I can help you more." She returned to her chair and stared into the fire. Several minutes passed while she watched the dust dance in the beams of firelight. She lost the war without firing a shot—her fleeting, infant dreams of choosing her own man to love died with her father's disclosure. Her spirits sagged to a new low. "I will agree to wed Charles Henry, but I must ask for a concession in kind. Please let me give him my answer and choose the time to announce our engagement. Gentlemen don't always understand a woman's feelings, and for mother's sake, let me announce it once the parhelia paper is finished."

"I don't see why—"

"Please." She rose and leaned over to kiss his cheek. "I cannot explain now, but you have my word. I have always done my duty by you, so I promise to announce my engagement before we return to London."

Fourteen

"FATHER HAS ARRIVED? *MY* FATHER?" IF SOMEONE HAD told Boyce that a trout had happily walked out of the nearest stream and enjoyed a chat with Lady Buxton in the library, he would have believed that before he would have believed the marquess had left his country seat during a grouse-shooting party.

"He is actually very sweet," Eve said as they stood in the hall in front of the dining room door. "Seems years ago, he and Lady Buxton's husband had been business partners in a canal venture. The two have even met numerous times before, so they had plenty of catching up to do."

Boyce's head continued to spin. "How come you know so much? Sounds like you were in the room." She smiled, and the lovely sight caused his spinning wits to become even more disordered.

"I was," she said. "Lady Buxton invited me to join them. She was anxious that the marquess should be introduced to the young lady who had ensured the safety of his youngest son. I must say, at first he seemed just like one would expect from a marquess. You know, full of propriety and aware of his consequence. But after ten minutes of polite conversation, I was pleasantly surprised to find your father so amiable. By the time we left to dress for dinner, we exchanged jests like old friends."

Boyce felt the earthquake caused by the words *father* and *amiable* used in the same sentence. However, she seemed unconcerned and failed to clutch the walls for support, but he could have sworn the whole house shook.

"I, of course," she continued, "told him all about your courage during the flight. How after such a harrowing ascension, you bravely refused to land immediately…"

"You do have a talent for a good tale. Really, you must write a novel."

"I saw no evidence he ignores you. He was very interested in your efforts to assist me with the experiments and sounded very complimentary." She stopped and colored. "Maybe we all think our parents ignore us. Oh, I hear someone coming. How about you take me in to dinner?" She placed her arm on his sleeve.

Several members of the household approached the dining room door. Deep in conversation, Mr. Mountfloy and Mr. Henry entered the hallway. When they reach the door, Mr. Henry stepped forward to address Eve. "May I take you in to dinner tonight?"

Boyce's shaken wits returned in enough time to object to this plan. "I asked her—"

"Of course you can," Lydia said, descending the staircase in a cloud of sky-blue silk. "Dear Boyce will escort me in to dinner."

As soon as these words were spoken, Lady

Buxton and his father arrived in the hallway. The marquess offered his arm to the older woman. "May I have the honor?"

Boyce had never seen Lady Buxton's stunning smile. The happiness crossing her countenance made him believe the rumors that she had once been the toast of London, the brightest star of her season.

"Nothing would give me greater pleasure," Lady Buxton said, nodding for the footman to open the dining room door. As she and the marquess strode into the room, she said, "I am afraid we are an odd number tonight. I invited our neighbor, Mr. Sackville, to join us. Unfortunately he was unavailable, so we will just have to make do."

Boyce led a beaming Lydia into the cavernous, formal dining room. One wall was dominated by an open hearth big enough for a man to walk into while the longest mahogany dining table he had ever seen appeared like dollhouse furniture under the high ceilings. With room for at least twenty people on each side, only one end had been set for dinner. He pulled out Lydia's chair.

She patted her hand on the chair next to hers. "You will sit here next to me, dear Boyce. Now, isn't this pleasant."

His father lifted a brow, and Boyce tried to imagine how much tittle-tattle he had heard or imagined about his son's behavior in Sussex. More than likely, Boyce would need to provide explanations later.

Unfortunately, Eve sat on the other side of the table, next to his father. Since Mr. Henry had claimed her hand for dinner, her apple pout continued to linger.

Strange feature, that pout. He had never witnessed any feature that demanded to be kissed more.

After the service of clear turnip soup liberally doused with fragrant sherry, the conversation lagged. Except for Lady Buxton and his father, who seemed like a pair of whispering children at the end of the table. In an attempt to free Eve from the humdrum conversation of Mr. Henry, he said, "Did you tell your father all about the technical details of our discovery?"

She failed to answer him and shook her head; a small smile appeared.

Mr. Mountfloy admonished her with a single glance.

Lady Buxton leaned over and whispered something to the marquess again.

"Tell me about the earl's race," his father addressed him. "Since I understand it was the reason behind your remarkable balloon flight."

"Oh, yes," Lydia said. "I would like to hear about the earl's wager too. I am sure the courage he has shown in accepting the challenge will be to dear Boyce's credit."

When young, there were many times Boyce had eyed the tablecloth by his knees and thought about lifting it up to spend the dinner under the table—out of sight and unable to respond to any remark. This time, he dreamed about how wonderful it would be to crawl under the table and lay his head on Eve's lap. Glancing back at his father, Boyce found his father holding his spoon full of soup suspended in the air, waiting for his reply.

"Please, let me tell the story," Eve said, turning to speak directly to his father. "Your son's modesty might cause him to leave out the parts of the story where he was indeed a hero."

Boyce remained speechless as Eve continued to describe his honorable intentions to ensure the future happiness of Lady Sarah. Right now, right here, he desired nothing more than to kiss her senseless. Then she continued to praise the intelligence behind his decision to hire the most forward technology of the day to get him to France, and the generosity of spirit he showed helping her complete her experiments under difficult conditions. By the end of her speech, he had become the only person who could have helped her, his efforts the sole reason for their success. She obviously needed him, and from her description, he sounded like one of the finest fellows on the planet.

The ladies of the priory both cooed over the tale of his adventures, while his father sat silently ruminating over his beef joint.

Boyce stared at Eve, and she winked—*winked*. A song bubbled up, but one glance at his father's expression and the song died before he had the chance to give it life.

Lady Buxton and his father once again started to whisper to each other.

Lydia sighed. "Oh, there really are so many great men in England, are there not? I do wish my dear Buxton was here tonight."

Mr. Mountfloy turned to his daughter. "The parhelia data will cement our position in the sciences and ensure future donations. You must write up the parhelia's observed distances from the sun while the events are still fresh in your mind."

This caught the marquess's attention. "I am sure Lady Buxton would allow my son to help Miss Mountfloy compose, as you say, their observations here at the priory. Two memories are better than one, so there would be no chance of any important detail being lost."

"I do not mean to insult your lordship," Mr. Mountfloy said, "but your son is not trained for this type of work. Despite a single balloon ascension, his life has been frittered away on frivolities."

"I think my son can remember enough to assist your daughter, sir," the marquess pronounced. "He may give the appearance of a high-spirited, carefree fellow"—he looked at Boyce—"the singing comes to mind, inherited from his grandfather on the maternal side. But of my eight sons, my relatives always believed his amiability would guarantee his success in life." The marquess turned to Lady Buxton. "I have recently learned he played an instrumental role in turning his older brother's publishing business into a profitable one, solely from the acquisition of a popular novel. I firmly believe that Boyce has the abilities to surpass all of the accomplishments of his brothers, except Richard's, of course. Perhaps by winning this race to France? The point of the matter is, my friend Gunstone collects butterflies. He discovered some orange monster that proved to be of interest to the Royal Institute of Great Britain. I can't tell you how impressed I was to hear Gunstone speak at an afternoon lecture. So there is precedence for amateurs contributing to discovery."

Lady Buxton nodded. The gesture was a small

one, but it caused the two tall feathers on her ornate turban to move dramatically. "Yes, he must assist Miss Mountfloy. Dear Boyce is quite capable." She leaned over to address his father. "He has your dear wife's charity too."

Boyce gulped. He had never heard such praise or his father speak of his future with such optimism. A song instantly came to mind, but he suppressed it for the time being. He'd sing later, by himself.

Mr. Mountfloy laid down his fork. "With my respects, I must disagree with you both. You, sir, gave him the cut direct, and rightly so. Besides, I do not see how any man could contribute to science with the nickname Piglet Parker."

Several people gasped.

Boyce's mind whirled and the feeling of inadequacy returned. His failures once again paraded in front of his father.

His father ignored the insult to his son and remained silent.

Everyone focused on eating their meal.

Boyce became physically sick. Without any support from the others and lacking the presence of mind to defend himself, he excused himself with as much dignity as he could muster and left the room.

❧

Staring up at the high, square windows in the priory's library the following day, Eve sat at the long table waiting for Parker. Her father eventually had to agree with Lady Buxton that two heads were better than one when it came time to remember an event. Even he did not want to lose any important data, so he agreed to them writing the letter together. She inhaled deeply and smiled. Looking up, the round, stone room reminded her of a large dovecote. She wondered if, centuries ago, monks had walked endless circles in prayer in this room. She hoped not.

Someone neared, whistling an upbeat tune.

Parker entered the room and smiled at her. "Happy to be here and happy to see my brave aeronaut. Shall we start with a song?"

She laughed. "What kind of song? Getting our parhelia observations down on paper is serious and important, so the tune should reflect that."

"Funeral dirge?"

"Not quite that serious."

"How about that Handel dance tune with all those small steps a fellow can never remember? Step over here—step over there—in—out—up—down, then beg your partner's forgiveness."

"Minuet?"

"Yes, that's it." He glanced up at the ceiling and whistled. "This room is so perfectly round, I'll bet your balloon would fit inside. What do you think?"

Eve examined the dimensions of the room. "It's a hair too small; our balloon would become wedged between the walls."

"It's funny how I've come to love that balloon." He strode over to the table, moved a chair next to her, and sat. "I tell you, my friend, I really miss it. Yes, yes, I don't miss the cold, the brief rain shower that fouled your instruments and made you quite grumpy, not to mention the carnage of the butterfly. Yet, I do miss its freedom." He slapped his thigh. "Especially the soul-searing calm freedom of the universe above us."

She chuckled quietly. "With our fathers here, that sort of calm freedom becomes unobtainable, don't you think?" If she had used a ruler to measure the distance between them, it would reveal them to be significantly closer than strictly acceptable. For heaven's sake, his shoulder almost touched her. And if her heartbeat escalated any more, there would be no way for her to complete the task before them. They'd fall into a spell of kissing—an altogether pleasant thought—but the consequences of discovery could be severe. "I mean no offense, but I'd prefer you to sit on the other side of the table. Then we can address one another face to face. Put a list of our experiments out in front, so both of us can check the accuracy. That is our number one goal in completing this parhelia paper. We must be ruthlessly accurate."

He did not say anything at first, his profile inscrutable. "Right. Ruthless is the word. You're the captain, remember?" He jumped over to sit on the other side.

Eve miscalculated. The ability to see him clearly was not an advantage for keeping her mind on the experiments. His curly, unruly hair demanded her smoothing touch.

He gave her a smile that began as a simmering grin, evolved into a bright smile, and reached a beaming crescendo.

She sharpened an already sharp pencil. "Today, let's refresh our memories on the timeline of the experiments. I do not expect to include all of these results in the paper. But if we complete this first, we will not leave anything of significance out. A small detail about the type of clouds seen before the two parhelia appeared might become important when you present our paper."

"If I'm invited to speak, I wonder if my father will be in the audience. I have to admit complete astonishment to see him walk through the door. I initially wrote to my brother Richard for assistance, so I did not expect to see the pater. I suspect he hurried down expecting to extract me from some imbroglio I had gotten myself into."

"Maybe that is why he came, but he did seem genuinely interested in us writing the parhelia paper together before our recollections faded."

He opened his mouth slightly and held his hands out. "Yes, yes, as soon as he said that, you could have knocked me over with a feather. He has a large circle of scientific acquaintants and is a fellow of many learned societies, so he is familiar with scientific letters."

His words reminded her that there were no guarantees the Royal Institute of Great Britain, or any other institution, would select their paper for presentation. Indeed, it might not be considered good enough even to publish. Yet Eve still had a small bud of hope that, with her name on the paper, she would solidify her reputation as a serious lady of science, whether she was able to present her data in person or not. "Our parhelia observation may not be significant enough for publication, so I do not want you to get your hopes up."

He groaned. "Is there any way to tell beforehand? I mean, if I cannot present in person, I will have to rejoin the race immediately, since I have less than a month left. My father was impressed by your tall tale of my heroics during our flight. So I must rejoin *and win* the race now that he is aware of my goal." He twirled his pencil. "I don't suppose *we* can try for France again?"

"In my opinion, you have already won."

"How so?"

"The earl would have to be a greater fool than I suspect if he awarded the Service to a Lady prize to anyone else. What other gentleman's story could compete with helping a lady save humanity?"

"Yes, yes, you have a point, but I don't think the earl will see it that way. I really need to reach Paris and tell my tale. Hopefully, my story will win more than one of the challenges. With two victories, I could not fail to make a name for myself. Besides, who knows what the other fellows are doing. My friend Drexel, for example, doggedly droll, but he always ends up victorious. He's one of those men who, when his valet quits, the best valet in Britain becomes available for hire. Or when his horse goes lame, some uncle dies and wills him the finest thoroughbred. So Drexel's participation in the earl's race means stiff competition. I really must win."

A wistful, aching feeling strangled her spirits. If granted one wish, right here and now, she'd wish his father had hesitated and carefully considered the situation before he had given his son the cut direct. The nickname Piglet Parker was unfair too. Together, these cruel circumstances had created his extraordinary urge to succeed and gain praise. "Let us write up the facts as we witnessed them. My father has suggested that once we finish, you present the paper after dinner, like a practice recital here at the priory. That way, any discrepancies can be cleared up before the letter is posted and considered for publication. You also should keep a copy, in case the institution invites you to present our results."

He tapped his finger on the table. "Right. What did we do first?" He winked at her. "I mean, after the tussle for the valve. You tussle very well, by the way."

For some inexplicable reason, this comment made her laugh. He had an extraordinary gift of setting her natural humor free. "Thank you. I mean, we did the bird experiments first: crow, pigeon, duck—"

"I wish I knew if they landed all right."

Happiness welled up from her heart and found freedom. "I do not recommend searching for the birds. Since you speak fluent duck, he may have a few strong words for you."

"Ha!" He jumped up, swooped her off her chair, and swung her in circles. Seconds later, they fell upon a sofa against the wall, and he plopped her on his knee. "Indeed he would, probably give me an earful too."

He wore a cream-colored linen shirt and a velvet waistcoat the color of claret, so being near him gave her pleasant thoughts of thick cream and strawberries. "I don't think this is proper," she said. "What if someone enters the library?"

"Then they will find two people hard at work saving humanity. Besides, recreating the tussle will help me remember."

Is he going to recreate every movement in the balloon?

Kisses too? "It's not necessary for us to relive every event. We need to concentrate on the facts."

A transitory wounded look shone in his eyes. "Right. You do the facts, and I will remember all the subjective bits."

"Since we are composing a scientific article, only the factual data is important."

"What exactly is the line between factual and subjective?" He cleared his throat. "There were some experiments I enjoyed very much. Isn't my enjoying them a fact?"

"Yes, but not an important one. If you said you felt cold when the temperature was eighty degrees, that is an example of where subjective data may be important. Now let us return to the table, so I can write all of this down."

"Go fetch your writing things and return here. I cannot remember the facts without you in my lap." He smiled, quite pleased with his nonsensical directive. "You spent a great deal of time there, so it will help stimulate my memory."

Even though it proved to be a weak excuse, she wanted to comply. Maybe she'd take a page from his book and claim that his fetching brown locks stimulated her memory. A rampant blush claimed her cheeks. *Blast.* She only had limited time in his company, so she needed to remember everything about him before he left. Gathering up her paper and pencil, she did her best to sit nonchalantly upon his knee. "Am I too heavy?"

"No, no. Light as a butterfly." He gasped. "Wrong choice of creature. We must do our best to spare our readers about the fate of the butterfly—too traumatic. And of course, leave out the details about what the duck said. We don't want to upset anyone."

Eve nodded. "Agreed." Together they discussed all of the bird experiments and reached a consensus on the details of each bird's flight. They also remembered every detail about the discovery of the parhelia.

Finally, they found discord over an old argument. "It must be 'living sparks tossed upon an inky vault.' It really must," he said.

"How would you feel if a learned society mocked you for that nonscientific description?"

He dropped his jaw. "Yes, yes, too unpleasant. A man must make concessions now and then. What boring, *factual* words did you use to describe the sky? I remember, *black*. The stars were…*white*." He smirked. "Who could mock that?"

"Perhaps we can keep the vault bit. How about 'black vault'?"

"I've decided to agree with you because I want to get to the huddle bit." He enclosed her in an embrace. "We need to huddle now, so we can accurately remember how it felt."

"In the library?"

"Why not? While I'm not a scientific sort of fellow, I do believe we should report that huddling, chafing, and kisses can prevent scientific investigators from suffering the effects of extreme chill."

Laughter gurgled up, and for the first time in her life, a song came to mind. She relished the thought of kisses being discussed in the lecture rooms of a learned institution. "That really is not necessary. Can you imagine gentlemen of science routinely kissing one another?" She laughed again. "Can you imagine father and Charles Henry kissing?"

"Not on the lips—maybe on the cheek—if they want to survive. Might have to kiss everything in sight to live. Kiss the grapnel, kiss the wicker—I'm sure there is a song there. Let me see… Kisses to warm you, my friend, too la la."

She joined in. "Kisses to warm you, my friend, too la lee."

He pulled her closer to his chest. "Yes, that is the idea. Second verse is always the toughest. Maybe we should do a proper recital and open with a song."

His lips were inches from hers, but leaning in for his kiss was out of the question. Why, then, did it sound so delightful? Though technically betrothed, she changed her mind and decided one little stolen kiss couldn't be of any harm. She stared at his slightly parted mouth. Seconds later, her only awareness was of the softness of his kiss, the hardness of his chest as she leaned full against him, and the smoothness of his locks as she entwined her fingers deep within his hair. The kiss seemed so right, neither of them made any motion to end it, so it continued for some unknown amount of time. It lingered lightly on their lips before the sound of their escalating breaths spurred a need to return to deep, wit-melting kisses. Then one or the other would chuckle in the middle of the kiss or sigh deeply, necessitating additional rounds of deep thrusts of tongue countered by a parry of kissing lips.

In the end, he was the one who finally pulled back. With his soft lips touching her cheek, he whispered,

"Eve, sweetheart, I heard a rumor today. I suspect it's false, but if not, give me your word of honor that you will never marry that damnable fellow."

She pulled her mind out of a sensuous haze and assumed a carefree expression. "I don't know what you mean. We really must get back to work."

"Trust your heart. Speak to Lady Buxton. She will be able to guide you."

His urgent plea pained her heart, but he did not ask her to marry him. Besides, she could never find happiness as the wife of an aristocrat. Her allegiance and duty belonged to her father and his needs. Fighting the beginning of tears, she turned to drink her fill of Parker's handsome face. A single tear fell anyway. She leaped to her feet and turned her back to him. "I'll send our letter to the Royal Institution in the morning post. Following luncheon, you will give your recital—"

"I promise it will be a success," he said, with a crack in his otherwise steady voice. "Facts only."

"You give your recital, and then we will say our farewells." After she spoke the word *farewell*, her tears fell in earnest. "What happens after that is not important." She left the room without glancing back.

Fifteen

WITHIN THE FIRST TEN MINUTES OF DRINKING MADEIRA in the company of Mr. Mountfloy and Mr. Henry, Boyce easily recognized the additional spirits that laced his glass of wine. The overwhelming smell of pungent alcohol fumes when he brought the glass to his lips coupled with a liquid the color of light claret, instead of the deep reds of Madeira, hinted at the possibility of dilution with clear spirits. Since Eve's father had requested this private conversation, Boyce concluded he—or Mr. Henry—wished him to become the worse for wine. Then once his mind was thoroughly muddled, his upcoming speech before the priory's occupants would fail. This evidence of ill will did not concern him much because he only drank a polite, single glass, despite Mr. Henry's repeated urging for him to drink another.

After an hour without either of the two men of science saying anything of significance, just exchanging speaking glances, they left the room in a huff.

Boyce's tongue felt like sand, so he headed down to the kitchen. Whatever form of liquor was added to the Madeira, it had left him undeniably thirsty.

In the hallway, he met Mr. Buxton. The MP had returned from London after dinner yesterday in time to join the men in drawing room. Today, he still wore his habitual city coat, gray trousers, gray waistcoat, and not a bright color or shiny fob anywhere. "Are you ready for your big speech?"

"Of course, but I need a glass of water first. Your Madeira, when it's poured by Mr. Mountfloy, can be a bit too strong."

"I don't understand. Mother drinks the weakest Madeira in all of England. She claims the strong liquor upsets her constitution."

"You missed the point—when poured by Mr. Mountfloy."

"Ah, stiffened it with extra alcohol, did he?" Mr. Buxton patted him on the back and led him in the direction of the kitchen. "Come, we'll get you some pure water straight from the tap. How did you know the drink was laced?"

Boyce laughed, wishing the housekeeper with the pitcher of water poured it faster. "*You* ask me that question, my brother Henry's boon companion?"

"Ah, Henry, he lived for practical jests when young." Mr. Buxton took two leaded cut glasses in hand, and the two men returned to the small parlor used as his study. "Frogs were his normal means of warfare against me. But I remember he swaddled a hedgehog once and put it in your crib. Evidently, your old nurse discovered nothing amiss for a whole day. The gig was up when a housemaid found you sleeping merrily in a cupboard. Your father, of course, was not pleased."

"Goes without saying that, as the youngest of eight brothers, I became a constant target. So a drink laced with excess liquor is child's play in my book. It normally takes two or three bottles before I'm in my cups."

Buxton sat in an overstuffed leather chair by the fire and stretched out his long legs in front of him. "All I can say is one of those gentlemen aeronauts is an amateur and a swine. Do you want me to expel them with haste?"

"No, no." He held the glass of water up to eye level. "See, steady as a rock." His hand shook, spilling water on his knee. "Steady as a pebble. Don't worry. It will take more than a little wine to sabotage my speech. I have no intention of boring anyone with drunken rants or raves. Besides, I refuse to let Miss Mountfloy down."

"I'd say you're more than just a little fond of that remarkable young lady."

Boyce gulped more water, contemplating his answer. Perhaps his brain had become muddled after all, since no suitable retort came to mind. "Yes, yes, she is remarkable, pretty too. My upcoming presentation of our data will be a great success and please her no end. I cannot wait."

❧

Just under an hour later, Boyce glanced around the room where—in fifteen minutes—he'd give his sun dog speech and tell everyone about his greatest triumph to date. It was an unfortunate circumstance that the music room was small and the Broadwood and Sons piano took up a quarter of the room. If that gleaming mahogany beast were removed, then the entire neighborhood could have been invited to hear his presentation. However, today's small audience didn't signify much, since once he presented in front of a venerable London institution and poured out his sage words, everyone in Britain would soon hear of his victory.

Being the first to enter the room, Boyce arranged the wood chairs to his advantage. Unfortunately, the music room's high ceilings necessitated a fire in the grate to chase out the damp, even though they were in the warmest days of summer. Not wanting his audience to become overheated, he pulled the chairs around a small podium moved in from the library. On the podium's front gleamed the priory's arms in painted wood. Heraldic ermine and stars composed the family's arms, yet two greyhounds rampant supported the shield. The dogs stood on their hindquarters, forepaws raised, staring straight ahead with a fierce expression, their tongues sticking out. Boyce straightened. He too felt rampant and ready for the chase.

As he waited for the others to arrive, he sang a few words of a new song brewing in his head, a song about remorse. He anticipated his father's impending remorse upon giving his youngest son the cut direct. Even if, a year later, his father had forgotten the cut, Boyce's successful speech could only go a long way toward making him proud.

Eve entered the room and immediately joined him at the podium, looking neat as a ninepence in her wool gown. "Did you study last night? Do you remember the degrees observed from the main sun?"

"Yes, yes, twenty-two degrees. I wonder if there is a word that rhymes with degrees? Knees?" He smiled at her wide eyes. "Lately I've thought about our discovery and how best to express its meaning. I've also written a new song."

"No." She clutched his arm. "This is serious business. You must understand your speech is not a lark. You must present the results exactly as you would before a learned institution. Then everything will be at stake—my father's reputation, our livelihood—"

"Don't worry, I'll include all of the details." He inhaled a sharp breath, causing her pout to appear. For a moment, his brain became muddled by thoughts of apples and suns and kisses and kittens. He patted the top of her hand. "I won't let you down. We should talk afterward, alone. There is something I wish to tell you."

Her pout vanished, an unspoken question appeared in the gleam of her eyes. "Tell me?"

The priory's occupants began to enter the room. On the right side, Mr. Mountfloy and Mr. Henry sat and spoke in hushed tones.

On the other side, Lady Buxton sat in the only upholstered chair while her maid fussed with a footstool.

"Later then." Eve flashed him a smile, then moved to sit next to Lady Buxton.

The older woman quickly claimed her hand and patted it. "I am so looking forward to Boyce's speech. Aren't you, my dear?"

"Yes, although I'm worried some of the others from the priory may become bored." She flushed. "The speech has a lot of numbers, so it may not be meaningful to everyone. Mr. Henry and my father will comprehend the importance, but I fear the remainder of his audience may not fully understand. Then with the room so hot, they may fall asleep."

Lady Buxton chucked her under the chin. "My dear, whatever Boyce says can be trusted entirely because he always speaks from the heart. I may not understand a single word, but I know the speaker says it with great sincerity. No listener could ask for anything more. Don't you agree?"

Boyce did not hear her reply. Instead, he became distracted by Mr. Mountfloy's fulminating frowns aimed in his direction. The older man clearly disliked him, and Boyce was at a loss to understand the precise reasons why. Yes, he refused to land the balloon before France, but that seemed like a small offense almost a week later. It certainly was not enough reason for the man to continue his glares, negative words, and a probable attempt to sabotage Boyce's speech using alcohol. Boyce glanced again at the greyhounds supporting the family's arms, rampant and ready to pounce.

Mr. Buxton and his wife entered the room. Today, Lydia beamed brighter than any raging fire, and her gaze never left Buxton's ear.

Buxton seated his wife on the other side of his mother and then joined Boyce at the podium. Still wearing a drab gray coat, Boyce thought Buxton should have been more fashionably dressed for such a momentous occasion. "Ready, my friend?" Buxton said with a wink.

Boyce had never seen his brother's friend wink and smile with such abandon. Obviously, the man was delighted to be back in the bosom of his family. "I am ready. But I must admit I don't think I have ever been as happy as you look today, old fellow. Yes, yes, marriage agrees with you."

Buxton gave him a back pat. "It certainly does. I tell you, a fellow can really get in trouble if he thinks too much about his wife. He must trust her unreservedly with his whole heart. I've apologized for abandoning her, and today the two of us are happy as Greeks. I recommend marriage, Parker. It can try a man at times, but as a soother of souls, there is nothing like it."

"Yes, yes, still young, not quite ready on the leg-shackle front."

"Time will come. As men, our hearts cannot escape the siren's lure. But now I hope you're ready on the speechifying front. I'm excited to hear all about this amazing balloon adventure. I must admit I never would have pegged you, old chap, as the scientific sort. I expect you more on the creative end of things. That book of songs from the Coal Hole, for example." Buxton needled him with an elbow. "Funny those, eh?"

Boyce furtively glanced at his father.

It was time to begin, so Buxton motioned for Boyce to take a seat in the front row. The host faced the small assembly in a half circle before him. "All of us here at Duddleswell Priory are honored to have the Marquess of Sutcliffe's company. I would also like to welcome all of the members of the ballooning party. First the distinguished man of science, Mr. Mountfloy, and indeed, we are happy to meet his lovely daughter and young assistant too. I personally would like to thank all of you for your efforts to amuse my mother, Lady Buxton. I know you have all been treated well, since no lady keeps better house than my wife." He nodded at Lydia. "Thank you, my dear. And I also wish to thank the ballooning party for providing a stimulating distraction for my wife from her worries arising from my temporary absence."

Resplendent in deep-red silk and a gold shawl, Lydia cooed and clapped.

"Today, Lord Boyce Parker," Mr. Buxton continued, "one of the younger brothers of my good friend Lord Henry Parker, will give us a brief presentation of some sort of abnormality involving mock suns." He held his arm outward. "Ladies and gentlemen, may I present Lord Boyce."

Boyce took his place behind the podium and glanced at his audience. Besides the guests, his audience included the addition of several housemaids, the butler, and a footman. A fine grouping, even though it was a small one, because they all sported a smile and wore a look of expectation, like a card game where everyone stares at you seconds before you reveal the winning hand. "Yes, yes, I would like to thank the Buxton family for saving Miss Mountfloy and myself after the balloon crash, not to mention the warm hospitality of everyone here at the priory. Mrs. Buxton and Lady Buxton are indeed fine hostesses." He bowed. "Thank you, ladies. So here goes." He inhaled deeply then began his speech. "Our journey started with the magnificent hilarity of our ascent. A very rapid one designed to impress me, eh, Mr. Mountfloy?"

The aeronaut's pinched lips made him appear quite sour.

Boyce paused; perhaps best not to begin a speech by teasing your audience. "After our ascent, we performed the experiments using birds, so that one day, we might better understand the weights and type of wings necessary for humans to fly. I personally cannot wait for this event, since I'm sure a fellow will be able to choose the size and material of his wings, the way he does a good hat."

Mr. Henry coughed and exchanged nods with Mr. Mountfloy.

Had he misunderstood the reason behind the experiments with the birds? He'd ask Eve later; best to get on with it. Should he start with the observations of the other animals or skip to the sun dog discovery? "Before I continue, I would like to thank the birds, bee, and the butterfly for assisting us with our understanding of the brilliant-blue air. I also apologize to these fine animals for throwing them overboard and giving them a nasty scare." He glanced over his audience and found them no longer smiling. He coughed. "Ah…by late afternoon, we finished the experiments with the birds…" He focused on his notes.

The silence stretched.

"Right. Don't need to hear the story of the duck, tragic that." He looked up from his notes to discover his audience's stony faces.

Some were staring at the fire, others picking at their clothes or winking at their neighbor.

He had made a perfect hash of this speech and lost his audience. Perhaps he should emulate the Vicar

Wigby's remedy for a sleepy Sunday congregation by using emotional words that are shared by all humans. "The story of our sun dog sighting began after an afternoon of joyous calm. The world was about to be tucked into bed for the night, and the next promised to be even a better day." He waved his arms to increase the dramatic effect. "Before us the most magnificent of God's creations, the sky high above us, robed itself in the dusk colors of blue, like a cornflower, orange... like an orange, and gray, like the skies above London." He spread his arms wide. "An hour later, the stars appeared, like living sparks floating upward through the abyss of an inky vault, illuminating the splendor of life." Expecting a small, enthusiastic response to his emotive speech, he glanced at the crowd.

Lydia adjusted her shawl, his father had pulled out his pocket watch, and the servants whispered softly in the back of the room.

His aeronaut sported a rosy blush, more than likely not pleased with his performance so far. Perhaps the Madeira had muddled his mind after all. With the memory of Eve's warning about the seriousness of his speech, he decided to stick strictly to the facts, and soldiered on. "Pardon me. We observed the sun dogs—I mean parhelia—before the inky vault bit. So I'll talk about that now."

Mr. Mountfloy leaped to his feet. "This young man here obviously lacks the seriousness required to present such important information. I say we—"

His aeronaut stood to face her father. "Lord Boyce has a firm grasp upon the facts, and since he has never spoken publicly before, any hesitation on his part is likely due to lack of practice before a real audience. Let him finish, please."

Boyce beamed at Eve. *Bless his aeronaut.* For the required tone of utter seriousness, he must now alter his strategy and resume his speech with the same solemnity Vicar Wigby used when he mentioned the local Quakers. "Right, here goes. The barometer, hygro…I mean several o-meters read thirty-four and sixty. The parhelia, or two mock suns, danced… appeared in an immense halo. These were first seen at half past seven in the evening, when the sun kissed…touched the horizon. The halo's two Brobdingnagian…" He glanced over to Eve to find her brows knit. *Right, no waxing lyrical.* He must be ruthless and avoid all those frowns by not using pesky adjectives. He never realized how a little thing like an adjective could be so dangerous to a fellow. "The halo's two giant…large arcs of light spread vertical in relation to the majestic…magnificent…the real sun." He needed to take a deep breath.

His audience watched him intently; two house-maids wore silly smiles.

"The enorm…plain arcs were measured with a sextant and discovered to be just shy of twenty-four degrees. The halo arcs were red on the side closest to the real sun and blue-green on the farthest side. In the center of each arc shone a mock sun, perpendicular to the arcs of the halo. The two mock suns appeared within fleecy cotton…white Cirrostratus clouds, ninety degrees from the real sun. They were almost round and orange in color when at their brightest. The real sun measured twenty-two degrees in altitude. The parhelia lasted forty minutes and changed in intensity before fading away into an extremely delightful…an extreme evening. There, I'm finished with the science part of my speech."

Eve focused on her lap, but he held the attention of the other members of his audience. Perhaps he might, for the benefit of this audience only, express what this balloon flight meant to him and how it had changed his outlook on life forever.

"Before I finish, there are a few observations about balloon flight I would like to tell you about." He took a deep breath. "I had always gazed up at balloons and wondered if our world would appear changed when viewed from above. But our world below appeared as I would have expected—roads, woods, and cities spread out in the fashion of a chessboard. The most notable parts of our everyday life that caught my attention were the sounds reaching my ears, the racket of dogs barking and bells ringing. Even the odors we create, like cattle fields and chimney smoke, rose up to us in the balloon. Now after my flight, it is not our world on the ground from another viewpoint that amazed me, but the brilliance of the universe above us that took my breath away. I got the impression of being lifted into the heavens and my worldly cares remained earthbound. High in the sky, I felt total freedom. Hanging suspended hundreds of feet in the air, I could not hear painful words or the sounds of mankind's suffering. I became embraced by a feeling of total happiness and will always remember my flight as one of the greatest moments in my life. This memory I will cherish close to my heart until the day

I die. Thank you for your attention." He made a brief bow then studied his audience.

Most of them clapped rather randomly.

Lydia and Lady Buxton clapped with enthusiasm.

Eve clapped slowly, wearing a troubled brow and biting her lower lip.

His father's expression looked exactly similar to the one he wore immediately before giving Boyce the cut direct.

Another failure, in front of his father too. He sighed and stared at his feet to regain his composure without witnessing everyone's disappointment. Regardless of his negative reception, he believed the science part of his speech went quite well. Eve should have no complaints. With a little more practice, his speech would be as bright as a penny. Granted, at the beginning, in a moment of unbridled enthusiasm, he had burst out with the "inky vault" bit, and there was one time when he got an "o-meter" wrong. Thermo, hydro, baro—they all sound the same. He also forgot to mention the temperature and something else measured by whalebone instruments. However, he did remember all of the other tricky parts, even the twenty-two degrees—the most important information in his speech. In the end, he hoped his audience came away with a better understanding of the excitement of newfound discoveries and the poetry expressed in the sky above us every day.

Mr. Mountfloy rose and turned to address the others. "I refuse to let this man ruin all of our reputations. His mind is too unfocused for serious study. Hysterical ascents, fleecy cotton clouds, irrelevant nonsense—"

"Father, please."

"That is the second time you have interrupted me, my girl."

The marquess stood, his consequence providing unspoken gravitas. "My son has disappointed me in the past. His efforts seem to do nothing but bring embarrassment to our family name. We do not need additional shame created by a botched speech before England's brightest men of science. The failure would create a scandal equal to his lurid books. I forbid him to speak to any institution until he has more practice. Then, perhaps, he might be able to present a responsible speech that would be considered adequate."

After his father's censure, Eve was his last hope of someone who would defend and support him.

He stared at his aeronaut, but she remained silent.

Mr. Mountfloy almost yelled, "It's clear he possesses almost no significant knowledge on the subject whatsoever. In fact, I strongly believe that, if asked a question, he would not be able to give a coherent response. He'd likely wave his hand, twaddle on about inky vaults, and end the answer with bad poetry or a lamentable simile. 'Freedom from words that hurt,' no sane person could understand the meaning of that phrase."

Eve glanced at her father. "We cannot take the risk of letting him present our data in a speech like the one we have just heard, since any failure before a learned institution might end funding for our research forever." She glanced at Parker. "I had previously warned Lord Boyce on the seriousness of the matter, but he did not follow my advice, so he might not follow it again in the future."

The coup de grâce delivered by Eve herself. Boyce swallowed with difficulty. No one truly understood him. He firmly believed that every human accomplishment contained some poetry. His audience even failed to realize that all "bad poetry" sprang from intense, poorly expressed emotions. *How can they condemn emotions?* For the first time, he questioned his ability to pull off an acceptable scientific speech. Perhaps if he tried again, he'd be publicly mocked, as he had been too many times before.

Lady Buxton slapped her fan shut and stood. "I've had the good fortune to attend many scientific speeches. However, none of them proved as interesting and enjoyable as the one delivered here tonight. I shall seek out my old friends from the Royal Institution and relay the importance of this discovery. Well done, young man. You accomplished one of the most difficult balancing acts of speaking before an audience, the balance of learning something new, coupled with the amusement of wit and poetry. I must say, I was not bored in the least. With a little coaching and assistance from Miss Mountfloy here"—she gave Eve a nod—"Boyce's speech will be even better."

He smiled at Lady B. and took a small measure of pride from her support. He had to; it was all he would receive, apparently.

Eve fussed in her chair, then gave an almost imperceptible sigh. "If it would please you, your ladyship, I will assist Lord Parker in preparing the speech again. He did have a fine grip on some of the important scientific parts, and with more coaching on removing the subjective parts of his speech, he might be a success. But—"

"I disagree," Mr. Henry said with a tone of terse finality. "This wastrel will never do. Lacking the seriousness and rigor of mind needed for a gentleman of science, he will embarrass and bring ruin to us all. I have no intention of letting my good name be associated with this hulver-headed poet."

Boyce spoke before he could check himself. "That's a bouncer coming from a man who embarrassed himself by stealing the *Results* book."

"The praise falls upon the servants who searched the woods," the marquess said, in a clipped voice. "I had hoped you learned a lesson from your previous boasts."

Boyce froze, pained by his rash claim. "Please forgive me. Neither Mr. Henry nor myself found the book. My father is right. The priory's servants deserve the credit."

"Enough!" Turning to address his daughter, Mr. Mountfloy said, "You will coach your fiancé, Charles Henry, to give the parhelia speech instead. That way, we can depend on an accurate representation of the data."

"Father!" Eve jumped out of her chair. "You promised to let me announce my engagement."

Mr. Mountfloy ignored his daughter's stricken expression. "You should only be concerned about the advancement of your future husband." He turned to the wide-eyed, startled audience. "While we planned to announce the official engagement before we left, my daughter has formally accepted the hand of Mr. Charles Henry. I hope you will all join me in wishing the couple happy."

Eve hung her head on her chest, as though her

spine had turned into aspic. After a single wipe of her eyes, she ran from the room.

Boyce's legs felt wobbly, but that was nothing compared to the feeling of Gentleman Jackson delivering a full blow to his stomach. He focused on the coat of arms again and on the armorial greyhound supporters. He no longer felt rampant by any means. The pain in his torso reminded him of one of those armorial half animals, the kind with the bottom part of their bodies cut away and missing. *Demi* was the preface to the word they used in heraldry. That described him perfectly, a demi-greyhound, suffering from the loss of his lower half. His armorial motto sealed forever: "Piglet Parker."

Sixteen

E<small>VE</small> <small>FLUNG OPEN THE DOOR AND RAN FROM THE</small> recital room. Tears blurred her vision, causing her to bump into a table in the vestibule, upsetting a china vase of yellow roses. Fearing additional damage to the priory if she remained, she fled outside, heading toward the fields. She ran as fast as she could on the longest stretch of pathway she could find. Her heart physically hurt. Like some wounded animal, she needed time alone to heal; time to try and understand why Parker had disobeyed her wishes; but most of all, time to find the understanding behind her father breaking his promise and announcing her betrothal.

Her vision eventually cleared, and she found herself breathing hard, standing on the path to the turnip field. She thought she heard rapid footsteps behind her, but when she glanced around, nobody appeared. Desperate to be alone, she ran toward the stand of trees marking the beginning of the woods. She stepped about twenty feet into the cool canopy of trees and stopped, not wanting to repeat the calamity of becoming lost. All around her stood dense woods. On her right, the gold earthen pathway, bathed in sunlight, provided her with an anchor to the outside world.

She found a flat area of fallen leaves. Then with the intention to escape the damp earth, she tried to break off a large fern to sit upon. The prickly stem failed to break, so she repeatedly twisted it. This effort failed too. After a long glare at the evil frond, she stomped on the large leaf until it lay flat. Surprisingly, the exertion left her feeling relieved. She took a deep breath, sat carefully, and exhaled slowly.

She needed to think—think—not feel. In the last few days, she had been beguiled by pretty gowns and happy thoughts of a blissful life with the man she loved. Yes, she had come to realize that she loved Parker. And the heart is not an organ that can be easily silenced once given free rein. Hers seemed to be speaking louder than ever this past week. For her own future happiness, she had to ignore these enchanting feelings, be ruthless, and only think. Somehow, someway, she had to forget Parker—consider her allegiance to her father's needs, not hers. She had to decide upon real, achievable choices from now on. Either marry Charles Henry or become a governess or companion. Perhaps Lady Buxton required a companion? No, she dismissed that thought, because it did not solve the problem of her father's constant need for research funding and failing eyesight.

"Yes, yes, hiding from us all. Don't blame you myself." Ten feet to her side, Parker stood, illuminated by the sunshine, both hands on his hips. He appeared to be breathing hard. "I need to hide too. May I join you?"

Like most women, she suffered from being overly polite. No, she didn't want his company, but she couldn't be cruel enough to tell him to go away. His presence would only upset her sense of balance. She'd end up fighting her own feelings as he tried to talk her out of marriage to Charles Henry. "How did you know where to find me?"

"I saw you run in this direction." A tentative grin crossed his masculine face. With long strides, he stepped over several shrubs until her reached her side. "I also know you have a fondness for hugging trees when you are in difficulty."

The unseen hand squeezing her heart released its grip a little.

He easily pulled and arranged several large fern leaves before sitting opposite her, face to face. His long, elegant legs in gleaming black top boots stretched along her side. He bit his lower lip, perhaps hesitant to speak first.

She welcomed the silence, since she had no desire to speak either. She needed time and solace to allow her brains to take charge. The minutes of silence stretched. She picked up a fern, kept her head down, and started pulling small bits of the fronds off, trying to formulate the words to kindly ask him to leave.

Finally, he scooted closer and reached for her hand to stop the frond's destruction.

The touch of his warm hand melted the immediate worries clouding her mind. She took another long, deep breath, realizing she welcomed his touch.

He squeezed her hand softly. "That's better, more like my fearless aeronaut."

While her anxieties had lessened, she still had nothing of importance to say. Or if she did, she could not summon the words.

He filled the silence first. "I apologize that my speech let you down. Buxton asked to hear about my adventures, so I attempted to please him, but that was a mistake. I truly planned to withhold the subjective parts when I presented it before the Royal Institute." He paused.

"I'm sorry my criticism was so harsh," she said. "You presented the data rather well for a beginner. And I really shouldn't blame you for the desire to please your audience." She lapsed into silence.

He took the hint and carried on the conversation by himself. "Created quite a rumpus with our fathers and Mr. Henry. I guess fleecy cotton clouds is not appropriate scientific terminology."

This time an audible chuckle escaped her.

"Yes, yes, you sound much better. I enjoy your laughter; you don't do enough of it."

She grinned wistfully. "I should have expected you to embellish your speech a little, but emotional descriptions would never do in front of a scientific audience. Still, you actually did remember most of the scientific details, so I guess my anger was unjustified."

He grinned.

"I said *most* of the details. Several important facts like the hygrometer readings were omitted. I cannot say my attempt would be any better." She smiled. "Perhaps I would mention less ink and fleecy cotton."

"Thank you," he said softly, squeezing her hand again. "Seems Lydia insists on your party's removal again. Do you want me to smooth the waters?"

"Thank you, no. It's just as well we are on our way back to London."

"I'm on my way too. Pater brought my horse, Charity, with him. I plan to head for Dover immediately. Only after your party leaves, of course. I cannot bear the thought of facing him ever again without some grand accomplishment. Besides, if I return with him, he might insist I help run the estate or do some other occupation under his eagle eye. I like the publishing business and have plans to continue editing and composing. My efforts also benefit my brother, and there is nothing like entertaining, informing, and amusing people. You know, lighten a mood with a song or two. So once I arrive at Dover, I'll continue my journey to Paris, ready to tell my amazing story." He smiled and nodded.

His obvious relief, brought on by the thought of victory, spurred a question she had always wanted to ask. "Tell me, I understand at the beginning how important it was for you to win the earl's race. Once we discovered the parhelia, the goal of winning was replaced by speaking before a learned institution. So it is clear that gaining your father's respect is important to you, but I do not fully understand why. He obviously cares for you; otherwise, he would not be here. Most of us get horrid nicknames when young, so I don't understand why your unfortunate moniker drives you to seek fame. Lydia told me something went wrong in a piglet race, but she didn't know the details. Just why, then, do so many people remember Piglet Parker?"

He remained silent for a minute or two, looking

in the direction of the golden sunlit field. He sighed deeply. "It was meant to be a lark—a piglet race to amuse my sisters-in-law, nephews, and nieces." His smile returned. "With seven older brothers, I'm a wealthy man in the nieces and nephews business. Anyhow, everyone enjoyed a pleasant day in the park. The piglets squealed as they raced around a small circle lined with bales of hay. The ladies clapped and the children seemed to squeal as loudly as the piglets." He started to pluck a frond to pieces. "Then one piglet escaped the hay wall. His tiny hoof slashed the leg of an eight-year-old boy who happened to be watching with his mother." He looked directly at her and shook his head. "You would not believe the amount of blood."

She nodded, biting the corner of her upper lip. "Yes, I can. Hooves are quite sharp."

"Thank heavens, my brother Richard was there. He's a war hero, fought the Americans in New Orleans, then in a blink, found himself at Waterloo, imagine that. Richard knew precisely what to do. Stopped the bleeding in no time."

She exhaled. "What happened to the boy?"

He gave her a radiant, broad smile. "Small scar on his leg, but I think his mother is permanently scarred the most. She lost her husband in the war and Alfred is all she has. I've called upon him every year since the accident. We go boxing or fishing or whatever masculine pursuit he chooses. Of course, I keep him away from all hooves. Sometimes Richard comes along too. Alfred has heartily forgiven me by now, but his mother always sends a footman along. I don't think she'll ever forgive me. Yes, yes, I suppose I don't blame her."

"So that's the reason you're called Piglet Parker and the trouble started with your father."

His smile evaporated. "You're right, that's how I got the nickname and when my troubles began." He appeared crestfallen.

She reached out to cover his hand with hers. They both moved at the same time to sit closer, side by side, still holding hands. She dropped her head on his broad shoulder; no feeling could ever soothe her more.

"Before the race, he wrote off my peccadilloes to youthful high spirits, but the piglet race changed his mind. I instantly became the new black sheep of the family, the one to watch, the one most likely to bring shame to the family name." He lowered his head to rest on hers. "Then three years ago, I talked two of my friends into writing a lighthearted, satirical book for my brother's publishing firm—on a lark, you understand. The book's called *The Rake's Handbook: Including Field Guide*. It became an immediate bestseller, and my brother was quite pleased with the profits. But when my father came down on his yearly visit into town and walked into our club, one of his friends read aloud a colorful passage from the handbook. My father's face turned as red as a radish and…" He sighed, caught her gaze, and paused. "Right then and there, in our club, in front of all of London, my father—*my father*—gave me the cut direct." He stopped speaking. Wrapping his arms tight around her, he dropped his chin on the top of her head. "He failed to acknowledge me, turned his back to me, and walked away. My father." He choked on a word. "Walked away."

Both his pain and his warm breath against her forehead were palpable. "So your dream is to make him proud of you once again."

She felt him nod, and they lapsed into silence.

"We have a lot in common then, because I too have a similar dream," she said softly. "My father does not believe women have the rigor of mind for science. He believes that women who hope to contribute to knowledge are wasting their time and effort. And the only proper employment for a female of intelligence is to run a household well. He accepts my efforts only because my brother died and he could find no one else to assist him without pay. But even my accomplishments these past years have failed to change his mind. To him, I'm just an extra pair of hands he orders about."

He nodded.

"Just now, when I saw you up on the podium, I realized that I too desired nothing more than the chance to prove myself, prove my worth before an audience, prove that women can contribute to society in many ways. Maybe even change my father's mind with respect to female capabilities and force him to realize both men and women can contribute to the betterment of mankind. It sounds silly, doesn't it?"

"No, perfectly reasonable." He lifted his head and gave her a light kiss on the cheek. "I've never heard of a proper lady speaking about science before an audience." He chuckled. "Bet that would make all of London's tongues wag."

"Normally in front of an audience, females are only allowed to sing or play the pianoforte, and many do it well. Perhaps a few other accomplishments, but our dreams are limited to that."

"If you spoke in front of the Royal Society, I'll wager it would create a huge scandal, what?"

"Yes, but if our paper is accepted, you will have to give the speech, I suppose.

He paused, raised his head, and widened his eyes. "Your name is Eve."

She turned her head to look directly at him. "I don't understand."

"Eve! Your name is Eve. You know, Adam and Eve."

Smiling, she glanced around them. "And we are in a garden too, but I have no apple to tempt you with and get us evicted from Eden."

He focused on her mouth. "I wouldn't go that far."

"Pardon?"

He enclosed her in a full embrace. "No more lessons, no more kittens, no more innocence. Do you fully understand the consequences of marriage to Mr. Henry? You will be transferred from being your father's servant to your husband's. Any hope that you would be recognized for your efforts to contribute to humanity would be lost. Or even worse, claimed by Mr. Henry in the same manner he claimed his discovery of the *Results* book." He lowered his head. "You lack understanding of the role you will have to play every day." He kissed her. No glancing peck this time but a full kiss.

Like every time they had kissed before, she started to analyze the touch of his warm, moist lips and the heat created by their movement. But this time, she successfully stopped herself from the restrictions of logical analysis and gave her heart free rein to feel. She let go. She let her heart feel the languid joy of his kiss, feel the unusual but not unwelcome messages sent throughout her body—feel the supreme sense of well-being, silent comfort, and her sense of a growing, pleasant urgency.

They gradually leaned back onto the greenery, the leaves cooling her warm cheeks. The delicious kiss lingered and teased and quickened and slowed.

Her kisses expressed what he meant to her, that she loved him. Did he understand this message?

He touched her breast over the fullest part, and she sighed upon the joyous sensation this created. Wrapping his arms around her, he rolled her on top of him and buried his kisses on her neck and under her ears. Sitting up, he scooted to lean against a tree. "Come here," he said, his voice taking on a deep rumble. He pulled her up onto his lap. Then he reached under her bodice and kneaded her breast, all the while raining hot kisses on her neck. The earthen pathway in front of her blurred into a golden halo of light.

She relaxed fully, sinking lower onto his torso, pushing her breasts against his palms. Her attention seemed fixed upon her physical responses from the caresses and kisses delivered under the heated spotlight of the sun, just above. Soon, however, she felt his reaction, a stiffening member directly under her backside. Logic returned, since she was unsure of his control over the situation. She hesitated, waiting for him to move first.

He must have sensed her reluctance. "You cannot marry that fellow. Please reconsider what your betrothal would mean."

Logic prevailed; they were not speaking the same language. His tenderness did not bespeak a marriage proposal, while her responses put voice to an unspoken acknowledgment of her love. His behavior was meant as a lesson in contrast, the differing sexual proficiencies between two men. His kisses were merely a gesture to wake her up, persuade her not to wed Charles Henry. Each kiss said, "Here is what I can do for you, versus the ineptitude of the other man." She concluded his heart was likely hidden, inaccessible, or jaded due to a lifetime of easily available women.

"You are the one who does not understand me," she said, a tear forming. She turned around again and lay with her back on his chest, so he couldn't see her tears. Before her stretched nothing but the darkness of the impenetrable trees.

"So you will wed this jackanapes, Mr. Henry. How could you?"

"I've always done my duty to my family."

"Duty?" He leaned to the side to stare at her directly, and she glanced away.

Eve's mother had wanted her to be happy. She needed to persuade her father to allow her to remain unwed, and the three of them continue their research as before. Happiness with the man she loved was not her fate. "Come, let's return to the priory and say our farewells. We are needed elsewhere." In the future, whenever she felt alone or frightened, maybe even witnessing others share an embrace, she would hold dear this one blissful memory of passion, under a canopy of trees, hidden away.

Seventeen

WHAT WAS WRONG WITH EVERYONE? FUNNY THING
how a single day can lead to a fantastical change in
your life. Yesterday, Boyce's future stretched before
him composed of nothing but promise. Today?
Today, after a sleepless night and a hurried breakfast
before anyone else at the priory had risen, he entered
the quiet stables to saddle Charity.

With his small collection of belongings and a few
necessities loaned by Buxton, he planned to rejoin the
earl's race. His ribs, right leg, and back, injured from
his fall out of the balloon, pained him more today than
yesterday, but this gave him strange comfort, because
it complemented his feeling of being ill-used and
allowed him the luxury of suffering in silence.

Damnation. Before him, outside the stable doors,
the day proved to be another blasted sunny one. A
perfect summer's day had never irritated him before,
but it did now—birds yelling, bees buzzing, stable
hands being cheerful.

Charity became difficult to saddle, perhaps dragging
her from a warm, cozy stall made her grumpy this

morning. For the fourth time, he tried to tighten the strap under her belly, but she scooted out of the way.

"Boyce dear."

He let his head fall to rest on Charity's flank and closed his eyes.

Lady Buxton sighed. "I apologize for disturbing you, son. For the sake of your dear mother, please let me have a word with you before you leave."

What should he do? Have a conversation with a lady who deserved no disrespect from him, or hang himself with Charity's bridle?

"I know why you are leaving us so soon."

"I gave my farewells yesterday. It's all settled."

"I wonder if a groom is awake to fetch me a stool?" She stepped back to peer down the row of stables.

He turned to face her. "Why do you need a stool?" He wondered if Lady B. planned to climb upon Charity.

"To stand on, of course. Under the circumstances, I believe your dear mother would approve of me boxing your ears."

He turned back to resume securing Charity's saddle. "Please leave me. Please." Perhaps if he ignored her, she'd return to the house. He could then apologize for his ill spirits on another visit.

Even though the stable floor was covered in straw, her cane hit the ground with such force, it made a loud tap. "You're a sulky puss, now attend me."

Resisting the urge to lift her physically into his arms and return her to the house, he spun to face her and straightened. "You have five minutes," he snapped. "I apologize; it's early."

The fight in her seemed to leave as her shoulders

sagged. All of a sudden, her countenance expressed every one of her sixty-plus years. She carefully and slowly approached him until she stood at a distance suitable to box his ears. Then she sighed and waited.

He had no intention of speaking first.

After a longer sigh, she said, "Tell me about this Lady Sarah. Are you in love with her?"

He shook his head. "Pardon? What gave you the idea I was in love with the woman? I only met her once, and that interview lasted a full minute."

"What about Miss Mountfloy? What are your feelings for her?"

A good question. Yesterday, he had not lingered after his aeronaut confirmed her betrothal. His mind had instantly become hopelessly muddled. Now his blood boiled whenever he thought of her engagement, so he vowed never to consider it again—ever. He needed to flee this place, rejoin the race, and put his failures and her mistaken choice of a husband behind him. If not, his heart might pain him forever. He doubted they would ever meet in the future.

He then remembered his father's expression after she accused him of not being able to take his presentation seriously, the pater's tight lips, head held lower than normal, and the all-too-familiar expression of disappointment. Was his father disappointed with her too? The marquess had only known her for a few days at most, so he couldn't have been upset from the news she planned to marry Charles Henry. Was his father blaming her for *his* less than perfect performance of the sun dog speech? He remembered his father using the word *adequate*, and despite Eve's misgivings, her offer to help make his next speech more credible. But perhaps his father had only said it because he did not want to appear overly critical of his son in front of Lady Buxton. Boyce knew for certain that, had he remained in the room, his father would have belittled him even more for his failure. He might even be waiting for him this morning with some colossal scold. Boyce must flee.

"Perhaps you do not consider your feelings for Miss Mountfloy. So you leave me without a notion in my head why you are so eager to leave us, leave the people you love, for some trifling race."

"It's not a trifling race. With my ballooning adventure, I truly believe I have won at least one challenge. Why would I leave a race, abandon the winnings and acclaim, if I have already won?"

She squeezed his forearm. "Don't you understand that winning the race will not ease your difficulties?"

He stared at her wrinkled hand still squeezing his arm, possibly as hard as she could. "I'm not going to listen. Leave me alone."

"Although you hide it with your enthusiasm, you are an intelligent young man. Look past your father's words and into your heart. What will this race accomplish? What do you fear? What matters the most to you?"

He pulled his arm away. "You are acting like a female, all empathy and consideration, but my father is a typical gentleman, a man who desires successful sons. He was so proud when Richard faced American bullets like a man in New Orleans. But to him, I'm just Piglet, the youngest and the one always in trouble.

With my victory, I will win respect and thousands of pounds. That matters the most to me."

Her eyes became shiny. "No, upon reflection, you will realize that is not what matters. You have won already in a different sense—*think*."

"I can't."

She paused, shoulders stooped. "I cannot stop you from making a grave mistake, so you must learn it for yourself." She stepped close.

"See, like my father, you too think I'm defective— broken." He understood why she stepped near, so he lowered his head to give her the opportunity to box his ears.

She kissed him on the cheek. "Come back when the race is over. I want to have the pleasure of boxing your ears." A fond smile appeared on her ruddy face.

"Thank you," he said, with a slight bow. "I don't know exactly when I can return, but I give you my word." He resumed saddling Charity, aware of the sound of her footsteps leaving the stables.

෴

Darkness had fallen by the time he reached the small town of Uckfield. His day's progress was unremarkable, since he'd spent the morning wandering around an old Saxon church admiring the stonework. Then the following day, after traveling a few miles in the afternoon, he had stopped at the Wayward Lion. The rest of the evening, he had spent obscuring his recent memories by means of copious ingestion of the local ale.

It took him four days before he rode into the small town of Dover late in the evening. The packet would not sail until just after sunrise tomorrow, so he had plenty of time to drink himself to the blue devils. He engaged a small room at the local inn, The Fair Breeze, brushed the obvious dirt off his clothes, and attempted to tie a decent cravat knot. In the middle of a halfhearted attempt at a Maharatta knot, his thumb became stuck in the middle. He yanked his thumb free, messing up his almost-perfect folds. Following a long sigh, he tied a simple knot, adequate to join the locals in the taproom.

At the bottom of the grimy oak staircase, he heard the loud voices of an unnecessarily happy crowd—an irritating sound. Then directly in front of him, a pretty young lady dressed in pink sarcenet walked through the door in the company of her proud mama. He gave both women a respectable bow, but even the calming loveliness of the fair sex failed to soothe his troubled spirit. Realizing he lacked the ability to enjoy, or even be civil, this evening, he ordered a pitcher of ale, a mutton pie, and retired to his room. Sitting on a rather ugly sofa in front of the fire, he stared at the coals glowing in the hearth.

Before he became lost to the blue devils, he needed to write a letter to his father and explain his motive in rejoining the earl's race. Except ready words escaped him. He became lost in contemplation of the random hiss of hot coals in the grate. Why did one silly race and a few ribald books turn him into a disregarded son? He drank the pitcher of ale and ordered a second without bothering to wipe away the heavy foam lingering on two days' worth of whisker growth.

Soon his ale-addled mind fixed upon his aeronaut,

Eve. He could not think of her—too painful—even
now. Unshed tears pooled in his eyes, blurring the
hot coals into a smudge of red light. Best to put her
out of his mind entirely if he wanted to complete the
earl's race. Maybe someday in the future, he could
think of her again. Think of her without tears. Think
of her happy. But until that day, if his mind strayed
or remembered her in any manner, he'd force himself
to sing.

He put two fingers into his ale and flicked some
brew into the fire. The liquid sizzled before it vaporized into acrid steam. He repeated the gesture; the
noisome smell of sour vapors suited him. By the time
he finished the second pitcher, a wet trail of ale stained
both trousers along his thigh, while puddles of brown
ale spotted the floor.

The next morning, he rose late, paid his bill, and
chatted about the probability of a smooth crossing
with the innkeeper. Standing at the bar, in the middle
of the crossroads of humanity, waiting for the packet
to sail, Boyce ignored the commotion around him.
Then over the hubbub, he heard someone shout his
name. Turning, he saw Buxton struggling through the
crowd to reach him.

"Lord Boyce, it's a pleasure to find you. I thought
you'd have sailed by now, but I'm delighted to be
proved wrong." Buxton placed his hands on his knees
to recover his breath.

"Buxton, well met. Let me help you to a chair.
Landlord."

"This way, your lordship." The burly innkeeper
created a pathway for the men and their baggage

through several large parties, into an almost-empty back parlor.

Old-fashioned and on the small side, the private room had giant oak beams holding up the walls and ceiling. In a corner, under this low-beamed ceiling, a wealthy, respectable gentleman and his son waited for the packet.

The landlord showed them several oak chairs around a small table. Once they were comfortably seated, Boyce ordered coffee before the landlord left the room.

"What brings you all the way to Dover? Is there an emergency at the priory?" Boyce could not think of any reason his friend would set out on a journey of eighty or so miles. At least, not a good reason, so he began to panic over the welfare of his friends.

"No, not in the least. Let me catch my breath—I ran all the way from the stables—and then I'll tell you the purpose of my visit."

"Right ho." Boyce watched his friend regain his breath. After his first mug of coffee, Buxton returned to his usual self. Except, Boyce noticed an extra-wide smile shining on his friend's face, wide enough to make him suspicious that Buxton held some good news. "You seem happy today. Happier than I've ever seen you, in fact."

"Bliss, Lord Boyce. Bliss."

"Bliss is a rather strong word for a fellow to use. What has caused this overwhelming happiness?"

"Actually, you had a hand in my good spirits. After Drexel's field guide became published, I talked myself into a spot of bother. Saw my wife's initials between the pages and jumped to all of the wrong conclusions. I firmly believed my worst fears, that my wife lied to me or was incapable of love. I even sent her down to my mother to punish her."

"Yes, yes. I say, rather harsh, that. For someone like Lydia to be isolated is a sure path to a strained marriage and unhappiness for you both."

Buxton chuckled. "And so I found out. She cleverly alluded to the consequences of the riot act, and I deserved it."

He nodded. "I think you're a lucky man. She is a delightful companion and a good and faithful wife. I truly wish you both happy."

Buxton held up his mug. "To Mrs. Lydia Buxton."

"Mrs. Lydia Buxton," Boyce said, smiling at his friend and touching their mugs in salute.

"Thank you." Buxton put down his coffee and then pulled a parchment letter out of his waistcoat. "This is why I came all this way to Dover." He slid the letter across the table.

"What is it?" Boyce felt his pulse begin to throb.

"I don't know the precise contents of the letter. But Lady Buxton urged me to place it in your hands immediately."

"What did Lady B. say it was?"

"I doubt Mother knew for sure, but she indicated that she had good feelings about it and urged me to find you with all haste."

Boyce gulped loudly. Not expecting a letter and unsure of his readiness to face censure in a missive from his father, he opened the letter and immediately read the valediction: Mr. Thomas Harrison, Secretary of the Royal Institution of Great Britain. He yanked and pressed the letter flat with his hands, almost tearing it in half.

"Steady on," Buxton said.

Upon a rapid perusal, Boyce learned Mr. Harrison wrote to inform him that the recent paper he submitted relating the observation of parhelia was interesting and important. Enough so, they accepted it for publication in their *Journals*. "Huzzah!"

Buxton patted him on the back. "Congratulations, I knew it would be of some importance. Important enough to justify my journey. What does it say?"

The innkeeper approached with fresh coffee. "Good news, your lordship?"

"Yes, yes." Moreover, the letter contained an invitation to relate his observations in person at a Friday afternoon lecture, at two o'clock, on the third of the month. "Huzzah! Our paper has been accepted by the Royal Institute, and they would like me to present my sun dog observations in person." He vowed to give a credible speech and make Eve proud.

"Congratulations, old man," Buxton said, clapping his hands.

To the amazement of everyone in the small room, Boyce rose to sing and dance a little jig, successively lifting and bending each leg at the knee. "Yes, yes, my man, good news, indeed. So off to London with Godspeed."

Eighteen

BOYCE CANCELED HIS RESERVATION ON THE PACKET. Then he headed back to his family's London town house at a record pace. Once he and Charity had set off on the return journey, he fully approved of the sun's choice of brightness, a perfect sunny day.

Standing in the front parlor of Sutcliffe House almost a week later, Boyce saw his brother Richard jauntily hopping up the steps of the family's town house on Portland Place.

Within two ticks, the famous war hero shook his younger brother's hand before landing a punch on his arm. "Guess what I have here, Whip?" He pulled out the afternoon edition and held the newspaper in front of Boyce's nose. "I see congratulations are in order."

On page four, under an advertisement for oil of rhubarb, was the announcement of the afternoon lecture at the Royal Institution of Great Britain.

For the edification of all, the courageous aeronaut, Lord Boyce Parker, will present his observations regarding his unusual atmospheric discovery of parhelia (sun dogs).

Boyce hoped the praise would continue, but the remainder of the announcement merely reminded all of their subscribers to arrive at the Albemarle Street entrance, with their horse's heads pointed toward Grafton Street, to avoid another tangle of carriages heading in two directions. He held the paper up to examine the size of the announcement, relative to the entire page, and found it satisfactory. A song bubbled up from his toes, but Richard stood next to him. Boyce had stifled the urge to sing so many times in front of his brothers, in order to avoid retribution, so he could easily do it now. Deep inside, however, he sang a merry tune. *Dream within my reach, my father will hear my speech.* "I cannot wait for my presentation; then I'll gain father's respect." He sat near the fire holding the newspaper high in the air to admire it again.

"What are you referring to?" Richard poured a brandy and sat in the opposite stuffed chair. "Of course he respects you. Don't be daft. What a notion."

"No, he doesn't, not really. After the race, General Hansen called me Piglet—"

"You have to admit you deserved that, ol' man."

"That is not the point. The point is, Father said *nothing*. He said nothing after the race and nothing after the publication of *The Rake's Handbook: Including Field Guide*. He just scowled and walked away, on both occasions."

"What did you expect him to do? He naturally blames Henry for egging you on, but father felt you should have known better. Publish and edit more respectable books, like that novel, or travel or adventure stories." Richard finished his brandy in a single gulp. "I also think he imagines Mother's response to your unsuitable books, her likely disappointment."

Boyce failed to swallow even a sip of brandy.

"Don't take it to heart," Richard said. "It's all just flummery. Pater will come around. Give him grandchildren—pleases him no end."

The mention of his mother's possible disappointment only pained Boyce more. "It's not flummery to me. After my speech, I know Father will be proud of me, and Mother…" He managed to swallow awkwardly. In a minute, he'd be in difficulties and a bothersome tear might fall. He jumped up, strode to the door, and on his way out said, "Mother would be proud too."

The next day, London sparkled. Boyce glanced up at the gleaming gray-and-white Portland stone buildings of St. James Street. It had rained last night, so some of the coal soot had been temporarily washed away. Even the windows seemed to sparkle like cut crystal in the morning sun.

He needed a new waistcoat from his tailor in Cork Street, but he decided to forgo the direct route and take a westerly route through the park. Up ahead, two gentlemen turned the corner. One tall gentleman he immediately recognized as his father, while the other, stouter man was General Hansen, his father's boon companion. Boyce winced, but the general had seen him, so there was no escaping the duo now. He must go through the perfunctory greetings and hope his father saved his usual dressing-down for another time and not in front of the general.

"Hail, sirs, well met." Boyce bowed to both men. "General, fine day." He wondered if either man had seen the yesterday's newspaper with the announcement of his speech at the Royal Institute. Boyce kept the newspaper tucked away under his arm, fearful that if he presented it to the men, his father might level another charge of attention seeking. However, if required, he could produce the edition in a second.

"Well met, Son," the marquess said. "Yes, it is quite a fine day." The two older gentlemen stopped on the pavement in front of him.

At the priory, Boyce had noticed his father appeared aged, his temples sported gray hair, and his shoulders bowed slightly forward. Today he looked younger, more lighthearted. The gray temples still revealed his years, but his broad smile, straight carriage, and green eyes expressing a rare twinkle—only observed when he was delighted with someone—reminded him of his father's appearance a decade ago.

"General, you are acquainted with my youngest. This is the son who will give a speech at the Royal Institution."

Boyce felt giddy, like the earth had started spinning faster, so he widened his stance so as not to fall on his nose in front of his father and the general.

The general was a short, rotund man, wearing somber mourning clothes, but even his severe dress failed to dampen his natural effervescence. The general tapped the marquess's upper arm with his silver-headed walking stick. "Congratulations are in order once again, Sutcliffe. Needless to say, the whole club is proud of the boy. Congratulations to you too, Piglet, quite an achievement."

The word *piglet* caused Boyce's spirits to flag, and the old feeling of failure returned. He couldn't slight both men by walking swiftly away. Instead, his mind started the infinite calculations of the appropriate excuses to do just that.

The general tapped his cane hard on Boyce's chest. "Ha, ha, can't call you Piglet any longer, can I, you young dog? The fact is, when Donkins showed us the announcement in the newspaper, your old nickname became obsolete. It didn't take very long for the fellows in our club to come up with a new nickname, and it quickly became fixed. Goes without saying that every gentleman in the club then enthusiastically discussed your discovery. The result is you are now called 'Parhelion Parker.' Quite the encomium, I can tell you. I suppose all of London"—he leaned close— "even the ladies, will call you that soon enough."

Boyce's spirit leaped so high that, if he were a bird, he'd have been in the treetops by now.

The general turned to the marquess. "It's the *helion* part of *parhelion*, you know. Sounds like hellion, hellfire, so the word makes Lord Boyce sound dangerous in the manner all ladies admire. So, Sutcliffe, gather up your best. You might find this young cub leg-shackled any day now."

His father winked—winked!—a gesture Boyce had never seen directed toward him. "So your letter earned you a chance to speak. Well done, Son. Both the general and I will attend your speech. We look forward to hearing your presentation. Right, sir?"

"Oh, yes," the general said, followed by a short huff. "Wouldn't miss it for the world."

Meanwhile, he noticed his father studying him. "We'll be on our way, then. I'm sure you will want to practice your speech. Do you understand me?"

"Yes, sir." He understood his father did not want the repetition of his failure at the priory.

A broad grin crossed his father's face. "Very well. Looks like the next we meet will be at your presentation. So, we both wish you well now. Come, let's continue on to the park. The boy has plenty to do."

"Oh, yes," the general said, tapping his cane on the pavement. "Farewell, Parhelion Parker. Best of luck." The two men walked past him down the flagstone pathway.

Lightning hit him. Boyce knew that was the only reason every nerve tingled, and he appeared to be glued to the spot. He wished Eve had heard the "well done" compliment. There was no cut. His father hadn't slapped his friend on the back in silent agreement when the general had called him "Piglet."

Boyce longed to give his speech now, since he couldn't wait to regain his father's goodwill and forever impress the world. But then he remembered his father's admonition at the recital. Worried about the family's reputation, he had forbidden Boyce to speak until he acquired more practice. Even now, he had stressed the word *practice*. Simple enough to do; Boyce would return to his room and practice.

Boyce strolled on, a new skip to his gait. He hoped Eve had seen the announcement in the newspaper. Perhaps she would be in the audience. Besides his

father, he couldn't think of a single person he wanted
to witness his victory more. When he returned home,
he vowed to send her an invitation.

At his first practice session that afternoon, he stood
before his mirror and collected his thoughts. When he
revised his speech, he must be ruthless and use only
logic. Write all the details down on paper and then
practice his speech over and over and over. He would
stop only when he could recite it in his sleep.

His first matter of business was to eliminate his
previous observations that were subjective in nature.
In other words, communicate the sun dog discovery as
if Eve were giving the presentation. Hmm, he would
have to mention her at some point, since she was a
beautiful aeronaut. He wondered what nonsubjective
word he should use. Scientifically, should he refer to
her as "the female" or "the woman"? Those terms
sounded heartless, but he soon recalled his purpose.
His heart was not needed now.

Right, ruthless it is.

The memory of his failure at the recital returned,
so "inky" vault and "fleecy" clouds were out. Instead,
he'd replace those inappropriate words with the ones
Eve used. The heavens... No, he must use the scientific term *sky*. The sky would only be referred to as
"blue" or "black," and he'd call the stars "white." For
the real sun, he'd dangerously wax lyrical and call it
"bright." Nothing like an inside jest to spur a fellow
on to his best and provide a bit of excitement. He then
practiced every day, all day.

When the morning of his speech arrived, Boyce
checked his coat and cravat in the vestibule's looking

glass. Pleased with his appearance, he contemplated a stiff bumper of brandy before he strolled over to the Royal Institute. Overwhelming memories of his first attempt at this speech kept him from finishing the entire bottle. With the first taste of the fiery brew, the thought of failure assailed him, so he put down his glass. He needed to be perfect today; he *must* be perfect today. He headed outside and turned south.

Once in front of the tall pillars of the Royal Institute, he took a deep breath and entered. A footman directed him to the offices of Mr. Harrison and several other members of the institution, for a preliminary interview and tour of the impressive facilities. After an hour or two of pleasant conversation, the members led him to the lecture room to ready himself for his speech. A wooden semicircle table marked the spot where he would stand, and he quickly visualized himself wearing victory's laurel crown. Surrounding the table were over a hundred tiered wooden seats. The commoners sat in the gallery, and the aristocrats in front. A small stove behind him kept the room warm and cozy.

As two o'clock approached, a crush of men and women milled about in conversation. In the front row, he observed the Royal Institute's secretary and several men of science he easily recognized. He greeted the officials he had not met before and then moved to welcome his father. "Good afternoon, sir."

The marquess smiled broadly, seemingly unable to respond.

Boyce was at a loss for words too.

The two of them stood in reverent silence, focused solely on each other, surrounded by a racket caused by eager subscribers greeting each other. His father reached out—and for the first time, shook Boyce's hand. "Son, with your speech today, you honor the name Parker."

His spirits soared; he longed to sing. Unable to utter a suitable reply, because he'd embarrass himself, Boyce nodded. But his heart sang and laughed and sang and laughed again. The oldest Parker and the youngest Parker stood there like tongue-tied idiots, so he excused himself and took his place at the lecture table. He pulled his well-practiced notes from his pocket and reviewed them. At two o'clock sharp, the lights were raised and everyone took a seat.

Mr. Harrison spoke first. He presented the general announcements, including several new books added to the institute's library and the names of twenty new subscribers.

During this prelude, Boyce examined the audience. Two-thirds were gentlemen, about a dozen of his acquaintance. The other third were ladies, many of whom he knew. He saw Mr. and Mrs. Buxton, several of his brothers and sisters-in-law, and two friends from Oxford. Drexel arrived late and climbed up the stairs to his seat during Mr. Harrison's introduction.

The secretary came to an end of the list of business, leaving Boyce to eagerly anticipate his introduction.

Then he saw Eve.

She sat with her father and Mr. Henry in the second row at the far end, the most beautiful woman in the entire room.

His heartbeat escalated from fast to pell-mell full gallop.

Their gazes met.

The pained, wistful expression in her eyes robbed him of breath. Speaking before a learned institution was her dream. He stood in front of her, his very presence mocking her life's ambition.

His thoughts raced. Glancing toward his father, who wore a smirk of extreme gratification, he became confused. His heart stopped; his throat closed. But unlike the butterfly, he could change the outcome. He could give her life, the chance to fly.

Mr. Harrison introduced him.

When the secretary finished, Boyce assumed his position at the center of the table. He took a deep breath; his mind cleared. "Thank you, Mr. Harrison, members of the institute, and assembled guests." He paused to focus on Eve again. "I would like to thank the members of the institute who reviewed our paper and presented me with the honor and the privilege to speak before you." His voice cracked on the last word; he needed to get this over with. "We have a bit of luck today. My fellow aeronaut in our balloon journey is here in the audience. This dedicated aeronaut has vast expertise in the discovery and description of atmospheric science."

One glance at the startled expression on his father's face, and Boyce almost collapsed. He swallowed and clenched his fists. *I must* do this. "Please allow me the privilege of introducing this seasoned aeronaut, so she can enlighten us all." He strode to Eve in the second row, then held out his hand. "Please, you must speak."

Her eyes widened; she failed to move.

Her father spoke close to her ear. "You wouldn't dare. You'll embarrass us all."

Boyce nodded and smiled at her. "You know this by heart. You can do this. Come with me."

In a perfunctory manner, she took his hand and followed him to the lecture table.

"Ladies and gentlemen," he said, "please welcome and allow me the honor to present the aeronaut E. Mountfloy. We are fortunate that she is in the audience today, since she is the first person to discover the sun dogs. Since we are all citizens of science, we value logic and experience, so she should present the data." He stepped behind her, slightly to the side. "I'll stand right here in case you need my assistance," he whispered.

She turned to look at him, her eyes wide.

With his brightest smile to give her courage, he nodded. "Time for you to sing."

Nineteen

EVE FOCUSED ON PARKER'S WARM HAND, A TANGIBLE anchor of support. To her amazement, her legs functioned, and she found herself standing. He gently led her all the way to the speakers' platform, probably unaware his warm hand fed her ravenous courage. She grabbed the edge of the speaker's table's and surveyed the crowd before her. Her racing brain remembered him say the words, "You can do this."

She *could* do this; that was a fact. She had helped Parker practice, and she knew all the details by heart. Now he gifted her with the delivery of her dream, the chance to prove herself and contribute to knowledge—in hopes that, one day, it would benefit others. "Good evening, ladies and gentlemen, I—"

"Your lordship," Mr. Harrison stood and addressed Parker. "Ladies have never spoken before an audience. This is highly unusual."

Two older gentlemen stood and spoke in agreement that no women should be allowed to address the audience. After all, they did not pay their subscription monies to listen to female twaddle.

After these pronouncements, everyone in the audience voiced their opinion to the person next to them or shouted directly at her. In the confusion, everyone seemed to speak at the same time.

Eve heard mixed opinions. Some accused her of scandalous behavior and demanded she instantly step down. Several others, including many women, voiced their support, although not quite as loudly as the objectors. A few even endorsed any decision made by Lord Boyce, because he must have a good reason to bring her forward.

Amongst all this confusion, Eve didn't know what to say or do. She stood frozen, her palms annoyingly damp, watching the secretary for instructions to step away and take her seat.

The marquess stood and moved to address Parker, but she did not hear what he had to say.

She did notice Parker's frozen expression, but then she heard her father in the second row. "We must show charity and forgive females from their natural arrogance gained by the acquisition of knowledge."

Maybe with all of the noise she heard her father's comment wrong, because it made no sense.

Parker stepped near her, then the crowd became eerily silent.

She spun to face the crowd, many of whom were now sitting. Standing in the center, directly in front of the audience, was a lecturer at the Royal Institute Eve recognized as Mr. Michael Faraday.

"The Royal Institute," Mr. Faraday said, with the practiced ease of a popular lecturer, "is unique among learned institutions because we believe every person, regardless of gender or class, can employ the gifts of intellect for the betterment of mankind. I am thankful that you have graced me—an ironsmith's son—with the opportunity to put before you the marvels to be found in chemical research. I might point out that ladies are not excluded in our charter. Indeed, hundreds of ladies make up our institute's subscribers, and we are grateful for your patronage." He gracefully bowed to the audience. "Females have also stood here before, answering our questions about certain medical symptoms. Females can also contribute in other ways, of course. The author Mrs. Marcet has provided many of us, myself included, the desire to make the study of chemistry our lifelong aspiration. I've spoken to Lord Boyce Parker, and I believe his lordship must have good reasons for his action. May I suggest a compromise? Miss Mountfloy will report her observations, followed by his lordship's additional observations. I sincerely hope all of you are as excited as I am and eagerly join me in anticipating the chance to learn new information about the wonders of our natural world." Mr. Faraday bowed and returned to his seat.

Most of the crowd applauded Mr. Faraday's words, and everyone took their seat.

She knew Parker resumed his position behind her and to the side, because he was the last person to stop clapping.

A feeling of immense strength welled up inside her. She thanked Mr. Faraday, the members of the audience, and began her speech. After Lady Buxton's response to Parker's recital, Eve understood the benefits of presenting the significant data interlarded with a few amusing details. She began with a question to hook her audience's minds into immediate focus. "When and where, and under what circumstances, do we witness the possible variations in the sky above us?"

She began to describe the majesty of the heavens, intertwined with information about the parhelia. As she spoke, she felt her feet firmly on the ground, her intellect the sharpest it had ever been, and her spirit soar above the crowd. "The parhelia, or two mock suns, were observed at half past seven in the evening, set in the middle of an immense halo. The halo's two giant arcs of light spread vertical in relation to the real sun. The arcs were measured with a sextant and discovered to be just shy of twenty-four degrees. The halo arcs were red on the side closest to the real sun and blue-green on the farthest side. In the center of each arc shone a mock sun. The two mock suns appeared within cirrostratus clouds, ninety degrees from the biggest sun. They were almost round, and bright orange in color. The altitude of the real sun was twenty-two degrees. During the appearance of the parhelia, the barometer read thirty inches, the thermometer declined from sixty-two degrees to fifty-six degrees, and De Luc's whalebone hygrometer rose from sixty degrees to sixty-five degrees. The current hypothesis is that the causes of the parhelia are similar to those of a rainbow, refraction, and consequent reflection of the sun's rays." She turned and smiled at Parker. "The parhelia lasted forty minutes before fading away into an extremely delightful evening."

At the end of her speech, several lecturers put forth detailed questions, which she was able to answer with ease. She also provided observations made by others to support her interpretation of the findings. "Only two suns were observed—not four, as previously seen by Hevelius at Dantzic in February 1661. Are there any additional questions?"

Some of the audience glanced at each other; no further questions were tendered.

"Please allow me to thank the Royal Institute for allowing me to speak, and to all of you for your generosity and attention. Thank you."

The room erupted in applause—perhaps more vigorous from the general public up in the balcony than the aristocrats sitting in the front rows. But most important to her, many scientific members of the Royal Institute seemed pleased and enthusiastically clapped.

Then several gentlemen and ladies stepped forward to surround her at the table. Some had additional questions, while all offered their congratulations. It was the greatest moment of her life. She was treated like a colleague and spent the next few minutes in blissful discussion of atmospheric science. But her greatest triumph was recognition that she had been given the chance to contribute to mankind.

As the people milling on the floor started to thin, she noticed Parker standing off to the side. How could she ever thank him? Then she saw the marquess move to speak to his son. Parker's face became ashen, and he left the room before the marquess could reach him.

She started after him and stopped at the door, not knowing what to say if she caught him.

When she returned to the table, Charles Henry

stood front and center. He seemed to be answering all of the questions, even the ones addressed to her father. As she approached, Charles Henry said, "You've had your say. Let the experts handle the questions from here. His lordship was wrong to let you speak, but we won't say any more about that."

Unwilling to create a scene, Eve did not press the matter and stood beside her father. She saw Lydia approach, stepping through a slight gap between the scientific gentlemen. Wearing a gold overcoat trimmed with fox fur, a turban ornamented with white ostrich feathers, and a white opera muff, she reminded Eve not of a confection, but of a pampered pet. "Lydia, I'm so pleased to see you and Mr. Buxton here this afternoon. Thank you for coming."

"Oh, I could not possibly stay away. Someone I know, giving a speech, and then it turned out to be the first speech by a female too. I'm pleased I told dear Buxton we had to attend." Lydia grabbed Eve's hand. "I must say how much I admire you so, dear Eve. The presence of mind you showed stepping forward like that. I'm afraid my delicate nature would never allow me do something so courageous."

Eve squeezed Lydia's hand and smiled. "I know you well enough to say that, under any circumstances, your courage would never fail. Regardless of what you believe, I know you will always arise victorious."

Lydia slapped her fan open to hide a giggle. "That is so very kind of you, very forgiving. Let me apologize now for my—let's be generous and say—poor behavior at the priory. Fearing the loss of the affection of my dear Buxton and desperate for good company, I behaved rather badly. I am grateful you can overlook my ill nature at the time."

"Dear Lydia, what I remember most about you is your kindness."

She tilted her head and appeared weepy. "Ah, thank you."

Mr. Buxton joined his wife in front of the table and gave her a brief, one-armed hug. Whatever difficulties the couple experienced were behind them now. They resembled the perfect picture of connubial felicity. His features softened whenever he glanced in Lydia's direction. "Congratulations are in order, Miss Mountfloy. I am very impressed. However, I am concerned about some of the older members of the audience. They might not be as accepting of a female giving a speech. If you experience any difficulties in this direction, don't hesitate to inform me. I have some influence with the newspapers, you understand."

Eve reached out and grabbed a hand of each Buxton. "Thank you again, both of you. I think you are wrong, however. One or two gentlemen seemed miffed, but I doubt they will remain that way long enough to create a scene."

"Let's hope so." He took his wife's arm. "And, remember, you have a standing invitation to return to the priory soon. Lady Buxton's health kept her from traveling up to London at this time of year, but I know she will want to hear all about your victorious speech from your own lips."

"Yes, I will visit her as soon as I can. In my many years assisting my father, there is no place we have landed that has shown us such excellent hospitality under awkward circumstances." She chuckled. "Many people on the ground chase aeronauts away with pitch forks, fearing they are monsters from the skies. Lord Boyce and I were fortunate, indeed, to land near such a hospitable household."

Mr. Buxton stared lovingly at his wife. "I have learned from my mother that, during your visit, Lydia did everything within her means to make you comfortable and was an excellent hostess."

Lydia beamed and squeezed his arm. "Oh, thank you. Your praise means the world to me." She turned to Eve. "Such happy times. We all look forward to your return."

When the couple finished with their felicitations and started for the door, more people stepped forward from the audience to offer their congratulations. Many of these stayed long enough to engage her in scientific discussion, even, to her amazement, members of the Royal Institute.

Her father joined her in some of these conversations, and he too spent the remainder of the afternoon in the pleasant exchange of scientific ideas with serious, knowledgeable gentlemen.

By the time they stepped outside onto Albemarle Street, all of her father's previous misgivings about her presentation had flown. He had gained the promise of monetary support from a number of the institute's subscribers. Moreover, several ladies and gentlemen had congratulated him as a progressive man for educating his daughter. As a result, a great number of the institute's female patrons thanked him personally, and he may have earned even more promises of research funds from the ladies than the gentlemen. His earlier reasons for opposing her speech, and his harsh words, he now seemed to have forgotten entirely.

Up ahead, they spied the Buxtons waiting for their carriage to be brought around.

As they approached the couple, Eve's father and Lydia exchanged pleasantries for the first time.

Mr. Buxton leaned toward Eve and spoke in a low voice, close to her ear. "Remember my offer in regard to the press. Any hint of trouble over your presentation must be nipped in the bud immediately. Otherwise, it could quickly become blown out of proportion and your name sullied. Please, do not hesitate to seek my assistance. Promise me?"

Twenty

HAD PARKER STEPPED ASIDE BECAUSE HE BELIEVED SHE could give a better scientific speech? Had his courage failed him? Had he planned for her to speak before yesterday? The next morning, Eve lingered for hours and hours in the front parlor drinking strong black tea with a light odor of moorland grasses. Her thoughts seemed fixed on Parker's selfless act. He stood before an audience, confident in his well-practiced abilities to impress them, his dream almost within reach, and eagerly anticipating the accolades. Then he sacrificed it all for her. The precise, logical reason for him stepping down escaped her, but he had appeared unconcerned and sincere when he had taken her hand. She had then presented her data.

Warm rays of sunlight dazzled in through the small window, while a chorus of songbirds serenaded her. She laughed and joined them. "Twiddle de dee, twiddle de do." Whatever her future had in store, her victory yesterday would lighten her heart forever. In times of trouble or stress ahead, she had this one great moment to remember when her efforts mattered.

Regardless of her inability to comprehend Parker's exact motive for stepping aside, she must find him today and fully express her gratitude. She planned to call at Sutcliffe house, seek a private word with his lordship, followed by the communication of her sincere thanks. All, of course, delivered without revealing any hints that would betray her unspoken love or her despair with the thought of their eventual estrangement. Her throat closed, so she sipped some more hot tea. Attempting to formulate a pleasant opening for their conversation, she thought about asking him to join her sometime for a future balloon flight, but she had no confidence he would agree.

Eager to be on her way, she asked her housekeeper to assume the role of chaperone. Her housekeeper grudgingly agreed. By the time they were ready to set off for Portland Place, Eve had thought of a serious variable. What if her presence at the Royal Institute that day had forced Parker to step forward with his offer to speak? His generous act of stepping aside merely that of a gentleman showing deference to a lady. He might, even now, harbor resentment or anger over her attendance that afternoon—maybe even blame her for not achieving his goal. Eve hooked her arm around her housekeeper's for comfort. Surely Parker would not be angry with her?

Once the duo were admitted into the great library at Sutcliffe house, Eve and her housekeeper were announced to the marquess. They curtsied in unison.

Boyce's father stepped from behind a massive mahogany desk and eagerly strode forward to greet them, his green eyes alight. "Please come in, my dear," he said, turning to his butler. "See that Miss Mountfloy's companion is given tea and perhaps Cook still has a few of Sutcliffe house's famous apple cakes."

Her housekeeper followed the butler out of the room.

The marquess held his arm out toward two gold jacquard sofas in front of massive, arched Palladian windows. The older man exhibited Boyce's simple yet elegant style in dress. Clothed in dark blue superfine, his only hint of luxury beyond the common means was his cream silk waistcoat and a large intaglio ring of cut citrine surrounded by diamonds.

Eve's stomach performed somersaults. Without knowing the marquess's opinion about Boyce's gesture at the Royal Institute, she didn't know if he supported his son's action in bringing her forward or if he vehemently opposed it. *Best to get this interview over with.* "I've come to see Lord Boyce. I'd like to thank him for his generosity yesterday." She swallowed awkwardly. "Thank him for allowing me to present the parhelia data, I mean. Thank him for his kindness."

"I am sorry you have taken the trouble to journey all the way up here to Sutcliffe house. Lord Boyce is not residing here at the present. He packed his portmanteau and left home before I returned from the Royal Institute. I imagine he's living with Mr. George Drexel, a close friend of his. Drexel's home has provided many a temporary refuge for Boyce when his older brothers go on a binge of *tease the youngest*." He grinned, but the effect was very unlike his son's open, friendly expression.

"I am sorry to hear that his lordship is not at home, since you are right, we traveled far this afternoon."

Her anxieties lessened. She saw no evidence of the marquess's disapproval of her, or his son's, behavior at the Royal Institute. "Is Mr. Drexel's house nearby? Perhaps I might get directions. I really must thank him for his generosity in allowing me to give the parhelia presentation."

The marquess leaned forward. "Allow me to thank you, my dear. I believe your presence in the audience caused my son to step down and encourage you to give the speech. I cannot thank you enough for being there."

"Pardon?" She did not fully understand him. Did the marquess believe Parker's presentation would have failed and embarrassed the family once again?

"While I do not begrudge my son's efforts to make a name for himself, I find his previous motivations similar to many of his other endeavors: bold-faced hunger for attention. In this case, by stepping aside and giving you the chance to benefit, he showed evidence of newfound maturity."

"I beg your pardon, sir. His actions are not bold-faced. The word I'd use is…*earnest*. He only wants to regain your respect after the cut and…" She wrung her hands, unsure of how the marquess felt about his cut. "Forgive me."

"There is nothing to forgive." The marquess sighed and gazed up at the ceiling, painted to resemble a blue sky with gilt cherubs peeking out from behind puffy clouds. "Funny, at the time, I never realized how seriously he took it. I was angry, of course, but that is no excuse."

She smiled at him. "Since the cut, his only goal is

to impress you. Everything he does is to achieve that. His misfortune is that with each of his failures, his goal appears farther away."

The marquess nodded in understanding. "You are wise beyond your years, my dear. In the last week or two, I have come to realize, I am the one who let him down. My actions, even if created in a moment of anger, were unforgivable. Do you have regrets in your young life? My advice is to avoid creating regrets by all possible means. They lead to behavior with irreversible consequences. In Boyce's situation, his need for repeated approval and a life of less-than-humble character. In my case, not recognizing the damage from my cut and not immediately seeking forgiveness. I never fully understood this until his speech at the priory. Today, we are two stubborn men, each wanting the other to capitulate and apologize first. Men! Your scientific mind must have realized we are creatures consumed by masculine pride, indeed."

Blushing, she kept her gaze on her yellow skirt and the green sash embroidered with blush-colored roses. She remembered her father's pride in hiding his blindness from everyone, and Charles Henry's pride in assuming they would fall in love upon the birth of their firstborn. "I don't always understand gentlemen, I must admit."

"Well, I would greatly appreciate if you would go and smooth the waters, urge him to return to his family. I fear my son is hurting, Miss Mountfloy, and I want him home. I need a chance to make amends."

After promising to do what she could to bring about reconciliation between father and son, she said her farewells to the marquess. Eve and her house-keeper then walked at least a mile to the Drexel town house close to the river. The home's owner, Michael Drexel, Esq., was one of England's greatest engineers, so it wasn't difficult to pick out Drexel's home from amongst the row of identical town houses. The home in the center of the northern block had a baffling iron structure just under the first-floor window, likely an engineering project for the transfer of coal or some other commodity to the cellar.

The Drexel's housekeeper, Mrs. Morris, greeted Eve and her chaperone. The two housekeepers quickly recognized each other as potential best friends, with similar stories to tell. So once Eve was announced to his lordship in the front parlor, the two women scurried downstairs for tea, both chatting away at the same time.

Eve examined the dark parlor and discovered a large room with only one window facing the street. The day was a gray one, and very little light penetrated into the back by the sofa and chairs. She stepped gingerly around numerous models of mechanical contraptions to reach a chair by the fire.

Parker lay on an upholstered straight-back sofa with toupie legs. Surrounding the sofa were two comfort-able bergère tub chairs and several canterburies filled to the brim with papers. Another chair close to the fire had a built-in wooden desktop pivoted upward and out of the way.

During this time, Parker remained silent, reclining on the sofa, one leg draped over an arm.

Every item around her was so extraordinarily

different from what she had ever seen before. Curiosity compelled her to spend several minutes examining the odd wooden models and strange bits of iron. Then she sat in one of the tub chairs. "Greetings."

Without taking his eyes off the ceiling, he waved his arm and then dropped it to his side.

She waited, hoping he would begin the conversation first.

He remained silent. Some sense of decorum must have finally overwhelmed him, because he slowly sat straight and greeted her formally with a slight bow of his head. "Greetings to you too."

With his words, she caught the scent of an unidentified alcohol beverage coming from his direction.

Wearing a hard countenance marked by a tense jaw and narrowed eyes, he turned to stare at the fire.

After his look of contempt, she no longer doubted his anger. Her courage failed her entirely and without knowing precisely how to deliver her thanks, she played it safe and started a neutral conversation. "What are you thinking about when you stare into the fire?"

Did he have to be polite to the female responsible for all of his troubles? Boyce kept his stare fixed on the glowing coals. Perhaps he should forcibly march her out of the room this second. "No, no, not thinking, thinking got me into trouble. Today, I'm only feeling underrated feelings. You should try them someday." He felt marginally better. His insult directed toward the author of his downfall gave him a manly jolt of satisfaction. "Thinking is your job, and me? No doubt my future will be defined by today's headlines about my failure to deliver a learned speech and your victorious rendition. I can hear the mockery at my club even now. I feel just like our butterfly—dead. So let the soft breeze take me..." He swallowed. "Let the soft breeze lift my corpse up to the *inky vaults*"—he shouted—"of heaven."

She did not respond.

"Struck dumb, my dear aeronaut?"

Her mouth opened, but ready words failed to come.

He tore his gaze away from her stricken expression and those all-too-kissable lips. If she hadn't been in that audience at the Royal Institute, his future would have been very different indeed. About now, he'd be the toast of London, invited to all of the best parties with the prettiest debutantes all paying attention to him. "You're obviously...struck dumb. Me too. Best to speak your mind and be on your way. The pleasure of your company has grown thin." He waved his arm toward the door, then scooted forward on the sofa in preparation to stand.

She blurted out, "I have come to thank you."

He froze before falling back onto the sofa's cushions. *Damn the woman, not now.* He didn't want to be forced into being grateful or honorable in accepting her thanks. He wanted her gone, so he could spend his day wallowing in the luxury of self-pity.

"I came to thank you for your kindness yesterday afternoon, allowing me to stand before the Royal Institute and communicate our results."

"Your results," he snapped. He paused, then shook his head to clear it of the lingering brandy. "I was perfectly serious when I asked you to leave. I'm not fit to be entertaining ladies." His rudeness left a sour, metallic taste in his mouth.

She gulped loudly. A single tear escaped her eye. She jumped up and fetched her pelisse. "Perhaps we can discuss this another time."

"No, no, no other time. Stay away. I don't need to be reminded of...failure." He locked his gaze on the fire. "Farewell." He then tried to convince himself never seeing her again would be the best for both of them.

She stumbled toward the door and then reached for the gleaming brass pull. The ornate lock fixed her attention. "A lock," she said in a low voice and then remained unmoving for a minute or two. She finally slid the brass bar into position with a loud clunk, locking the door. Draping her pelisse on the back of a tub chair, she returned boldly to sit next to him on the sofa.

In his current mood, all he wanted was her absence. He caught her scent of some happy flower, and his heartbeat escalated. "Yes, yes," he said. "I apologize, didn't give you a chance to say your thanks. Well, you are very welcome." He nodded. "Pleased to assist you and all that flummery. Now leave." He offered his hand.

She straightened, watching him every second, but failed to take his offered hand.

"Miss Aeronaut, now that we have exchanged the appropriate thanks, our association is at an end. Please leave me in peace." He dropped his hand to his side. "Please."

Their glances held.

"Please," he repeated in a softer tone, taking his seat again on the sofa. This was one of those days when acting like a proper gentleman proved to be a bear.

She bit her lower lip and her pupils remained black, unfathomable pools.

"Are you really going to wed the toadeating, namby-pamby fool?" He focused on the fire and shuddered. "Even though you are ignorant of men, I expected you to use your intelligence and have better taste. The thought of your upcoming married life disgusts me. How could you love…?" He shuddered again. "And why? Tell me the reason you will put up with this. You sell yourself short, because I know you do not love him. Please, make me understand."

"I lack information about the relations between men and women, I suppose."

Silence.

His muddled mind struggled to understand her.

She gulped again. "I want to know," she said, picking up his hand.

"Are you daft?" He snatched his hand away. "Get that slug Charles Henry to teach you."

"You don't understand. It has to be your touch."

"Why?"

"You don't know why? The reason seems obvious to me."

"Then explain why my…*touch* exactly?" he repeated, his tone uncertain and mind whirling.

"You're an aristocrat with extensive experience of females." Her lighthearted smile was likely feigned. "All of the ladies desire you. Maybe it's your title, money, possible marriage, and the promise of a good life? Your experiences have given you the ability to please many ladies without engaging your feelings or allowing them to reach your heart."

He gave her a hard, fulminating stare. "I will ignore the insult, for your sake. My touch is just a part of some big experiment to you, is that it?"

She shook her head. "No experiments. No logic. No regrets." She picked up his hand and kissed it.

He widened his eyes and stared at their hands.

She kissed each of his long fingers, the center of his strong palm, and the tender inside of his wrist.

He did not make a sound; his jaw tensed.

She moved closer to softly stroke his cheek. Running her fingers over his rough whiskers, she opened her palm to turn his head to face her.

He pushed her away, searching her eyes for a motive behind her advances.

Scooting close until their hips touched, she sat, unmoving, staring at his profile lit by the orange glow of the coals and the fading daylight.

He ignored her.

Silence.

He considered whether or not to march her forcibly out of the door this instant or concede to her desires.

She moved her body closer, touching him full along his side—close enough to feel the warmth radiating from the skin around her cheeks. Then she pulled him into a slow, full kiss on the lips.

He pulled away and thoroughly examined her countenance. All he saw was physical desire.

"Boyce?"

He felt desire too, but he also struggled with his continued anger. His resentment strong enough to lash out, consent to her advances, and teach her a lesson. He'd teach her about being burned from playing casually with fires of desire and the consequences of her bad choices in choosing her partner in life. "Yes, yes, maybe you are right." He slapped his knee. "Change your mind, what?" He stood, removed his coat, and laid it on the carpet before the fire. "Come here."

She joined him on the floor.

He jumped up. "Must lock the door."

"I already did that."

He lay on the cool lining of his coat and then wrapped his arm around her waist. "Clever girl." He pulled her sideways a few inches. "Twist just this way so the top of your head is lit by the fire. I want to see you." He ignored her winsome smile. "Yes, see you. Do you agree to accept my advances?"

She nodded, not a speck of fear or worry appeared in her eyes. "There is nothing I want more."

He hesitated. "Right." He tightened his grip and started to kiss her hard—a kiss of demand marked by severe pressure of his lips and repeated stimulating thrusts of his tongue.

She did not faint or pull back. Instead, she mimicked his rough movements, learning about her pleasure and attempting to respond in kind.

Pulling back, he placed both hands on the top of her sleeves and managed to pull her gown off one shoulder.

Turning around, she reached behind her. "Unbutton me."

He obliged and quickly had her gown and chemise around her waist.

She gasped but moved to face him.

The firelight fell upon two lovely breasts covered in glowing bronze skin and set under a beautiful slim neck. Struggling for air, he could never remember another woman lovelier. At the sight of her willingness to love him, he became hard, and it drove away his anger in the flash of a second. With his mind clear, the gentleman returned, a man horrified by his resentful actions toward a good lady who did not deserve his harsh treatment. She had done nothing, nothing but desire him and offer her body to pleasure him, while he had acted like a cad, a scoundrel of the worst sort.

She scooted forward slightly. "Do you want to kiss me here?" She glanced at her breasts.

He died a little inside. All he could do now was to gather all of his skills and pleasure her the way no lady had ever been brought to ecstasy. While he would use every fiber of his being to check his desires and withhold his pleasure—all for her benefit. He vowed to make this moment truly lovemaking and special enough for her to remember him forever. He needed to give her that gift. "Did I ever tell you how beautiful you are?"

Twenty-one

Eve felt a tear well in her eye. "I don't think so."

"No, no thinking, remember?"

His mood confused her, biting mockery one minute and now his whole mien softened. When she took her place next to him in front of the warm fire, she feared he was too befuddled to understand her actions. Now with his pause and seeming change of heart, she gathered her bravery once again to make him understand what he meant to her. By giving herself to him fully, he had to understand the depths of her love for him. She vowed to express every fiber of her love until even he acknowledged it. Perhaps in her wildest dreams, she might determine if he returned just a little piece of her affections—some little sign or words to hold on to, because this was their last moment together, and she would never have the chance again. She focused on the seductive hollow in his throat, illuminated by the fire. "Yes, feelings only," she whispered just before a bout of long, heavenly kisses.

When the kisses stopped, he focused on her forehead. "Right now every inch of your skin lit by the firelight shines a bronze color. The rest of your features are shrouded in darkness. I plan to kiss and caress every inch of your body as it becomes revealed in the light." He moved to kiss her forehead, followed by dragging his cheeks and lips across her temples. Moving down to her nose, he kissed the top and then rubbed his nose backward and forward over hers.

She giggled softly.

He lifted his head. "Right, I'll return to those lips later." He pushed her an inch or two away from him. "Ah, now your chin and neck take on the light of the fire." His head turned as he moved his lips to her neck and kissed her long and lovingly.

As he kissed and licked under her ears, she sighed. When he lifted his head again to push her several inches to illuminate more of her body, she caught his glance. *Is he a man consumed by love or a man consumed by lust?*

"Ah, now I see that the orange glow of the fire landing on the top of your breasts." With deft fingers and a little help from her, he managed to turn her so that both breasts fell under the full illumination of the firelight. He sighed once, before sitting up on his knees. "Let me look at you. Beautiful, beautiful." He repeated the word until his mouth covered the top of her breast. With a rhythmic move of his torso, he kissed and licked and kneaded her breasts, his tempo increasing.

Arching her back to increase her pleasure, she moaned in enjoyment, an odd sound, so she couldn't help but giggle.

"Are you all right?" he asked.

"Only if you do that forever."

A deep, rumbling chuckle escaped him. "Good." He resumed his caresses.

She became aware of the rising, languid urgency of unfamiliar desire. "Please," she said. Her reason seemed obvious; her love had to be written on every feature; her passion expressed by her every move and every word. Did he recognize it?

He pushed her another quarter turn, so her lower half now received the light of the fire. Lifting her skirt and spreading her legs, he began to kiss the inside of her thighs—a strange feeling, not uncomfortable but one that evaporated her early ease. She rose on her elbows. "Boyce."

He paused and glanced up.

She threw out a small lure to determine his affections. "Do you love me?"

"That's what I'm doing, sweetheart." He began to kiss her intimately between her legs and the soft urgency returned.

She had to tell him now, before she became lost. "I love you."

"Yes." He kissed her full on the mouth once. Then he unbuttoned his falls and penetrated her. Without moving, he said, "Do you feel me inside you? Do you feel us as one? Do you feel our love?"

She found herself in the mortifying position of being in the presence of the man she loved without being able to string two words together. She only registered a new type of pleasure. Their glances held, and she saw something new in his eyes. He loved her, and this was his way of telling her—his gift, this one time.

He pushed forward and pulled back slowly before accelerating his thrusts.

She rose on a cloud of warm urgency. The cloud lifted her, suspended her, her awareness only punctuated by the sounds of slapping flesh. Without warning, her feeling vaporized, leaving her shuddering and slowly falling back to earth, eventually landing on the carpet in front of the fire in his embrace.

He withdrew from her and remained lying facedown on his coat.

Relishing her newfound experience, she stared at the plaster ceiling, vaguely aware of his continued movement.

Minutes later, a slight groan escaped him. He remained facedown on his coat and did not move.

They remained still for a long time; the scent of sex filled the air.

Finally, he made a small noise, like a choke.

She turned to face him and reached out to stroke his back. "Boyce?"

He kept his face hidden in the smooth lining of his coat. "How could you do this with Charles Henry? How?" The tone of his voice sounded wounded, confused.

He had proven his love by his actions—or was this a dance solely to persuade her to call off her engagement? He spoke no words of love following their lovemaking and made no proposal of marriage. Her heart seized and a dull pain centered in her chest. She had expressed her heart by fully giving herself, but she remained unsure of his reasons. A single tear fell on her cheek. She faced the inescapable fact that her life would be lived without him. She would try to make a happy life for herself after this little moment of bliss, never to be repeated.

"Make me understand, please." He kept his face down, away from her view.

She attempted to enlighten him by wrapping her arm over his torso and whispering into his ear, "Duty to my family."

Silence.

"I think you should leave now."

She squeezed him in desperation, letting her tears fall onto his back. "For other reasons too, but I gave a promise to keep them secret."

"To you, I'm just a variable to evaluate, nothing more." He turned away from her, then stood. "Now I've ruined a favorite coat." He carefully folded it into a tight square. "I'll wash it myself."

She rose and put her gown to rights with his assistance. In the fire's glow, she could see evidence of a tearstain on his cheek. Rising her hand to wipe away the tear's trail, he batted it away.

"Leave me. From now on, you do what you must, and I'll flee far away. Maybe Italy where it's warm." He strode to the door, unlocked it, and held it open.

She followed and stood before him, focusing on his watery eyes.

"Look what you have reduced me too. See my tears; analyze the logic of that, Miss Aeronaut. You leave me like the butterfly, unable to sing."

Twenty-two

BOYCE REMAINED FOXED FOR A SIGNIFICANT PART OF the next couple of days. This state of mind calmed him, because when disguised, he forgot everything, even his name. Eventually, when the effects of the wine wore off and painful memories of Eve intruded, he resumed drinking until the brandy blotted his memories into oblivion. In his other infrequent moments of lucidity, he remembered the horrid afternoon at the Royal Institute. He stood before all of London, eager for his chance at redemption. The sight of Eve, sitting quietly close to the table, forced him to confront the fact that, in relation to her, he was a fraud.

She had discovered the sun dogs; she had taken the instrument readings; she had written the speech.

He had no choice but to step aside and watched her rightly achieve her dream. While his heart swelled in pride for her sake, the contemplation of his failure had caused a wayward, unshed tear to interfere with his vision. No gentleman could ever be seen with a tear. So he stepped behind her into the darkness, ready to assist her by any means. Then when she had stopped speaking, he overheard the first words of mockery aimed in his direction.

"So, Hatwell, is the youngest Parker nothing but a cuckold to this female?"

If Boyce hadn't fled, he might have started a row with every man in the room.

Now he existed as the man who fled to Drexel's house, a habitual unwashed lump on the sofa before the fire, waiting for the scandal to erupt in the newspapers. He only moved when Drexel's housekeeper placed the recent edition of London's newspapers in his hands. Carefully searching every page, needing to read each sentence three times, he dreaded finding the article announcing him as a fraud, hoping that when he did, the muted blow wouldn't kill him.

Then one afternoon, his father walked into the Drexel's parlor. The marquess cleared away a stack of papers on an ivory leather tub chair and sat. After a thorough perusal of his son, a grimace lingered on his aquiline features.

Unsure if his father objected to his odious scent, his untidy clothes, or his whisker growth, Boyce lacked the desire to inquire. Since his father routinely teased him over his fastidiousness in regard to his coat, the older man shouldn't have any complaints now.

"Son?"

Boyce gave his father a single nod. "Sir."

"I see I owe Mr. Drexel for the trouble of your upkeep," the marquess said, his tone light and with a cursory glance around the room. "Are the Drexels in residence?"

"No, the men have gone to Bristol to examine a

potential site for a new bridge." He sighed. "Father, please leave. I am not fit for company, and I have no intentions of speaking to anyone. I will, of course, pay the Drexels for housing me, but I won't leave here, not just yet. Let me have some peace."

"To lick your wounds alone?"

"Something like that." Boyce buttoned the top three buttons of his soiled linen shirt.

His father watched him. "No, it's been too long already. Your exile ends today."

"I repeat, please leave me alone. I am too old to be given a dressing-down."

"I have no intention of scolding you, and I don't know why you would think so."

"Routine." Boyce sat straight, now keenly aware of his father's presence.

The marquess paused, holding a strange bit of iron in his hands. "I suppose I deserve that."

Boyce waved his hand. "It's not important. What have you heard about Miss Mountfloy's speech? Was it mentioned in the newspapers? Was I…" His throat tightened. "Perhaps I missed the description in the papers, since I haven't seen it yet."

The marquess stood, put down the iron, and called the housekeeper. When she appeared at the door, his father requested the good lady to order a bath, as his son wished to bathe. He then returned to the tub chair. "For several days, I worried some scandal might erupt from her speech, but either her friends, her father, or even perhaps the members of the Royal Institute squashed any news of an unusual event that day. In my anxiety, I even asked the secretary about it, but he just smiled and informed me that three subscribers expressed private complaints, but none of them canceled their memberships. As far as that day is concerned, you remain on the official record for presenting the afternoon lecture."

Undecided if he should be pleased or angry, Boyce realized he had been waiting for news of a scandal that would never come. Perhaps it was time for him to sober up.

"It is in regard to Miss Mountfloy's speech that I called upon you today."

The mention of Eve's name caught his full attention. "I don't understand. Let me guess. Despite the lack of scandal, you're blaming me for stepping down and making a mockery of our good name?"

His father paused; a sad, sympathetic expression entered his eyes. "I should've known you'd feel that way."

Boyce shook his head dismissively and focused on buttoning his brandy-stained waistcoat.

The marquess spoke softly, staring into the fire. "All of my sons possess extraordinary courage. By stepping aside to let Miss Mountfloy speak, you exhibited the courage natural to the males of the Parker line. But your sacrifice revealed something else too. You showed a good heart, one filled with empathy for others. Moreover, you also revealed a keen sense of justice. Those qualities are rare in most gentlemen, believe me."

Boyce stared in wonderment at his father. He had never heard words like these spoken to him or to any of his brothers.

"I can rightly say," the marquess continued,

addressing him directly, "your sacrifice impressed me. I consider your selfless act of courage similar to that of Richard's, standing before the guns of those concealed Americans in New Orleans. You have always been a favorite of mine, in all probability because your temperament resembles your mother's in so many ways. As a favorite son, I had great hopes of your success, so I reacted badly when your behavior did not credit the man you truly are. My temporary disappointment, however, did not justify a public cut. Forgive me."

Boyce's ears rang. Some affliction of the nerves must have overwhelmed him, because unshed tears welled up. He nodded. "I suppose all parents tell a child they are a favorite, but it really can't be true. When I was young, you did your best to avoid me on account of my foolishness. At least to me, you seemed always to show preference for the company of my older brothers."

The marquess gently shook his head. "Some lack of attention on my behalf may be due to you being the youngest, of course. But then again, whenever I went to look for you, I found you hidden in your mother's skirts, embracing her knees."

"It was always warmer there." His throat closed. In a home filled with obstreperous brothers, his loving, nonjudgmental mother was like a fire that warmed every member of the family equally.

"Why don't you start your own household, Son? Settle down and marry that nice lady aeronaut."

"She essentially referred to me as an unfeeling aristocrat," he said in a low tone. "Not a person who contributes to society. I'm not a gentleman with a profession, like politics, the law, science, or engineering. In her eyes, I'm of no value." If tears began to fall on his cheeks in front of his father, he planned to run from the room.

The marquess nodded. "Her sentiment is becoming more common. People admire gentlemen who make achievements. The heir has responsibilities to the estate, of course, but now you understand why I have always pushed my younger sons into respectable professions. You, without recognizing it, have much to offer a serious woman."

"I don't know what you mean."

"Your brother has defended you and tells me you are a gifted editor who quickly became a vital member of his publishing house. Perhaps she can use your assistance in that field. Or maybe something will come of that rotary press you and Drexel are working on. I understand one of your models has shown limited success. With a little thought, I firmly believe you will come up with an idea where your services could be invaluable to her. Explain what interests you, and she will understand that you contribute in your own way. Trust me, you will be surprised."

"I don't believe you."

The marquess chuckled. "I have my reasons for you to wed Miss Mountfloy. I have become very attached to the young lady, and I do not want to see her hurt. Blame it on the sentimentality of old age, if you must."

Boyce's heartbeat began to race. "What do you mean by the word *hurt*? What do you know of her feelings?"

"I'm not aware of her feelings in the least. I only know my own." The marquess pulled a rolled up newspaper from his coat pocket. "Turn to page six and read the article on the bottom of the page."

Boyce snatched the paper from his father's grasp and read voraciously. The story described a ballooning accident and the death of the aeronaut. One sentence in particular stopped his heartbeat. He mumbled and read the words again aloud. "The aeronaut landed in a flower garden, his body driven into the earth." His wild mind raced to the thought of Eve meeting a similar fate. He became light-headed before blinding panic seized him. He stared at his father, holding his arms out. "Ah!"

"I don't understand." The marquess tilted his head.

"That's it! The very second. When the mere allusion to a person's death is unbearable, that's the moment you realize you are in love."

The marquess did not answer. Instead, he sat in the tub chair, holding his watch fob, and gazing tenderly at the rock crystal containing a finely crafted lattice-work of his wife's auburn hair.

Only now did Boyce understand the pain his father must have felt over his mother's death. If his heart broke with just the thought of Eve's death, how could his father summon the fortitude to continue his existence? How could a person remain alive with a heart broken by the death of a beloved spouse?

"Yes," the marquess whispered, "that is an unfortunate way to realize the full extent of your affections." He dropped the fob, brushed his trousers with one hand, and faced Boyce. "Of course, I knew you were in love with Miss Mountfloy the first minute I saw you together at the priory. For all the teasing you receive from others, you really don't sing that often. Only when you are truly happy."

"So the reason I felt like singing all of the time at the priory was because of love?"

"You sang almost every time I witnessed you in Miss Mountfloy's presence. And if my knowledge of the fair sex has not failed me yet, she feels the same about you. I believe the two of you were besotted with each other without knowing it, or at least, you were unaware. Still, your obvious admiration made conversation in the presence of the two of you a little awkward, what?"

"I acknowledge my love for the lady, but I do not believe she returns my regard." He paused, remembering the warmth in her eyes on the floor in front of the fire. "How can she be in love with me if she refuses to cancel her engagement? I mean how can she even considering marrying that inconsequential, niffy-naffy, oafish toothpick?"

"I do not have the wisdom of Lord Chesterfield, but I do understand that you can never know a person's motivations for their actions. The lady is intelligent, so she must have her reasons. You must be generous and allow her to keep her purpose behind marrying Mr. Henry private."

Boyce rubbed his itchy whisker growth, struggling to understand how he was going to persuade her to marry him instead.

"Have you told her that you love her?"

A bout of coughing overtook him. "How could I tell her if I didn't know the full extent of my love until a second ago?" He stilled. While he didn't recognize it at the time, in hindsight, the moment stared him straight in the face. It was the moment he had called her beautiful. *Beautiful*—not pretty. *Pretty* was the word he used for all women. But he called Eve beautiful. "What do I...how do I...when do I... demonstrate my love?"

His father laughed. "Oh no, you must tell her yourself, but not in a letter"—he smiled—"not by singing, but by honest, sincere words. And because you are the gentleman, you must reveal your feelings first and risk the consequences that she might not feel the same. And whether or not she reciprocates your affections, you must grant her the privacy of her decision."

Boyce suspected Eve loved him. She had said the words to him in front of the fire during a moment of passion. But how she would respond to his earnest declaration of love, he had no idea—no idea because he didn't fully understand her meaning behind the word *duty*. With a groan, he rose to pace in front of the mantel. "I never realized females had so many variables. Ha! Did you hear me say that? I used the word *variable*, just like Eve, funny that."

"I can well imagine it. Because of your natural good looks, not inherited from me, unfortunately, you've had too easy a time with the fairer sex. As a consequence, you are spoiled. Therefore, you must summon the fortitude of your ancestors, men known for their bravery in battle and showing the courage to stand tall, even when outnumbered in front of a rushing horde. I've said it many times before, but that is the type of men we Parkers are and why our family motto is *Stand fast*."

Boyce rolled his eyes. "You're being gothic."

His father burst out laughing, a rare moment for the marquess. "When you grow older, you will be gothic too. It's part of being an English gentleman of a certain age, no doubt."

Boyce looked down at the newspaper again. "I may never get the chance to tell her that I love her. Something horrible—I cannot bear the thought."

"What do you mean?"

"Yesterday, the papers said her father planned a balloon ascension for today. I assume Eve will join him. It's the first flight since the crash, and it will be carried out using their newly repaired balloon. I mean what if it was not repaired properly? What if the silk tears during the ascent? What—"

His father straightened. "Now I'm quite worried about that young lady. You must stop her from getting into the basket now and forever. Pull her out of the basket if you have to."

Boyce smiled and shook his head. "I cannot do that. It's her life's wish to prove females can contribute to the pursuit of knowledge. My fears for her safety are not reason enough for her to end that dream and ask her to step out of the basket."

"Wasn't it enough that she demonstrated female worth when she gave a successful afternoon lecture at Royal Institute?"

"Perhaps. But you were right earlier when you said I had to think of what I might offer her, and I must do it quickly." He stood and grabbed his coat. Even if Eve refused him, he must tell her of his love and that she would always have it. "Regardless of whatever assistance I may provide, I cannot force her to accept me. She has to be the one to decide. By your analogy, she must be the one to take that step out of the basket."

Boyce asked his father to show himself out, ran upstairs to his room, tidied himself up as best he could, and then flew downstairs. *Thank the inky heavens above that love is blind.* His collar, waistcoat, and cravat had been set to rights, and he even managed a quick, if not thorough, shave of his troublesome beard. All of these ablutions he completed in fifteen minutes. His appearance failed to meet his usual standards, but he hoped his efforts were sufficient to propose to the woman he loved. Hopefully, if equally blinded by love, she should be able to forgive him for the current, deplorable state of his coat.

When he reached the first-floor landing, his father surprised him in the vestibule. "If you do not mind, I will join you on your journey."

"I prefer privacy." Boyce struggled into his coat, hiding his irritation. What sane gentleman wanted his father to witness his proposal? Eve had been as slippery as an eel when he mentioned the subject of her engagement before, so she might even do the unthinkable and refuse him.

The marquess chuckled. "I doubt you will find privacy around a balloon preparing for ascension."

His father's point rang true, although he really did not want to contemplate an audience for his declaration. "All right, then."

Before the duo headed for the stables, Drexel opened the front door and entered. "Ah, decided to join the living?" He caught sight of the marquess.

"Beg your pardon, Lord Sutcliffe. I didn't see you behind this great lump here."

"George, I am delighted to see you again. I certainly thank you for the hospitality your family has shown my youngest lump." The over-wide grin on the marquess's face, normally marked by numerous lines of experience, caused him to appear like a much younger man.

"Youngest lump?" Boyce spun to glance at his father. *The pater joking? The world must be coming to an end.* He pointed. "You made a jest."

His father ignored him.

"And you," Boyce said, addressing Drexel, "have been gone for weeks. I thought you must've abandoned that bridge and attempted a last chance effort to win the earl's race."

"No, the bridge is still in the works, but my father and mother needed my assistance. Besides, haven't you noticed the city of London is empty of young gentlemen?"

"Um, I don't understand." Boyce coughed, wondering if his days spent in his cups had affected his brain.

The marquess whispered to Drexel. "Inebrious lump for days."

"So I heard." Drexel laughed. "Explains his coat. Look at yourself, Whip. You let your standards down."

Boyce waved Drexel away from the hallway. "I am not going to stand here and listen to the two of you. I have plans for today, so you must excuse me."

Drexel stepped aside. "What's this rush all about then?"

The marquess winked at Drexel. "This day is a significant one in Boyce's life."

Boyce snatched his hat and gloves from the pier table in the vestibule. "Enough!"

Drexel leaned close to Boyce's father's ear. Then in a fake whisper, he loudly said, "Grumpy too."

The marquess's eyes gleamed. "In this day of Boyce's life, you might even say his very life is at stake. But it's a day every man, even you, George, must eventually face."

"Hmm," Drexel ruminated. "I doubt it. Whatever it is, I plan to avoid it, because just look at what it's done to him."

Boyce damned his shaking hands; closing the last button on his waistcoat seemed impossible. "Yes, yes, all very well. You two have had your dramatic moment. Now I must leave immediately—preferably alone. There is something I must do."

Drexel looked at the marquess. "I'll wager you know what this is. Tell me."

"Let's just say his future happiness is at stake."

"I've had enough of you two." Boyce closed the buttons on his coat.

The marquess laughed. "Do you think you'll have steady hands, George, on the day you openly declare your love to a woman?"

"No! Well, I'll be damned. I am too old for that fustian, sir." He shuffled awkwardly about. "I'm made of different stuff altogether. Troublesome things, females—not like a bridge—all emotions a fellow can never understand."

Boyce did a final check of his appearance in the pier glass next to the door. "I cannot offer marriage to the woman I love dressed like this." He turned and held out his hands. "Look at me. Stains on every piece of clothing and half-shaven. She'll run away at first sight."

"Yes, I would if I were her. You're very ugly," Drexel said.

"You could come home," the marquess said, "and have your man do a proper job of it. Of course, Miss Mountfloy's ascension may take place before you are finished." He lifted an eyebrow.

Boyce's heartbeat began to gallop. "I'm wasting my time. Where's Charity?"

"Saw her in the stables when I arrived," his father said. "George, are you ready?"

Ignoring his father and Drexel, Boyce headed downstairs in the direction of the mews.

A rushed twenty minutes later, and the three men galloped out of London, toward Islington.

Once they slowed to give their horses a rest, Boyce embraced his optimism created by the glorious, sunny day. How could she justly refuse his suit with such a beautiful world surrounding them? The sun warmed his face; the grass field shone that distinct bright green no paint could reproduce—*the perfect backdrop for a song on a journey to propose to the woman you love*. "'The fair of my fancy whisk'd into the room, All lovely she look'd like a May morning's bloom. Her form was, but forming a simile's flat, think all that you can think, and she was all that.'"

Drexel twisted around to shout at the marquess. "Lord Sutcliffe, what do you think this foul songbird did with the money?"

The marquess brought his horse up even with the

two men. "I beg your pardon, George, I don't understand. What money?"

"The money you gave him for the voice tutor."

"Ha, ha," Boyce said. "Very amusing." He refused to let anything dampen his spirits. "Drexel, the day you tell a funny jest is the day rocking horses poop."

"Jingle brains."

"Dulpickle."

"Gentlemen, please," the marquess said as they turned down Frog Lane.

Boyce once again found himself surrounded by vegetable gardens. Up ahead, he could see a crowd gathered around the wooden platform built for balloon launches. Nothing seemed to have changed from last month. A young boy and Mr. Henry fiddled with barrels and tubes, while Mr. Mountfloy stood in the basket and shouted directions. He didn't see Eve at first, but when they grew near, he noticed her in the basket fiddling with the ballast bags.

With his first sight of her in the balloon, Boyce feared he might be ill.

His father chuckled. "You should see your face, Son. It's the color of white soup. I knew you failed to understand my point about courage. What you are about to do takes courage, because now you risk your life's happiness, and failure here is irreversible too."

Drexel whistled. "There is no possible way for you to steal a private moment. All I can say is, it takes bollocks to declare yourself in front of a crowd. And from the looks of the rabble in front of us, a large number of people will more than likely thoroughly enjoy your declaration."

Twenty-three

EVE DISTINCTIVELY HEARD HER FATHER SWEAR. SHE stood up to discover him shielding his eyes from the sun and looking into the distance. Glancing past the crowd and the vegetable field in front of her, she saw three men on horseback approaching the platform.

"Looks like that lordship of yours has come to witness our flight. I hope he has no intention of interfering with our research again."

Eve gulped and focused on the three men. At this distance, she could not identify any of the riders, other than getting the impression that they were gentlemen. "How do you know it's Lord Boyce approaching the platform?"

He ignored her and continued to scowl at the riders.

She forgot her preparations for the ascension and strained to identify the three men. It did not take long before she realized her father was right. Parker was indeed one of the horsemen, along with another large, tall man she had never seen before and his father, the marquess.

The three gentlemen dismounted, tied their horses next to the others, and then strode through the grass. They stepped onto the corner of the wooden platform, a mere ten feet away from her.

Charles Henry approached Parker. "Your lordships must leave this instant."

"Yes, yes," Parker said, smiling, "just a word with Miss Mountfloy for a minute, and then we'll be on our way."

"I urge you to leave now." Charles Henry glanced at Eve, scowled, and addressed Parker again in a lowered voice. "You have repeatedly stolen the acknowledgments rightly owed to me. If you don't leave here immediately, I will take measures to ensure your reputation as an honest man is ruined forever."

Parker and the other man wore frowns and stepped close to Charles Henry.

The marquess rose his brow.

Charles Henry continued to address Parker in a voice too low for Eve to hear.

Eve could not take her eyes off Parker. Their lovemaking had created days and days of the utmost despondency. No longer cherishing any hope of finding happiness with the man she loved, she clung to the knowledge that, with time, she might become a suitable, more good-humored wife for Charles Henry. Now she stood mute, drinking up the rich sight of Parker standing before her. She greedily committed it to memory and stored it alongside so many others: she'd never forget him.

"I hope for the sake of our experiments today," her father said, leaning forward to hear the men's

conversation, "their lordships are not going to interfere with our flight. I am going to find out what this is
all about." Her father stepped out of the balloon and
joined the four men in heated conversation.

Then Charles Henry said something, and the blood
drained from Parker's face.

The large, tall man Parker called Drexel became
restless and appeared to be barely restraining himself.
"That's blackmail, sir."

"You will do no such thing," her father shouted
to Charles Henry. "No account of her speech will be
told to the newspapers. We do not want to lose the
precious support we gained that evening."

"But the man is a failure, sir," Charles Henry yelled
in reply. "To this day, he takes credit for giving a
successful speech when he obviously did not. He's
done this before, taking credit where it is not due. It's
wrong, and he must be exposed as a fraud. Of course,
I wish no harm to your daughter, but the truth must
come out. She did behave in a scandalous manner by
stepping onto the stage that evening, so she must bear
the consequences too. Surely even you do not believe
a gentleman's daughter should speak before the public."

All of the gentlemen started shouting at each other.

Eve could hardly believe Charles Henry, a man
who claimed her as his fiancée, would expose her to
censure and scandal. Perhaps she heard wrong, because
she knew him to be an honorable man, but his threat
did not sound honorable in the least.

Parker's face became bright red, and the other man
in Parker's company seemed to be physically restraining him.

"Enough," the marquess shouted, stepping between Parker and Charles Henry.

Each of the four men stepped backward, and the crowd hushed.

The marquess faced her father. "I believe you have an ascension to perform. The two of you must have plenty to do."

Charles Henry strode to the tube containing the gas, now rapidly filling the balloon.

Her father walked over to her in the basket.

"Does Charles Henry want to create a scandal in the newspapers?" she asked. "Why would he do that to me?"

Thomas Mountfloy shook his head. "Charles said some rash things, my dear, but I'm sure he did not mean them. He is in a difficult position and wishes to—deservedly, I might add—discredit his lordship's claim of giving a well-received speech."

"Did his lordship claim he presented our discovery that afternoon?"

"Not that I am aware. But he did not refute it either, and he remains the speaker on record that day. We all know his lordship seeks credit where it is not due. Consider the discovery of the *Results* book. I do not want your name, and hence my name, blackened by Charles's exposure of his lordships behavior. For many, it remains scandalous for a woman to put herself forward in such a manner. If Charles writes an article for the newspapers, as he threatened his lordship, I fear it will greatly reduce our financial support and goodwill amongst the scientific community." Her father surveyed the crowd before speaking to her.

"Let's ignore his lordship's party and get the balloon off the ground. I do not believe the man has anything of importance to say. Do you know the reason why we have the *honor* of his visit?"

"No, I do not understand why Lord Boyce and his father are here today." She glanced at Charles Henry, bending over the gas tube filling the balloon, and realized that she could never marry him. Time would not heal her poor opinion of him. She returned to examine Parker again.

He stood surrounded by his father and the other man, all deep in conversation.

The other gentleman, dressed wholly in black, elbowed Parker in the ribs.

"Yes, yes," Parker said, removing his hat and brushing those curly locks away from his enchanting green eyes.

A mere five feet in front of the basket stood her favorite Tulip of the Goes in his prime—the most beautiful male specimen on earth. Her stomach performed somersaults, but the rest of her body froze like a startled animal's. All she could manage was a smile that must have appeared as an idiotic one.

"Miss Mountfloy," Parker pronounced, straightening his shoulders even more. "I seek permission to have a word in private."

"No chance of that, gov," someone shouted.

The audience voiced their amusement and agreement. "Speak up, sir!"

Parker glanced around him, evaluating the crowd. "Right ho, Miss Mountfloy. In front of these good people then, I'd like to offer a declaration."

Did Parker say the word "declaration"? What sort of declaration? She glanced at her father.

Thomas Mountfloy dropped the *Results* book on a chair and strode to the group of gentlemen lined up in the center of the platform. "Your lordships must leave this minute. You have no business being here, and we have work to complete before our ascension."

The marquess spoke directly to her father. "I understand you, sir, but I request you show my son the deference owed to a gentleman and allow him a minute or two only. Please, Mr. Mountfloy, let my son speak."

Surely her father must agree, in deference to Lord Sutcliffe's consequence.

Her father waved a hand in dismissal. "No, I want the three of you to leave now." Then he turned to Charles Henry. "Hurry up. Let's get the balloon airborne."

A tear began to form in Eve's eye. She stepped away from the edge of the basket and turned her back to the crowd, hoping everyone would go away. She needed time to contemplate the nature of Parker's declaration. Marriage declaration? What other type was there? *Think, think, think.*

"Yes, yes," Parker said, "my brave aeronaut. I know you are currently thinking hard with that beautiful brain of yours, but listen to me, please."

After a swipe of her watery eyes, she turned and stepped to the edge of the basket, facing the crowd squarely.

"Do we have enough gas for ascension now?" her father yelled at Mr. Henry.

"Yes, but we won't get far." Charles Henry glanced up at the balloon, only a quarter filled. "A few minutes more before we are able to rise safely above the trees."

Parker turned to face the audience and directed them to stand back. "Lord Sutcliffe, Mr. George Drexel, ladies and gentlemen, prepare to witness my declaration of love," Parker said, bowing first to Eve and then the audience.

The mob laughed heartily. The women wore smiles, while many of the men slapped their knees and laughed aloud.

Eve's heartbeat escalated to a million beats per minute, and there was every possibility her lungs no longer functioned. Air became a precious commodity, and for some reason, she could not get enough of it. She needed to clutch both edges of the basket to steady herself.

"Miss Eve Mountfloy," Parker said, in the tone of a formal pronouncement, "I love you."

The crowd roared; many clapped.

She forgot her lack of air and became fixed by Parker's earnest expression. Without doubt, she wore a Cheshire cat smile just as silly as the one on his face.

Parker turned to his father.

The marquess bowed to his son.

Many in the crowd wore foolish grins.

Parker then turned to wink at her. "You will notice that, while I feel like singing, I am not at the moment, my dear, dear Miss Mountfloy. I'm perfectly serious. Will you do me the great honor of accepting my hand in marriage?"

The entire crowd erupted in applause and whistles. Many of the men threw their hats in the air. The women clapped daintily, and everyone, old and young, sported broad smiles.

Meanwhile, Drexel laughed so hard, Eve thought he might do himself an injury.

"Stop this! All of you. My daughter is already engaged."

"Before you give me an answer," Parker continued, completely ignoring her father, "I must inform you that upon marriage, I will support your father's current studies. As my wife, I will encourage you to publish your father's discoveries. I'll be your publisher and editor, and you'll write away, like that Mrs. Marcet woman." He held out his hand. "She taught the world about the wondrous discoveries to be found in chemistry, and you can contribute by instructing us all about the amazing properties of the air around us."

Parker paused, and the marquess vigorously patted him on the back. "Congratulations, knew you could do it, of course. I've never been more proud."

Parker smiled, nodded, and the two men exchanged congratulatory back pats.

While her heartbeat raced, Eve stood still, amazed that her dreams now dangled before her. Her life could be lived without the sacrifice of her happiness. Parker was the only man who could satisfy both of her dreams. She'd marry the man she loved, and with his promise of publishing their atmospheric results, he presented her with the chance to spread the word of their discoveries beyond her wildest expectations. Of course, upon his mention of Mrs. Marcet, she instantly thought of the title of her book. *Conversations on the Atmosphere* sounded suitable, but first she would suggest the title *Conversations on a Cloud*. She smiled at the thought of children rushing to choose a book with that enticing title. She focused on Parker. Despite her overwhelming love for him, and the warm, good feelings now spreading throughout her body, she remained still in a sort of stupor.

Her father climbed into the balloon. "Mr. Henry, give me a shout the moment we can ascend safely."

"Of course. Not long now." Charles Henry nodded and continued to hold the tube entering the bottom of the balloon.

Her father grabbed Eve's arm and spun her around to face him. "Now listen to me. You will politely decline his lordship's offer and send these people away. Tell them it's all a mistake."

"Why? Didn't you hear him? His lordship will help with our research and pay for us to spread the news of our discoveries worldwide." She knew this argument would have to sway her father's resistance. How could her father refuse the accolades and additional support publication would bring? "We need him—I need him."

Seizing her shoulders, her father shook her violently. "You're a fool if you believe he'd put forward our discoveries. More than likely, he'd claim them himself. Besides, he's an aristocrat, remember? Do you honestly believe he will let his wife fly around in balloons? Of course not."

"If you lay another hand on her, sir," Parker said in a stern, steady voice, "I'll—"

Charles Henry began to wrestle with Parker alongside the basket.

The marquess and Drexel managed to pull Parker off Charles Henry, then restrained him.

"This is not your concern," Parker shouted at the assistant.

Charles Henry bowed at the waist to catch his breath. "Miss Mountfloy has given me a promise that we will marry. She eagerly anticipates our union and understands her duty to both her father and myself."

"No!" she shouted. "I know my duty, but I must withdraw my consent. We are no longer engaged."

Thomas Mountfloy shook his head. "This is not the place to discuss such matters, since we are all a little heated at the present. I suggest we wait until cooler heads prevail and continue our flight as if nothing has changed, for all of our sakes." Her father nodded in her direction. "Right now it is your duty to remain in the basket and help complete our experiments for today. In the future, you *will* wed Charles Henry. We all know his lordship speaks to gain false praise only. You have realized he is an embellisher of tales before this and that his word is not to be trusted. Refuse him immediately and send him on his way."

"No," she repeated, shaking her head. If she were to believe her father, that Parker desired praise above all else, he would have given his speech at the Royal Institute, instead of stepping aside for her. She addressed Charles Henry. "I apologize for my outburst, sir. We will never marry, but my father is right. This is neither the time or place for this conversation."

Her father's face reddened. He approached, slower and more measured than before. "Evie, remember what I told you. My failing eyesight demands that you remain here with me and Charles Henry. Think of your mother."

Her mind cleared; she straightened. "I do think of her—and Tom. *Always.* I remember her wishes for my future as long as I live. She prepared me well, taught me every talent I needed to be happy as a wife. But most of all, she desired I find happiness with the man I love, as she did."

Her father stilled.

"She loved you, and her desire for me was to find a man I truly love as a husband—and now I have found him. Please don't decide my fate on the inevitability of your failing eyesight. If you fear only I can help you, I believe you are wrong. We'll hire another assistant, so you will not be abandoned. But I *will* follow my heart and wed Lord Parker. It is the duty I owe to my mother, to Tom, and to myself."

"Yes, yes." Parker strode to the edge of the balloon and grabbed her father's coat from behind. He started to pull him to the edge, and several men joined him to haul her struggling father out of the basket.

The crowd shouted approval, surrounded Thomas Mountfloy, and restrained the aeronaut from climbing back into the basket.

She glanced at Parker, and he gave her a single nod. Her heart soared into the heavens.

Parker started to climb into the basket, but Charles Henry flung himself on his lordship's back. In one swift, elegant motion, Parker spun and delivered a bare-knuckled facer to the assistant.

Charles Henry fell back on the platform, sporting a bleeding lip.

The crowd cheered.

Drexel pulled the struggling assistant to his feet and restrained him. "Neatly done, Whip. What took you so long?"

Several members of the audience shouted for Drexel to release Charles Henry in heady anticipation of fisticuffs or an out-and-out mull.

Drexel flung the assistant into the crowd. He then ran to the marquess, and together they gave Parker a hand up into the basket with such force, he landed on the bottom in an upside-down lump.

The audience roared with approval.

Parker stood and gave Eve a formal bow. "My lady?" He held out his hand.

She clasped his warm palm and squeezed it. "Thank you." They remained holding hands, and she clung to this simple, much-appreciated reassurance of his affection. More than likely, they both wore foolish smiles.

Her father managed to free himself and shouted, "Evie! Your duty is to me."

Parker's eyes widened. "Duty!"

"Why did you say duty in that startling manner?" she asked.

"Step out of the balloon at once, sir," her father shouted, heading in their direction.

"Stand fast," boomed the marquess in the very tone that ordered his ancestors' troops into battle, the ghosts of those soldiers standing behind him now. His father took one step toward her father, and the men stilled.

Her father wore a menacing scowl, while the marquess held his stiff posture.

"Yes, yes, *duty* is a troublesome word." Parker

turned her swiftly, lifted her into his arms, and held her high off the floor of the basket, in the same manner as their first tussle over the gas valve in the balloon. "I don't want to take the chance you will run away."

"Put me down, madman."

"Is your lady proving troublesome, gov?" someone shouted. More laughter erupted.

"You shouldn't hold a lady like that, now should you, sir?" another voice chimed in.

Parker smiled and turned his head to face his audience. "I do beg your pardon. What did you say? Am I holding something?"

A member of the crowd shouted, "You're holding a lady, sir. In a most indecorous fashion."

Parker looked down at her and winked. "Well, look at that. Yes, yes, indeed I am holding a lady. And I plan to hold this one until she agrees to be my wife. But all of you are making such a racket. Did any of you hear the lady say yes? I am certain that with all the hubbub, I must have missed it."

"But the lady could be injured, sir."

"Put her down at once," Mr. Mountfloy shouted.

"Hmm, did you hear your father, Eve? I must say I disagree." He raised his voice. "Well, ladies and gentlemen, as a logical gentleman, I plan to hold her until she agrees to be my wife."

Her shock wore off, and now the absolute absurdity of her situation started her laughing.

"Are you injured?" Boyce whispered.

She laughed in whoops.

"Are you injured?" Boyce repeated.

She shook her head, unable to stop laughing.

The entire crowd started to laugh.

"Since I am unable to get down on one knee to propose for fear that you will run away, I must ask for your hand once more in this very awkward position. But so be it. Ladies and gentleman, a minute of silence please."

The crowd became mostly silent.

"I love you, Miss Mountfloy." Parker then whispered, "Perhaps the words 'I love you' are too simple. How about you filled my inky vault of a soul with the living sparks of love?"

Besides his silly words, she detected something else in his voice. A tone, a wish, an intangible sound that rendered the sentiment truthful—he loved her. He truly desired her to be his wife.

"And just to be safe"—he chuckled—"I love you with my heart, my head, and of course, let's not forget our Sussex horse, Brutus, my stomach. I'll even be generous and throw in all of my organs. I love you."

"Put me down." When her feet hit the bottom of the basket, she began to sing, "Yes, I will marry you, and together our love will ring true. Gammon tum doodley, I do."

The audience cheered.

He coughed once. "You're singing—singing!"

"Yes." She started laughing again. "I plan to sing every day of my life from now on."

"Ladies and gentlemen, it is my pleasure to announce that the lady has accepted my offer."

The crowd erupted in cheers and laughter. Everyone seemed to rush forward to express their congratulations.

She and Parker leaned over the side, shaking every hand offered.

Her father strode up to the edge of the basket and scowled. "We will speak of this scandalous scene later this evening. Now the two of you must get out of this balloon. We have a flight planned for today."

"Of course." She stepped away from the crowd, then perfunctorily reached for an instrument to pack.

Parker nodded in the direction of Drexel, who then whispered something in the marquess's ear. The two gentlemen separated and headed in opposite directions.

"Evie," her father repeated, "your lordship, step down immediately."

Seconds later, the right side of the basket lifted. Her father and Charles Henry moved to stop Drexel from releasing the ropes holding the balloon. Before they could regain the ropes to anchor them, the left side of the basket freed itself. The marquess and Drexel had untied the ropes holding them earthbound.

The balloon gracefully rose upward.

Below them, the audience screamed and shouted and laughed.

Parker held Eve tight, both of them laughing the entire ascension, until their upward movement slowed. "Away from my view fly the world and its strife, the banquet of fancy's feast is my wife," he sang.

She joined his serenade. "My spirits are mounting, my heart's full of glee. In your eyes, true love do I see."

Parker wrapped his arm around her shoulder and repeated his declaration into her ear before thoroughly kissing her. "I love you."

"I will never tire of hearing those words." She sighed, still under the heady effects of absolute bliss.

"Are you well? Your eyes appear glazed."

"There is something about the mesmerizing tone of your voice I enjoy, a sort of rumbling perhaps."

"Rumbling? I don't know much about noises, but my father can imitate every birdcall. Does my rumbling voice bother you?"

"Oh no, not *bother* exactly. It gives me a funny feeling everywhere inside my body though."

"Rumble is good." Parker gave her a sly smile that lingered on the corner of his mouth. "May I request permission to kiss my intended again? There. Did I rumble that time?"

She chuckled and nodded.

Parker proceeded to kiss her thoroughly once again—an experiment she truly enjoyed and returned, if not with great finesse, at least with all of her heart. "I love you too," she managed to whisper when the opportunity arose.

Glancing up at the balloon, she noticed hundreds of what looked like little pieces of paper flying around the basket. "Look."

They stood and discovered hundreds of white and colored butterflies hovering near their basket. The air seemed alive. Some flew upward, some downward, and some even flew into and around the bottom of the basket. They became surrounded with hundreds of gleaming wings appearing to fold upon themselves, shimmering like a moving cloud.

"How beautiful," he said, lifting his hand and holding it steady to see if a butterfly might land. "Have you ever seen this before? Is this a new discovery that you must report?"

She slowly twirled, absorbing the beautiful sight. "Yes, I have seen this twice before, but not this many butterflies. Funny thing, birds are frightened by balloons, and I've never seen a bird at this elevation. But insects don't appear to be afraid." She held his free hand, and they waited until a tiny creature landed on Parker's hand. The animal flexed his wings. "I think they have come to wish us well, like the guests at a wedding." She leaned close to the creature still on Parker's hand. "Thank you, little one." The butterfly rose in the air to join the others.

He grinned broadly.

They held hands and watched the butterflies circle and dance, until they dispersed and flew away some ten minutes later.

"I suppose we must land before we go too far," he said. "And because we are under circumstances that are not ideal for romance, I can promise you much more *rumbling* in the future, when we are alone." He placed his forehead on hers. "Then one day, soon I hope, I will demonstrate my love all night long until you know what happens?"

She smiled. "I cannot imagine. Let me guess: I sing?"

He lowered his eyelids until he appeared almost sleepy. "After our nights of lovemaking, I promise you will want to sing every day we are married."

She absolutely believed him. "I'm not much of a songstress, but I can make a sound of *apparent satisfaction*."

His eyes widened before they both burst out laughing.

She wrapped her arms around his waist, silently vowing to never let go. "And besides my testimony, you can use my singing as proof."

"Proof of what?"

"Proof that you won the earl's race, because your actions have been the true definition of Service to a Lady."

About the Author

Sally Orr worked for thirty years in molecular biology research. One day, a cyber-friend challenged her to write a novel. Since she is a hopeless Anglophile, it's not surprising that her first series is Regency romance. She lives with her husband in San Diego, surrounded by too many books and not enough old English cars.